Also by George D. Shuman

Lost Girls
Last Breath
18 Seconds

SECOND
—SIGHT
A NOVEL OF PSYCHIC SUSPENSE

GEORGE D. SHUMAN

SIMON & SCHUSTER

NEW YORK LONDON TORONTO SYDNEY

Simon & Schuster
1230 Avenue of the Americas
New York, NY 10020

First Simon & Schuster hardcover edition August 2009

SIMON & SCHUSTER and colophon are registered trademarks of Simon &
Schuster, Inc.

For information about special discounts for bulk purchases,
please contact Simon & Schuster Special Sales at
1-866-506-1949 or business@simonandschuster.com.

The Simon & Schuster Speakers Bureau can bring authors
to your live event. For more information or to book an event
contact the Simon & Schuster Speakers Bureau at
1-866-248-3049 or visit our website at www.simonspeakers.com.

Manufactured in the United States of America

10 9 8 7 6 5 4 3 2 1

Library of Congress Cataloging-in-Publication Data

Shuman, George D., 1952–
    Second sight : a novel of psychic suspense / George D. Shuman.
       p. cm.
1. Moore, Sherry (Fictitious character)—Fiction. 2. Pharmaceutical industry—
Fiction. 3. Psychics—Fiction. 4. Blind women—Fiction. 5. Psychological fiction.
I. Title.
    PS3619.H86S43   2009
    813'6—dc22   2009009140

ISBN 978-1-4165-9979-1
ISBN 978-1-4391-0978-6 (ebook)

On July 27, 1995, forty-two years after the cessation of hostilities in Korea, a most haunting war memorial was unveiled in Washington, D.C. It was a memorial to the 36,940 Americans who gave their lives from June 25, 1950, to July 27, 1953, in the war that never happened.

This book is dedicated to the 8,176 Americans still missing in Korea and to soldiers and agents of every American war and conflict that were ever left behind on foreign soils.

Source: Office of Secretary of Defense, Washington Headquarters Services, Directorate for Information Operations and Reports (WHS/DIOR); Defense Prisoners of War/Missing in Action Office (DPMO). Data released January 10, 2000.

It is now clear that we are facing an implacable enemy whose avowed objective is world domination by whatever means and at whatever cost. There are no rules in such a game. Hitherto acceptable norms of human conduct do not apply . . . long-standing American concepts of "fair play" must be reconsidered. We must develop effective espionage and counterespionage services and must learn to subvert, sabotage, and destroy our enemies by more clever, more sophisticated, and more effective methods than those used against us.

—Herbert Hoover Commission, 1949

SECOND
SIGHT

1

New York State Hospital for the Insane
New York, Catskill Mountains
1950

Rain pounded Mount Tamathy, melting snow into white patches that dappled the sopping brown leaves. Men formed lines along the ridges, wearing winter coats and fedoras, carrying shotguns that poked the brush behind the misty fog of their breath.

An eerie siren wailed faintly in the distance, warning residents of nearby Stockton that an inmate was still at large and that they should lock their doors before they turned in for the night.

"Jack?" a voice crackled loudly over the radio. "Jack, you trying to raise me?"

Jack McCullough put the cold device to his ear and raised the yard-long antenna on his radio.

"Emmet." The big man removed his hat to shake off the water.

"I'm under Chimney Rock. I need you up here."

Static hissed over the radio waves, finally broken by the words ". . . copy . . . help . . . all right?"

"Yeah, I'm all right," McCullough growled. "It's the boy Emmet, he's going to need a backboard. You copy?"

McCullough listened, but there was nothing more to hear, nothing but the steady rain, and now and then a chunk of ice falling from the boughs of the evergreens. He let the radio fall carelessly on its sling and cursed.

McCullough didn't much care for the army's gift of surplus radios, thought them cumbersome and unreliable in the mountains. He cared even less for the army itself or at least for Alpha Company, which had taken up residence on the mountain last year.

It wasn't enough that he had to deal with an insane asylum and all the problems that came with it. Now he was chasing soldier boys around the mountains.

The radio crackled after a minute and he heard Emmet say, "Backboard, Jack, I got it."

McCullough leaned with his back to the trunk of a tall pine, the long needles shielding him from the rain as he looked down at the body lying at his feet.

He'd thought they'd been tracking a mental patient all day. They all had. You just didn't see people running around these parts of the mountain on foot. Not unless they'd gone over the wall of the asylum.

He slid to a squat and leaned over the boy. The kid's eyes might be looking at him, but with so much blood streaming out of the sockets it was impossible to tell.

"Can you hear me, son?" McCullough leaned over and put an ear to the boy's lips.

"Can't . . . on," the boy whispered. "Can't . . . on."

"You understand me, boy?"

"Can't . . . on," the boy said, "Can't . . . on."

McCullough tugged the canvas hunting jacket up to cover the boy's eyes. Then he stood.

Mount Tamathy parted clouds at forty-two hundred feet, visibility good enough to make out the jagged black line of the Delaware River Gorge to the east. Elsewhere the sky was growing dark and closing in around him. The kid wouldn't have made it a night on the mountain alone. The temperature would drop again tonight and rain would turn to sleet before snow. Then the coyotes and wolves would have come in for the smell of blood.

McCullough had never looked upon the Catskills without wonder. The mountains never looked the same way twice to him and few men had laid eyes upon them so often. He chopped wood here in the fall and tapped maples in the spring. He hunted for the family's meat and gathered roots and herbs for his grandmother's medicines. He was, as all generations of McCulloughs and Groesbecks, Ver Dooks, and Van Dycks before him, dependent upon the mountain's bounty.

But Jack was hardly a country bumpkin. He had experienced the sordid nightlife around military bases south of Washington, D.C., and had seen action in France and Belgium during the Second World War. Jack had met boys from every corner of the continent, and in 1946, when he was discharged from Fort McPherson in Atlanta, he was left with fifty dollars to make his way home. Instead he drove west to visit a buddy from the Twenty-eighth Infantry who lived in Arizona, and then north to Wyoming before he crossed the Badlands on his way back home to New York. In a mere twenty years, Jack had seen more of the world than all of his American ancestors put together.

The urban world held little fascination for McCullough. He was a country boy at heart, so he returned to the farm of his ancestors and married Carla Woodruff, the first girl in his high school ever to matriculate to a university. Two years later she joined the Stockton public school system and Jack applied as a security guard at the New York State Hospital for the Insane.

The locals still referred to it as "the asylum," originally named Van Buren for the first president to have been born a citizen of the newly formed United States. Van Buren's father had once been a popular tavern owner in the upstate village of Kinderhook, and memories in the Catskills ran long.

A mammoth institution, the asylum was built at the end of the Civil War and consisted of a half-million-square-foot main building with six annexes on 338 acres of land. Seventy of those acres had been cleared for farming so the asylum could supply its own beef, grain, and dairy products. Thirty were devoted to hospital wards, and the remaining stand of timber provided a buffer to the world beyond Mount Tamathy. It currently housed 4,300 inmates and employed a staff of 264.

Escapes weren't uncommon; the thousand doors or windows were sure to be left unlocked at one time or another, and inmates sometimes came into possession of tools left behind by maintenance workers.

Not that there was anywhere to run. Dogs patrolled the only road in and out. Which left only the mountains to hide in, and while many went in, fewer were known to return. The Catskills were as inclined to swallow a man as spit him back out, the old-timers said.

This of course must have been the reason the asylum had been built in this remote region of the state following the Civil War. Tens of thousands of soldiers had lost eyes and limbs on the battlefields, suffered ball and shrapnel wounds to the brain; endured disfiguring burns from black powder explosions. Thousands more had been pinned down in no-man's-lands between enemy lines, covered by body parts and the dying who cried out for water or their mothers. And then there were witnesses to the carnage, all the nurses and sawbones and civilians who had to pick up all those body parts and put them into graves.

The psychological toll was overwhelming.

The government needed some place where the hopeless

could live out their lives in peace and segregation. And the Catskills were no less secluded a century later when the United States Army came looking for a place to conduct secret activities.

McCullough shook a Chesterfield from a pack, caught it on his lower lip, and lit it with a silver Zippo.

He looked at his watch. The search had entered its seventh hour.

He blew smoke through a heavy beard that matched terra-cotta freckles on his wrists and big hands. He looked down at the boy's body again: the polished black boots that had been badly scarred by the fall to the rocks; the army shirt punctured by bones where a compound fracture splintered his elbow.

McCullough kept wondering what in the hell would have possessed the kid to go out on the edge of Chimney Rock. The formation was little more than a sixty-foot spire and there was hardly doubt in daylight up above that you were stepping out into space.

McCullough had a feeling it had something to do with Area 17. The locals never doubted that there were strange things going on in that place. They'd seen the heavy trucks passing through Stockton on their way to Mount Tamathy. They knew the military was putting sophisticated equipment on the base and they knew that three-star generals and barb-wire outer perimeters around heavy-gauge security fencing meant but one thing. That whatever was inside was important enough to kill for. Not even the usually cocky teens demonstrated bravado by sneaking around the perimeter of the base.

Some thought Continental Air Command chose Mount Tamathy as one of the four strategic radar installations that would make up the new North American defense initiative. Some thought the government was concerned about things far scarier than Soviet aircraft. Just two years earlier, a farmer in Roswell, New Mexico, found the remains of an unidentified flying object in his field and there had been speculation ever since that the government had an alien body inside Area 51.

Whatever was going on inside the compound on Mount Tamathy, the cows were the first to disapprove. Within a year of the facility's construction, the large dairy herd at the mental asylum stopped giving milk. Then one of the Luxors' prized steers was found dead in a pasture six miles away off Fox Ridge Road. Two different vets who came to look at it could not explain its demise, although one later told a preacher that its eyes had been burned from their sockets.

Rumors of diseased cattle, however, were bad for business; even a hint of healthy animals collapsing in fields affected market profits for hundreds of miles. So a grave was dug and the steer and story were quickly laid to rest.

One night in June there was an inexplicable earth tremor shattering windows on two fire towers on Kawahita Ridge. The town's elders proclaimed they had never even heard of a quake in the history of the Catskills and the only agency that documented such things in those days, the New York State Police, concluded it was an act of vandalism, most likely teens playing with dynamite.

Then night lights started appearing over Mount Tamathy, yellow and green bands that shimmered like the Aurora Borealis. A small group of Native Americans said it was the Algonquin Indians' Manitou, whose spirit had been awakened by the earth tremors in June. Others were convinced that UFOs were conducting surveillance of Area 17. Everyone agreed it was the last time in twenty years they had been able to get AM radio reception near Mount Tamathy.

Then there were suicides. An orderly leaped from the water tower on a sunny afternoon. A patient was found hanging by a light cord in a storage closet.

No one could say definitively that the army was to blame, but then no one could say that it wasn't, either. No one really knew what went on behind the gates of Area 17.

The boy at his feet continued to mumble incoherently, the

result of a concussion, perhaps, but that wouldn't explain the fiery red color of his skin or the heat rising from his face. There had been no time for infection to set in and he sure as hell hadn't gotten a sunburn in the November Catskills.

McCullough heard the sound of brush snapping below him. His men making their way up the side of the mountain. He winced as smoke from his cigarette curled into his eye, and he ground the knuckles of his hand against the tears, muttering, "Damn." Then he spat and tossed the cigarette into the rain.

It was Thanksgiving, and he wondered if the boy's parents had any idea where their son was today. Could they have guessed he was lying broken at the foot of an obscure mountain in New York State? McCullough thought not. In fact, he doubted any of the enlisted men in Area 17 had mail privileges. Doubted that any of the families knew where their sons were.

The trees were nearly leafless now, forests colorless but for sprigs of wild grapes. The blood on his hands stood out in stark contrast to it all. He lifted the slicker and watched for the rise and fall of the boy's chest. The name stenciled clearly in black on the green army shirt read MONAHAN, T. He was no more than twenty.

It had started just after 9 a.m. this morning. An electrician repairing the spotlights on the main gates saw a man running toward the trees outside the asylum wall. That was how the call came in to security and how McCullough's men ended up spending Thanksgiving Day on the side of Mount Tamathy. He knew the staff back at the asylum was conducting a head count, trying to figure out who was missing from the asylum, but with four thousand inmates it was a job that took hours. McCullough saw no need to stop them just yet. His main concern now was getting the boy to the emergency room.

If the army was aware that one of their men went over the wall, they were keeping it quiet. No one from the base had alerted the asylum about such an incident and if they had, McCullough and his men would have been spared a day on the mountain. The army could have sent a search party off in the direction their soldier was last seen. Now he wasn't inclined to return the favor. The army would find out about their soldier when he was good and ready to tell them.

There was a long low rumble off in the west. Whether or not Private Monahan, T., knew it, he had picked a good day to escape. The storm had stalled over the mountain in the early-morning hours, drenching the Catskills with two inches of rain. There was too little snow left to track a man and too much water to wash away his scent. He might have gone on for days if he hadn't chosen to terminate his escape on the summit.

The boy kept repeating the monosyllabic words. McCullough could feel body heat rising from the jacket. He was tempted to lift the jacket again, but had no desire to look into those bloody eyes.

McCullough was not a man you would call squeamish. He'd seen plenty in his short time at the asylum. During his deployment in France and Belgium, he had the misfortune of watching a buddy die a horrible death in the sky over Bastogne. Medics had just airlifted them outside of the village when a mortar hit the tail of their helicopter, literally turning the craft on its side. His friend, thoroughly lashed to a stretcher—but not yet to the cargo bay of the helicopter—slid out the open door. Their eyes locked at that moment and he watched the stretcher fall until the helicopter righted itself and someone leaped to slam the door closed.

These were sights he would never forget, recurring nightmares that woke him in his sleep, and yet he was sure that there was nothing to compare with this boy's bloody eyes.

"Jack?" a voice called. "Jack?"

"Up here," he yelled.

A moment later Emmet arrived with three other officers, two of them carrying a backboard.

"Jesus," Emmet said. He looked up at the rock ledge and shielded his eyes from the rain. "He fell?"

McCullough nodded, grabbing the slicker and pulling it away from the boy's face.

Emmet stood frozen for a moment, then knelt and reached to touch a red cheek. "Shit, Jack, he's not one of ours. He's a soldier."

McCullough nodded. "Must have gone AWOL."

"What's he saying?"

"Sounds like can-teen," McCullough said. "He's been repeating it since I found him. He won't take water, though."

"His head's on fire. Maybe he's delirious with the fever?"

"Took a hell of a hit on the head," McCullough acknowledged.

Emmet leaned low and put his ear to the boy's lips. "He must have been laying here all day. Wouldn't have taken more than forty minutes to climb from the army base to the top of the rocks."

McCullough grunted, shivering himself, for the cold was getting to him.

The boy's voice was soft, the words monosyllabic: "Can't on, can't on, can't on . . ."

"You want me to send Billy down to tell his commanding officer?"

McCullough shook his head. "Let em keep looking. He needs an emergency room more than the army right now. Let's get some hands under him, boys," he said. "Put the board right there, Jimmy. Billy, help him push it up snug."

The men got their hands under the boy's knees, back, and neck and lifted him on a three count to the wooden stretcher. McCullough saw a green leather notebook lying where the boy had been and discreetly picked it up while the others were strapping him down.

"Lions slaughtered the Yanks in Detroit," Emmet offered.

"What was the score?" McCullough turned his back to his men as he opened the book and thumbed through the pages. There were dates and paragraph entries, neatly handwritten in ink toward the beginning of the book, but turning to scribble toward the middle where the writing ended. It was a log or journal of some kind, he thought, folding it closed and tucking it into his back pocket.

"Forty-nine to fourteen. The Lions had five hundred and eighty yards of offense."

"Jiminy Christmas." McCullough shook his head, looking up once more at the towering rock pinnacle above him. There was no way the boy could have missed recognizing the danger of walking out on it. He would have to have believed the fall would kill him if he jumped. So was this suicide?

"Hoernschemeyer ran ninety-six yards for a touchdown. I would have loved to have seen that one."

"Yeah, and I'd love to see New York put up ten thousand dollars for a decent running back." McCullough spat out a grain of tobacco caught on his tongue.

"What about Pittsburgh and Chicago?"

"Steelers twenty-eight, Cardinals seventeen." Emmet peeled off his outer jacket and tossed it to McCullough. "Here, Jack. You must be freezing. I've been walking all the time you was waiting here."

McCullough nodded gratefully and put it on. When they started down the muddy hillside—planting boots sideways to keep from slipping in the mud—McCullough patted his back pocket to reassure himself the book was secure there.

McCullough remembered the day the army first arrived to look over the adjacent property on Mount Tamathy. The asylum's administrator had asked him to meet an entourage of officers and guide them through a service road to the wooded property west of the asylum. He'd said they were looking at it as a possible site to place an air command monitoring station. He had also make it clear that the army wanted to bring as little attention as possible to their visit.

It was early on a Sunday and McCullough had met the

large black sedan at the main gate and escorted it to the edge of the asylum property before he left the army men to wander in the woods.

He could still remember the glitter of medals and gold epaulettes on the uniformed passengers front and back, but it was the man with the white homburg hat and white meerschaum pipe who startled him most. Dr. Edward "Buzz" Case, easily recognizable from newspaper stories and television appearances, might have been the last person he expected to see in the remote Catskill Mountains.

Case had been headline news around the country since the end of World War II, renowned for his work on the Manhattan Project, which produced the first atomic bomb. Case's connection to the army was well established prior to 1950, but publicly he was parting ways from the military, devoting himself full-time to the new field of nuclear medicine. Some said he was atoning for the millions of lives lost at Hiroshima and Nagasaki. Case himself suggested he was close to developing a "radioactive" magic bullet that would cure cancer, and there was much ado about his moving to California to be near radiological research at the Radiation Laboratory in Berkeley.

Then, without a whisper or a warning, he disappeared off the face of the planet. Reporters who had been following him and the esteemed biologist and physician Jonas Salk—the man who would conquer polio—across the country were left bewildered as to what happened to their photogenic genius.

When he didn't reappear at the five-year anniversary celebration of the surrender of Japan in Washington, D.C., the press began to ask questions. When they realized that Case's own family was stonewalling them, they began to speculate on everything from a Soviet kidnapping to alien abduction.

Jack McCullough had never mentioned seeing Dr. Case that day to anyone else, but was sure that he knew what the rest of the world did not. That Dr. Edward Case was living in Area 17 and that his work had nothing at all to do with cancer research or even the new strategic air command initiative. Case could only have been recruited to develop a secret weapon to combat the new superpower, the Soviet Union.

The Cold War was a time like no other. People in neighborhoods in the 1950s lived under the prospect of imminent annihilation. All across America the mournful sirens wailed to test their systems and evacuations to fallout shelters. Children were taught to crawl under their desks and avoid the flying glass from windows. Shelters were constructed in every basement and backyard. TV and radio broadcasts were regularly interrupted by earsplitting warning signals.

And rumors abounded: The Russians had a machine that could affect the thoughts of entire populations. The Russians were testing a death ray in the city of Novosibirsk. The Russians were using high-voltage electricity to control the world's weather.

Whatever was really going on behind the Iron Curtain, no one could say, but it was clear the United States was in an arms race with the Soviet Reds and the world had already seen proof—in Hiroshima and Nagasaki—that mankind was becoming capable of anything.

McCullough didn't know what happened to the boy, but he was sure it had something to do with what went on behind the gates of Area 17. He was equally certain that the army would not have wanted civilians finding their soldier alive and talking.

He thought about the journal in his pocket. None of his men had seen it, he was certain. It was probably personal and should be returned to the boy's family. But something else told him that whether harmless or not, it would be a mistake to mention it to the military. That to mention it would only bring trouble to the finder.

2

NAZARETH HOSPITAL
PHILADELPHIA, PENNSYLVANIA
2008

There was too much time to think in this place, to relive past mistakes and reflect on the truth of age-old maxims. Too much time to consider what grim news the machines surrounding you might be collecting.

It didn't matter that she was blind. Nothing could alter the clinical milieu of the place. Forget about counting to ten, inhaling and slowly exhaling, focusing on "happy thoughts" rather than the needles in your arm or the array of wires that found their way to your arms and head.

Sherry Moore had always considered the possibility of an early death. She'd suffered major head trauma as a child. Cerebrally blind since the age of five, a condition of the brain not the eyes, she suffered retrograde amnesia, unable to recall events before the accident in 1976. She also could visualize the last memories of dead people. If that didn't tell you something was wrong with the wiring in her head, then nothing would.

Now she had been exposed to deadly radioactive cesium 137.

It had started two weeks before in the Four Corners region of New Mexico. A maintenance worker curious about the rotting smell in a rest area Dumpster found the decaying body of a young female. The unidentified girl, five or six years old, had what appeared to be burn marks on her hands and face and was taken to Albuquerque's Presbyterian Hospital, where she was autopsied by a forensic pathologist. The pathologist found no evidence of sexual assault, and toxicology screens ruled out common poisons or pathogens. In fact, but for profuse bleeding of the gums, she looked perfectly normal.

Then in the dark of the night a tractor-trailer ran over a woman lying on Route 491 near Newcomb, New Mexico. The driver said that by the time he saw the outline of her body in his headlights it was too late to bring the fifteen-ton rig to a stop. An elderly physician in Shiprock—who sometimes filled in as coroner—conducted an autopsy of the sunburnt-looking body and concluded the woman had died of cardiovascular collapse brought on by an overdose of methamphetamines. It really wouldn't have mattered if the truck had stopped or not, he told the sheriff. The woman was already dead when the tires rolled over her.

He ruled her death an accident.

Eagle Junction's weekly newspaper announced that the thirty-eight-year-old woman, Victoria Spencer, was the daughter of Carl and June Spencer of Sheep Springs, New Mexico. Although she lived across the Colorado border in Ouray, police in the Four Corners area of the state knew Victoria—who sported tattoos of barbed wire around her throat and wrists—well. Victoria was the property of the Mongols, a California-based motorcycle gang that sold drugs at truck stops in New Mexico, Colorado, Utah, and Arizona.

New Mexico's various state and county law enforcement officers would all have agreed that Victoria was destined for a life of crime. Everyone in the Spencer family had been in prison at one time or another. From drugs to assault to fencing stolen property, sheriff's deputies and state police officers had been visiting the Spencer scrap-metal yard near Sheep Springs for as long as they had been in business.

Except that when the sheriff of Sheep Springs went to the the Spencers' to notify them of their daughter's death this time, there was no answer at the trailer door. In fact, the only sign of life on the two acres of junk cars and rusting appliances was an emaciated Rottweiler that the sheriff had removed to an animal shelter.

Meanwhile, in the days that followed, two emergency medical technicians who had transported the child's body to Albuquerque were admitted to Presbyterian Hospital with severe abdominal pains. Then the elderly physician who performed the autopsy on Victoria Spencer in Shiprock came down with violent flulike symptoms.

Three days later the pathologist who performed the child's autopsy in Albuquerque began to bleed internally, and four days later both medical examiners were dead.

Albuquerque's director of environmental health was notified about the incidents and blood was sent to the CDC in Atlanta for testing.

No one needed to mention the obvious. Not around Albuquerque. New Mexico had just had a serious outbreak of the hemorrhagic virus called hantavirus in 1993, right there in the same Four Corners area. Now it was critical to find out what the Spencer woman and the child in the Dumpster had in common. If they actually had become infected with hantavirus, state officials needed to know where they had been when they inhaled the spores of the deadly disease.

15

The director of health and human services for New Mexico ordered DNA tests for both victims. Then he issued bulletins to every hospital and physician in the state, cautioning them to be vigilant for new cases of hantavirus. No one was going to contract the virus merely by treating flu cases, but extra precautions were required in handling clothing, hair, and bodily fluids.

A colleague of the New Mexico health director in nearby Oklahoma who had been reading about the two new cases in New Mexico called with a most unusual suggestion. He knew of a blind woman in Philadelphia who was able to envisage the final few seconds of memory in corpses. In other words, he told the director, someone like her might be able to tell you where his victims were before they died.

The director of environmental health was still chuckling over his colleague's odd suggestion when the Albuquerque hospital's administrator called to tell him that the Sheep Springs sheriff who went to the Spencer ranch to locate the parents was now in her critical care unit hemorrhaging from the bowels.

The health director stopped smiling and had his assistant place a call to the Oklahoma Department of Health to obtain Sherry Moore's phone number. Meanwhile, his staff arranged to locate and quarantine anyone who had come in contact with the two original victims' bodies or clothing.

What harm could there be, he thought, in bringing a psychic here and letting her do whatever she did?

Sherry Moore was having dinner at the Deep Blue Bar and Grill in Wilmington when she received the call from an official of the New Mexico Department of Health and Human Services.

She and Brian Metcalf, a navy SEAL whom she had been dating since they met during a rescue mission they collaborated on in Alaska's Denali State Park last fall, were on a romantic weekend getaway at the Hotel du Pont in Delaware. Metcalf had just invited her to his parents' home in Boston the weekend before, where she met the whole family at a Memorial Day reunion.

This was brand-new territory for Sherry. She had never before had what she would have considered a serious relationship in her life. She had certainly never been asked to meet anyone's parents before. And, yes, there were times she'd had strong feelings for a man, but the men she met in her unusual pursuits around the world always ended up living thousands of miles away or were themselves traveling professionals. Long-distance relationships were difficult under the best circumstances, but for people barely acquainted, the distance in time and miles took its toll. It never took long for conversations to get diluted for want of substance and then the calls came less often and inevitably ceased.

She remembered how empty she'd felt following these experiences. She wanted something more permanent in life, something she could count on in the months and years ahead. She wasn't delusional. She knew that life was uncertain. But why couldn't two people enjoy a mutual dream? What could be better than a life shared with another person?

She also knew marriage wasn't a magic utopia. She knew people were having more difficulty than ever staying together. And maybe she was kidding herself, she thought. It seemed there was a new world order when it came to relationships. People were still getting married at a fantastic rate, but now two and three and four times, until they were old and living single and dating into old age.

This thing with Brian Metcalf felt much different to her. It seemed important. Brian called daily and he traveled every weekend from wherever he was training. She knew he couldn't keep up the pace forever. He was about to be deployed overseas, and in his line of work there weren't always opportunities to make calls. But he was giving her every indication that he was committed to the relationship, and whatever her views on caution might have once been, she wanted to let down her guard. She wanted to believe in this. Brian was that kind of man, all that she had ever wished for. He was strong and he was honest and he had integrity. He was the image of the husband she had conjured her entire life and she was ready to hold up her end of a partnership.

At least that was what Sherry had thought then.

Brian wasn't happy when she told him what they wanted her to do in New Mexico, but he didn't get upset or in any way interfere.

"Is this what you really want?" he'd asked, after she'd explained the CDC's concern over the rare hantavirus. "What if you are exposed to something?"

Sherry had to admit she felt a bit defensive at the time. As if the idea of someone trying to protect her from herself was more than she wanted. Lord knew Mr. Brigham, her neighbor and longtime confidant, tried and sometimes succeeded, but that was Brigham, and Brian Metcalf hadn't entirely earned the right to tell her what to do. Of course, Sherry was also aware that she had a stubborn streak and that she didn't respond well to the word *no*.

"Brian, I'm not going to be doing anything their own doctors wouldn't do. And I don't have a death wish, believe me. Besides, this is what I do in life," she'd told him. "I'll be careful, but life is inherently dangerous. The flight to New Mexico is dangerous."

She sensed his uneasiness, but what could he possibly say? If anyone was living dangerously it was Brian, who had made a choice to have a career in the navy. And yet, behind all the blustering, she felt the slightest satisfaction that someone besides her neighbor was actually worrying about her when she was gone.

Sherry took a 5:30 a.m. flight out of Philadelphia, landing in Albuquerque before 10 a.m.

The state trooper who met her at the airport had just finished a night shift sitting on the lane that went into the Spencer ranch outside of Sheep Springs, to see if the dead woman's parents would return. Police were still trying to notify the Spencers of their daughter's death, but they were also growing more and more concerned that the Spencers had fallen victim to the virus themselves. Especially since a DNA test had determined the child found in the Dumpster in the Four Corners was Victoria Spencer's daughter.

There were no official birth records for the child. No medical records, no enrollment documents for any school. No one in Ouray, Colorado, where Victoria was last known to live, had ever seen her with a child, and for that matter, no one had seen Victoria for the past month. What if Victoria had given birth to a child on the farm and left her there years before and it was the Spencer farm that was the source of the deadly virus? What if the rest of the Spencer family were still inside that trailer?

Trooper Marsh didn't relish the idea of spending the night around the Spencers' ranch, not even at the distance of the road leading into the property and inside the relative safety of her vehicle. Seven health care workers and law enforcement officials who had come into contact with Victoria or the child in the Dumpster had by now died or were in serious condition. If the disease had originated here, police could not ignore the very real possibility that the Spencers had disposed of their daughter's and granddaughter's bodies in remote places to keep whatever they had contracted away from the property.

"Miss Moore?" The trooper approached the blind woman in the terminal tentatively.

Sherry turned toward the voice and nodded. Stuck out her hand.

"Trooper Marsh, Jane Marsh. Let me get your bag," the trooper gave her a firm handshake and grabbed the overnight bag from her hand. Sherry was sure the temperature outside was well above a hundred, and the trooper's hand felt as if she'd pulled it from an oven.

"Thank you," Sherry said to the young woman.

"Car's on the curb, ma'am, right this way."

This is where people had difficulty figuring out how to handle a blind woman, Sherry knew. Wondering if she should take Sherry's arm or if she was only supposed to lead the way.

"Go ahead," Sherry told the trooper pleasantly, "I can follow your footsteps."

Sherry used her walking stick to follow the trooper across the terminal floor, and when the automatic doors whooshed open they hit a wall of arid heat.

The police cruiser smelled of must and a familiar women's deodorant. Marsh set Sherry's bag in the backseat and got behind the wheel. Then she turned up the air conditioner and cursed, scratching her hand against the seat fabric. "Damned red ants must have got me." She wheeled the car into traffic. "Sure is hot around here, huh?"

"I don't mind," Sherry said. "I'm kind of a heat person myself."

"Well, I've been living here five years and this is the first time my shirt was ever wringing wet. Hottest day I can ever remember."

Sherry could hear the trooper still scratching the palm of one hand.

"I read about you in *People* magazine once."

"That was awhile back." Sherry adjusted the air vent away from her face. "I was still in my twenties, I think."

"You read minds," the trooper said.

"Not really. It's more about memories," Sherry said.

Something rolled from under the passenger seat and struck Sherry in the heel of her shoe. She leaned down and picked up a heavy metal cylinder the circumference of a thermos.

"Sharp edges," the trooper warned, leaning across to take it from her, then putting it under her own seat. "Darned thing sliced open my tire last night. I cut my hand on it twice."

"What is it?"

"Beats the hell out of me, but it sure is pretty. One end has this thick periscope-like glass on it, and the inside glows fluorescent blue like you've never seen. You know, the color of those tropical fish in the Caribbean."

Sherry smiled and shrugged. "Not really."

"Ah, I'm sorry," the trooper said. "I forgot. Anyhow, it's just this amazing color of blue. My husband keeps a metal lathe in our garage. He's a genius when it comes to metal. I want him to make a bracelet out of it for me. Maybe a ring for our daughter."

The trooper adjusted her own air vents with her free hand. "Don't mean to be nosy, but are you going to look at all them bodies?"

"If I can."

"Yeah, that's what they said." She checked and adjusted one of the side mirrors. "Rumors fly around headquarters so fast they could knock your eye out. They've all been quarantined now, the bodies, you know," the trooper said. "Whatever it is, it must be highly contagious."

"I knew there was talk about a virus," Sherry said.

The trooper put her turn signal on and edged into the passing lane.

"The woman who died on the road, Victoria Spencer, was a junkie from Colorado. Her old man owns the ranch I was sitting on last night near Sheep Springs. We can't find the parents to notify them about their daughter and now we found out that a little girl found north in the Four Corners was a DNA match to Victoria. No one knew she had a daughter until now, but that's two Spencers with the virus. We're thinking maybe the parents were exposed too. Maybe even dead inside their trailer."

"Can't you break in to check on their welfare?"

"Our captain's talking with the Health Department now, trying to assess the risks once we're in."

"How about the house in Colorado?" Sherry asked.

"Troopers up there went in and no one was home. Victoria hadn't been living there for weeks according to her neighbors."

Suddenly the car began to slow. "I'm just going to stop up here at the gas station and hit the ladies' room. Maybe you want to stretch your legs or get something inside?"

The car wheeled off the side of the road. Sherry could hear the noise of gas pumps and a baby crying, a pneumatic wheel wrench in the background.

"I must be coming down with the flu or something," the trooper said, rolling to a stop. "My gut feels like I ate a bag of worms."

The Albuquerque Presbyterian Hospital administrator, Dr. Gladys Lynn, introduced herself when Sherry arrived and apologized for the confusion. "I'm really sorry, but I don't quite understand why you were sent to me."

Sherry explained who she was and said that the New Mexico Department of Health and Human Services had asked her to come at the behest of a mutual acquaintance. "I would have called first, but I thought you were expecting me," she'd said, explaining what she hoped to accomplish for the administrator.

Sherry waited through a minute of tense silence for a response.

But Dr. Lynn picked up the phone instead and got her assistant on the line and told him she wanted to conference with the health director. After two long minutes it was clear he wasn't available. When she replaced the receiver on her desk, she folded her hands and set her jaw. Sherry could feel tension in the air.

"Miss Moore, I don't know why the director thought it prudent to bring you here, but no one is going into that quarantine downstairs unless they are a physician and I mean one who is essential in identifying or treating this disease. I am certainly not letting any entertainers into that room."

Dr. Lynn bit her upper lip, shaking her head in wonder. "Miss Moore, I don't know what to do with you and I really have more important things to do. Please forgive me," she said, rising to her feet, "but . . ."

"Doctor," Sherry said softly. "You can either let me see your victims, or take me back to the airport. I can't help you without actually touching the girl's hand and I certainly don't want to be in your way."

Lynn hit the intercom. "Jeffrey," she said. "See that Miss Moore gets back to the airport and help her with any special arrangements she needs."

The door opened, her assistant entered, and Dr. Lynn slammed it on her way out.

"Sorry, but it's a little tense around here at the moment," the assistant explained.

Sherry wondered for the thousandth time if being blind worked for or against her. You couldn't help but think you were getting sympathy points from people at times, but then you were also quite easy to ignore. Sherry had perceived at quite a young age that there was power in being able to look into the other person's eyes. Not to mention the stigma that went along with being disadvantaged. The reality was that many people thought physical challenges made you less qualified to make decisions.

Blind or not, Sherry was conveying memories of the dead. Memories she retrieved through the deceased person's skin cell receptors. But if you couldn't accept the premise that Sherry was somehow tapping into human memory, there was but one other conclusion—glove, no glove, she wasn't going to produce what the administrator wanted to know.

She didn't blame Dr. Lynn. It would hardly be professional

to let a civilian get involved in a potential epidemic. And for that matter, if the administrator didn't know what kind of disease they were dealing with in quarantine, why should she be so willing to stick her hand in the hornet's nest?

The assistant led her to his outer office. "I'll start working on a flight for you," he said. "May I get you water or coffee?"

"I'm fine," Sherry said softly. "But please try to get me back to Philadelphia this evening?" she said. "I really don't want to spend the night here if I don't have to."

"I'll do everything possible, Miss Moore."

Sherry waited, thinking things happened for a reason. Brigham had told her often enough to be careful what she wished for. And now with Brian in her life, she had another reason to be concerned for her safety. Maybe she'd been too quick to take on new risks, with a potential partner in her life. Maybe she'd let her defensiveness override a real concern for her safety.

The phone rang and the assistant put the caller on hold.

Thirteen stories below, the corpse of a child lay in a sublevel cold storage facility. The body of the child's mother was on its way from the coroner's office in Shiprock, which by now had also been quarantined.

The cold storage facility in the hospital's basement was currently being used by the city's Office of Emergency Preparedness to preserve food and medical stores. Now a biohaz remediation team had been sent in to convert it into a temporary morgue.

The location had been chosen because it was already slated for demolition. In three months' time it would become the footprint of a new seven-story hospital wing. The only preparations it needed now were plastic sheeting on the walls and floors to segregate it from the remainder of the hospital. The room was large enough to accommodate fifty bodies should the unthinkable occur. Once the emergency was over they could simply demolish it and haul it away, rubble—walls, dirt, and all.

Sherry was halfway through a cup of coffee when she

heard heels striking tile and approaching the executive suite. The door opened quickly and closed behind Dr. Lynn's distinctive perfume.

"Would you please rejoin me in my office?" the woman said.

Sherry had the feeling Dr. Lynn was making some kind of nonverbal gestures to her assistant as she walked.

"Miss Moore," the doctor said, closing her door. She hesitated until they were both sitting, shifted her weight in the seat, and sighed. She seemed uncomfortable with what she was about to say, Sherry thought. It was something she was in conflict with.

"I must apologize," the doctor started saying abruptly. "I know you came a long way. I know you didn't ask to be here."

Sherry could feel the tingle of nerve endings the length of her spine. The doctor hadn't needed to bring her back into her office to make an apology. She could just as easily have let the assistant express any regret. Which meant the administrator had talked to someone and that she or someone higher had changed her mind. Sherry was going to be allowed to enter that room downstairs and all of a sudden she wasn't sure she wanted to.

"I'm afraid I'm a rather uninformed woman. I don't read much about the outside world"—she must have made a hand gesture, Sherry thought, during the interruption—"unless it's a trade journal," the doctor said. "Work is my life and my specialty is cardiology, not neurology. I have to say I've never heard of you or your rather unique abilities before. The health director and I spoke. I discovered, like him, that you have a rather esteemed following in our profession. I still can't say I'm happy with my decision, but I will grant you access to the child in our morgue. The mother's corpse is still in transit, so perhaps we can wait until tonight or tomorrow before you see her, and then only if need be." She sighed again. "So tell me. What will you need to do with the girl's body?"

25

Sherry rubbed the palms of her hands together, nodding in a moment of silence. She thought about Brian again and mused cynically that she didn't deserve to have a normal relationship. Of course he should have been worried about her. She was already blind, for Christ's sake. Did she expect him to take on someone with even bigger challenges than being blind? She had to accept that there were mutual interests at stake in a relationship. It was a responsibility to minimize the odds that anything bad would happen to her, and she was sure that Brian would do the same when the opportunity presented itself. In fact, he had been talking about taking an instructor's assignment once he finished his tour overseas.

Suddenly she felt guilty, as if she should be making a phone call and telling him about the risk she was about to take here.

But she didn't. She only needed to get through this one more time. She only needed to get home safely.

"I just need to hold her hand," Sherry said. "Just for a few seconds."

The administrator lifted the phone from the receiver. She placed a call and issued directions. Then she replaced it and stood.

"Someone will be in the room, Miss Moore, both to guide you to the body and to see that you enter and exit as efficiently as possible. I do not want you in that room long."

Sherry nodded.

"If you are limited to last memories, Miss Moore, I would be interested in bedding. Where did the child lie at night? What did the home look like, or, if it wasn't a home, was there a vehicle, a cave, a commercial building? Neither of the known victims had bites on their bodies, so they had to have breathed in the spores of the mice feces. Ventilation ducts from a basement or crawl space under a house. Insulation in furniture or vehicles, anywhere mice could nest."

"When can I get to her?"

"The room will be ready within the hour. They're rigging a

kind of airlock chamber of polyethylene skin between the entrance and interior. We've secured it like a decontamination tent.
It's hardly a real containment lab, but it will do. Use the restroom
or the phone if you like. I'll have my assistant bring you down
when they're ready."

Sherry nodded.

The floors were cold beneath her stocking feet. The suit felt heavy
and awkward, hooded mask pressing against her shoulders. The
technicians had improvised one arm by removing the glove and
duct-taping the material as securely to the arm as possible at the
wrist. Sherry would have five minutes in the room with the girl.
The administrator reassured her that the real risk of hantavirus
was airborne ingestion. If you weren't bitten or breathed it into
the lungs, you weren't likely to become infected. Not as long as
you avoided bodily fluids and the victim's clothing, which had
already been removed.

That in itself was a relief, Sherry thought.

Her feet were getting colder for lack of circulation or maybe
the floor was just cold. Sherry waited by the door, shifting weight
from one leg to the other. She could hear the rush of fresh fil-
tered oxygen as she breathed.

A minute with the child was more than enough time, she
knew. She only needed a minute if things went as planned.

Then the door opened and suddenly she was taken by the
arm and walked into the airlock, where she was helped into boots
that were sealed tightly around her calves. Someone else wearing
plastic gloves took her forearm and with a rush of cold air they
stepped through the heavy sheets of plastic into the makeshift
morgue and a moment later through a third. Sherry subcon-
sciously counted thirteen steps before a tug on her arm brought
her to a halt. The gloved hand lifted hers and placed a small bare
hand in it.

Sherry took a breath. Cool oxygen rushed noisily into her mask . . . *there was a man, unshaven, thirty or forty years old, he was shirtless and fat and he was standing in a cramped bathroom with his back to a sink. She was looking at him sideways, her head lying perpendicular on a kind of a bed. He was staring back at her, rocking drunkenly on his heels, trying to control a stream of urine splashing into a toilet; she saw a ring of orange embers pulsing under the ashes of a campfire, a red gas can next to the tire of a truck, a woman's purple backpack, a cracked red wallet on the ground, a key chain on a wine cork, a yellow T-shirt with stick people drawn on it. There was a black lump in the coals of the fire and a yellowed bone protruding through; she was holding a stick and using it to push a toy boat through a rut of muddy water; the boat was pink and there was a one-armed naked Barbie in it. Barbie was leaning sideways on the seat, a penny and a beer bottle cap in the stern. She saw an enormous woman jammed into an old fabric recliner; the side was torn and hanging like an elephant's ear over a filthy green carpet.*

The skinhead boy was pointing to something big and metal in the back of his pickup truck, a machine of some kind, or so it seemed. It was turquoise and as large as a refrigerator. It had a long pink plastic cushion on top as if it was meant to be lain on. There were dials and levers on the side and near the bottom at the wheels. There was an arm like a crane that reached over the cushions and from the end of the arm a black metal cylinder with a sealed glass end.

There was a large brown-and-black dog with one bent ear; it had a wide pale scar where fur refused to grow across one of its haunches; the dog had a collar with spikes sticking out and it came to the bed and licked her hand. The large woman again, still sitting in the recliner; she was biting down on an end of rubber strap, straining against the other that was cutting into the flesh around her bicep. The skinhead was kneeling next to her, wearing a sleeveless white T-shirt. He had swastika tattoos on both arms and was pushing the plunger of a syringe that was sticking out of the woman's forearm.

In the same narrow room the bald teen and the fat man were sitting opposite two long-haired men at a kitchen table. Cigarette smoke formed a gray halo over their heads. The men wore buckled boots and leather vests. They had prominent cheekbones and smooth dark skin; one had beads threaded into his black hair.

The kitchen table again, the men were laughing, the teenage boy was showing them the inside of the black cylinder she had seen in the back of the truck. One end was ragged as if it had been sawed from the machine. The other glowed electric blue, its light flickering eerily over their sweat-soaked faces.

The boy reached into the cylinder and withdrew his finger covered with the luminescent blue light and he drew an X on his forearm and the X glowed blue as he raised it over his head.

A young woman with brown hair; she was in her thirties, maybe forties, wearing blue jeans and a dirty blue bra. She was sunburnt and she was kneeling between the bumpers of two mangled cars, puking into the sand.

The little girl was lying on the mattress, staring at the empty bathroom. Flies were lighting on her nose, walking across a sticky spot of vomit by her face. The fat man was reaching for her, picking her up in his arms, and he carried her outside and put her into the back of the truck. Then something covered her and it was dark.

She was lying facedown in garbage, there were voices and the sound of heavy trucks coming and going. A sliver of light appeared above her. Something ran across her back. Cold water hit her face. She felt ice cubes lodging next to her eyes, something orange in the air, the light above her opened wide and went dark again.

Sherry waited, but there was nothing more. She let go of the hand and was immediately turned and led back to the door. A minute later someone was helping her out of the suit and then she was taken barefoot to a sink where someone scrubbed her hand until it was raw.

Dr. Lynn was waiting for Sherry when she came out of the storage facility. "Well, did it happen?" the administrator wanted to know.

Sherry nodded numbly as they walked to the elevator. The doors opened, then closed.

"She was in a house trailer," Sherry said. "I could tell by the windows. How they were wrapped around the kitchen."

"Who was there?"

"A woman in her thirties, maybe older, she was sick. Her face was burnt red and she was vomiting in a junkyard."

"Describe her?"

"Brown hair, rings of tattoos around her neck and both wrists."

Dr. Lynn punched buttons on a phone and lifted the receiver. "Jeffrey, get Captain Forrest on the line." She hung up. "What else?"

"A man was in the house, an older man; he had a very large stomach. There was a huge woman, she was twice as big as the man, and there was a skinny teenage boy with his head shaved. He had swastika tattoos on his arms. The woman used drugs, a needle." Sherry demonstrated using her forearm and finger. "The boy was breaking open a metal canister of some kind. It had glass on one end, round and thick. He was showing the big man and two others the inside and it glowed blue. He touched whatever was inside of it and drew an X on his arm and the X glowed blue.

"There was a dog, it was black and brown. There was a fire, and a woman's red wallet on the ground beside it. I think her body was in that fire. The dog had a spiked collar around its neck. I saw a machine in the back of a truck. It was large like a refrigerator and it had pink plastic cushions on one side, like you could lie on it or something. I saw . . ."

"Why do you call it a machine?" the doctor interrupted.

"It had gauges on one end of it, some buttons and dials, and this arm that went up over the top like a crane."

"Sherry," she said. "This machine with the cushions on it. Do you remember what color it was?"

"Like a bluish green, the color of jewelry . . ."

"Turquoise?"

"Yes," Sherry said quickly. "Turquoise."

"Where was it?" Dr. Lynn's voice had elevated a notch.

"In the back of the red pickup truck," Sherry said.

"No, I mean where was the truck?"

"I couldn't tell. The man with the stomach picked up the girl and threw her in the back of the same truck. It was empty then. She was covered and later thrown facedown in a large container. There was garbage all around her. She felt ice melting against her face. There was darkness and light and then she died."

The phone rang and Dr. Lynn snatched it up. "Captain, the ranch is hot! Remember the radiotherapy unit that was stolen in El Paso? I think it's in the Spencers' scrap heap. Whoever had it must have broken into the cesium canister."

Dr. Lynn listened for a moment.

"Yes, absolutely. It could cause the same symptoms, pulmonary and internal hemorrhaging. I'm calling the army medical corps. Anyone who went in or out of those trailers is dead and anyone who touched them isn't far behind."

"Don't hang up!" Sherry said excitedly.

"Hold on," Dr. Lynn told the captain.

"The trooper who picked me up this morning," Sherry said rapidly. "She has it in her car. She ran over it last night. She got a flat tire and cut her hands on it. Her skin was burning up, she was sick in the stomach."

"Wait, wait," the doctor said, holding the receiver away from her ear. "What are you talking about? What's in what car?"

"The trooper who picked me up at the airport. She was assigned to sit on the scrap yard last night. The place you're talking about. She ran over this cylinder and she said it glowed blue inside. It was in her car when we were coming here. I touched it."

"Oh my God," the doctor said. "Did you get that, Jim? Your trooper, she's got the cesium canister in her squad car. Don't let anyone near the machine or the trooper, and whatever you do, don't let her get into her house."

"The glowing light," Dr. Lynn hung up the phone and turned toward Sherry. "You're sure it was blue?"

"That's what the trooper said."

"But you, how do you know you saw blue downstairs when you were holding that girl's hand?"

"I had sight until I was five. I know blue," Sherry said, scared. "What does it mean?"

"You described a radiotherapy machine that was stolen from our clinic in El Paso a month ago. The machine was obsolete; it was on a loading dock waiting to be removed, but it contains a small amount of radioactive cesium and can't be scrapped by just anyone. They were waiting for a licensed hazmat dealer to come take it to Texas."

"And you said radioactive poisoning would have similar symptoms to the hantavirus you described?" Sherry's heart was pounding in her chest.

"Yes." The doctor sighed, punching a button on the phone console. "Jeffrey, get CDC on the line, tell them we'll need doses of Prussian blue. Lots of doses!"

"How is it transferred?" Sherry began to rub the palm of her hand.

The doctor grabbed the hand and turned it over. "Touch," she said, "or through the respiratory system. You touched it, you said?"

Sherry nodded. "What's going to happen to me?"

"You're going to be treated. There's a substance that will clean the heavy metals from your body, and you weren't exposed all that long."

"Am I going to get sick?"

"Yeah, you're probably going to get sick. Flu symptoms, but they'll be gone in forty-eight hours."

The doctor stood abruptly. "Just what in the fuck did they think they were going to do with a scrap radiology machine? There are warnings all over it. How stupid can someone be?"

She put a hand on Sherry's shoulder. "We're going to fix you, but I want you in our hospital lab for a workup right now. You can maybe fly back to Philadelphia at the end of the week, as soon as you start responding to the medicine, but right now I've got to find the state trooper who picked you up, and anyone else who came in contact with that canister."

"Jeffrey!" she yelled, running out of the room.

Within a day Sherry was experiencing fever, nausea, and stomach cramps. Then the strangest lights began to swirl and sparkle in front of her eyes. And it wasn't as if she could shut her eyes and make them go away. While the condition was painless, it was most disconcerting, even with her unusual abilities. Sherry had always been aware that her condition, cortical blindness, was a state of the brain, not the eyes, and that on any given day the condition could reverse itself. But she knew this wasn't sight she was seeing.

Prussian blue, discovered in 1704, is a dye that when ingested can reduce the half-life of cesium 137 by two-thirds in as little as a month. Sherry had been told it was highly effective if the dye was administered immediately and if the patient had received only a small amount of contamination. The dye has chelating properties that can cleanse the tissue and muscle where predominant distributions of the cesium tend to inhabit, all but negating long-term effects. Her first installment of a month's worth of doses would arrive within twenty-four hours from the Centers for Disease Control in Atlanta.

• • •

Something was different about her. She just knew it. Something was changing in her brain and she wished she could make it go away. She wished she could go back and reconsider her decision to go to New Mexico. Her only consolation was that because of her, the female trooper who had picked her up at the airport was stopped before she could reach her home and expose the rest of her family. That she was put on early medication and stood a good chance of surviving. But Sherry's dream of a life with Brian? Well, until she knew more about her condition, she considered that on hold.

If only she could forget. Sherry had recently read online, via her specially adapted computer, an article about the concept of neurological reconsolidation. It was the process of strengthening existing synaptic connections in the brain and forming new synapses—both of which express certain genes—to prevent transportation of painful short-term memories to the archives of our mind. In short, erasing unwanted memories before they became permanently stored.

She had laughed at the time, thinking it wouldn't be long before her ability to read memories was replaced by science.

"Are you comfortable, honey?" A nurse marched into the room and stuck a thermometer in her mouth before she could answer. A second later she clipped an oximeter on her finger and yawned out loud. "Chilly in here—you want another blanket?"

Sherry nodded with the thermometer still in her mouth.

In spite of her pleas, Brigham and Brian were on a plane to Albuquerque before midnight. He said that he'd noticed the change as soon as he saw her. In addition to the flulike symptoms that came as promised, he could tell exactly when she was seeing the lights because she kept placing a finger against her right temple. Sherry hadn't noticed her involuntary reaction until he mentioned it, but, yes, she had been doing that a lot lately.

Now Brigham wanted her to get brain wave tests when she returned to Philadelphia, only to be cautious, he assured, but she should be certain that the exposure to radioactive isotopes hadn't contributed to something in her brain as well as to the all too real possibility of dying of bone marrow cancer ten or fifteen years later.

Brian was worried too, but she knew he had little idea how tumultuous her life had been before he came along. How this little peculiarity was but one more big peculiarity in a long, long string of peculiarities that had been vexing her in thirty-seven years of living.

Sherry Moore would have scoffed at the idea of more hospital tests a year before, arguing that she'd been treated like a lab rat for the last time. That she had been to the bottom and back, and was content to remain who she was. The reality was that no one could really explain what was going on in her brain and that it might be another fifty or hundred years before anyone was competent to try.

But Sherry didn't argue with Brigham, and in fact, to his surprise, she would finally agree to let Brigham take her to Nazareth the day she arrived back in Philadelphia.

Part of it, of course, was that Sherry didn't want Brian Metcalf thinking she was the hardhead she was. But Sherry had to admit she was actually scared. She'd experienced the odd malady over the years, and she had gone through the endless bouts of night terrors before. Sherry had an acute awareness of the myriad sensations in her mind. She was like a marathoner, very much in tune with her body. But this time she wasn't convinced one way or the other. There might be something just a little bit different this time. Something infinitesimal might have shifted. Something in New Mexico could have altered her brain.

Here in the hospital, with all this time to think, she began to feel cheated.

It seemed so wrong, she thought. That this should happen after thirty-odd years of living alone. After such a great weekend in Boston with Brian's parents, and then the romantic weekend in Delaware before that fateful call from New Mexico.

Sherry had found Boston quite the complex affair. Everyone going overboard to be nice to Brian's new blind girlfriend: parents, siblings, nieces, and nephews. Nice, though you knew you were constantly under the microscope and that a critique followed every act and every scene. But she had pulled it off, she was sure, and without a hitch. The weekend had gone fabulously and after that she was one step closer to . . . what?

Now that she'd been exposed to radiation in New Mexico, she couldn't help but wonder if everything had changed.

She had already lost one of the most important people in her life when a bullet felled Philadelphia police detective John Payne two years before. She had already survived a year of self-medicating in a haze of severe depression. Wasn't it enough to be blind and without parents? she lamented. Couldn't she find happiness without all the doubt and fear of drawing someone who was innocent into her world? Of becoming someone else's burden?

She could actually see now why some people choose the solitary life. It wasn't the life she wanted, but then people don't always get what they want. It would be selfish to misrepresent herself, to occupy the dream of another without knowing if she was going to live.

But why now? she kept thinking. Why had she let Brian Metcalf rekindle her heart?

In a week or so, Brian would leave for Little Creek, Virginia, where he would deploy to Kabul. Time apart would do them both good, she'd decided. Perhaps a relationship wasn't the be-all-end-all she'd imagined it might be. Perhaps fate had something else in store, and who was she to doubt the cards?

She heard familiar footsteps in the corridor, which stopped at her door. A polite knock, a gentle whisper.

"Sherry?"

She turned to face her neighbor and confidant. "Come in, Mr. Brigham," she said.

"I didn't know if you were sleeping." He put his coat on a hook behind the door.

"I was just thinking," she said.

Brigham kissed her forehead and took a seat between the bed and window. "What did he say?"

"Something's changed in the EEG, he thinks. He doesn't know what it means. They never do."

"You're not in pain?"

She shook her head. "I'm thinking I should just try to live with it."

"Which would be like me living with random bouts of blindness. Don't be silly," Brigham said. "You've come this far. Maybe it's a good time to take your friend the neurologist up on his offer. Dr. Salix has been trying to get you back on his table for some time."

"To screw around with my head a little longer."

"What could it hurt? The weather's still cold. You're on medication for another month and not missing a ray of sunshine, I promise."

"He'd need months to set it up."

"You know as well as I do, he'll drop whatever he's doing for a shot at getting you on his table."

Sherry smiled weakly. She could feel tears welling in one eye. "You'll make the call?"

"That's better," Brigham said.

"I'm just making up to you for all the times I've been stubborn."

"Like in Haiti," he said sternly.

"I'm especially sorry for Haiti, Mr. Brigham," Sherry said meekly.

"And well you should be." Brigham took Sherry's hand. "I'll call the doctor and see if he can scare up some cadavers for you to play with."

"Oh, don't make it sound like a party."

"Sherry," Brigham said seriously, "maybe it's only a side effect of the Prussian blue. Or have you ever considered that the changes you might be experiencing are sight and that your night terrors are real memories fighting to surface?"

Sherry pulled the bedcover to her chin. She dared not speak.

The doctors would continue to take blood and urine every week. Those tests would provide the earliest indications of how well the Prussian blue was sweeping the deadly radiation from her body. But blood and urine tests wouldn't tell her how much radiation had been absorbed into her lungs and bones. That would take four more weeks.

In a month or so Sherry would undergo a whole-body scan at Boston Medical Center. The gamma ray test would be the final word on how badly her soft tissue and bone marrow had been dosed by radiation.

How likely she was to get cancer.

3

New York State Psychiatric Hospital
Mount Tamathy, New York

Mary Brighton was scratching a lottery ticket when she heard the dull tone of a monitor sounding in Corridor A. It was almost 4 a.m. and she was alone on the second floor. The state hospital could hardly afford overtime, let alone auxiliary staff on the graveyard shift. She brushed gray flakes from her scratch ticket and trashed it with a sigh. Then she stood and punched a button on the console as she reached for the box beneath the counter and tugged on a pair of latex gloves.

"Security," a man's voice came over the speaker.

"Checking out our friend in 1400 again, Jerome." She snapped on one of the gloves. "You got the phones."

"You can't convince him to wait another hour?" the man said with a dry New York accent. "I'm watching M*A*S*H."

Brighton rolled her eyes and disconnected, maneuvering her considerable weight past the counter as she started down the hall toward the flashing light over Room 1400.

Thomas Joseph Monahan had been acting up all week, if you could call a seventy-six-year-old man who hadn't spoken in half a decade acting up. Heartbeat low, blood pressure high. His breathing went from shallow to panting like a dog. For six straight days he had been tripping the monitors and running nurses to and from his room.

The nurse entered the dark room, thumbed up the light switch, and stopped dead in her tracks. Monahan lay in his bed with eyes and mouth wide open. His cheeks were hollow, his arm leaning on the bed rail, a finger raised and pointing in her direction.

She tried not to look at him as she picked up his wrist, simultaneously reaching to silence the monitor's alarm.

For more than fifty years, she thought, the entire span of her life, this man had been living in this asylum. His file, thick as a New York phone directory, recorded not a word of where he had come from or his next of kin. In fact, besides the routine records and various procedures he had undergone over the years, there was only a yellowed Kennedy-era document authorizing the U.S. Department of Veterans Affairs to accept all bills.

Monahan's end would be little more remarkable than his life, she thought. He would go to cold storage in the basement and then off to some medical school where students got their first experience with a scalpel. That's where all the bodies with pink slips stapled to their jackets went.

4

Case and Kimble had put most everything on the line when they focused early earnings and resources on a birth control pill in 1960. Then they moved on to C&K's antianxiety silver bullet, distributed as Sentinal throughout the last quarter century. In the nineties they released their first erectile dysfunction pill that broke records on all world pharmaceutical markets. Billion-dollar profit makers like these served to stabilize the gargantuan pharmaceutical concern from damage incurred through economic depressions and class action lawsuits. But Case and Kimble had a heavily padded safeguard against risk, even in an unstable economy. They had the United States government's largest black-budget grant to a private company in all history, and they had maintained it exclusively and secretly for the past fifty years.

The entity was DARPA. The Defense Advanced Research Projects Agency. The ultrasecret project was MIRA, which until 2008 was the linchpin of American weaponry. So advanced was MIRA's artificial intelligence that MIRA could have application in nearly every aspect of war and war machines.

Except that suddenly the newly elected president wasn't behind the defense department administration's spending, talking about cuts so deep they might even excise ongoing MIRA development, and that was something Edward Case had never anticipated. More than thirty-eight billion dollars' worth of research over the last twenty years was about to be shelved.

To an outsider it would appear that pharmaceutical companies could afford to take risks, since the profits in prescription medications alone were simply staggering. But no one stuck his neck out like Edward Case in speculation research, and no one had the nerve to question the company's surviving founder until the board of directors learned about the White House position on defense spending. Now at risk of losing their seven-figure bonuses, they wanted to know on record why he had been pushing so much of the company's holdings into research on MIRA. They wanted it noted that the company was already teetering on the FDA's approval of Alixador, which had passed its own billion-dollar mark in genetic research last year. The board wanted it made clear to stockholders that they were only following the lead of their founder, and that perhaps they had been misled themselves concerning future approvals.

No one ever knew what some jury might decide about how death or impairment was related to one of their prescription medications. Subjective though it was, major awards and ripples of consumer anxiety were enough to rock a company, even one the size of Case and Kimble. And C&K's legal bills were anything but incidental. Edward Case had always insisted that the organization send a message that Case and Kimble wasn't an easy target for every law school graduate who managed to add Esquire to their name.

Now a dozen competitors had eclipsed the wonder drug Sentinal, and the U.S. Food and Drug Administration was calling for a review of its progeny, Xendoral, which had been implicated in dozens of suicides in the last two years.

C&K's stocks were on the decline in a deplorable economy, and CEO Ed Case was getting vibes from his board of directors that they wanted a public audit. They were worried about their own asses, of course, worried and feigning disapproval of his own sixty-two-million-dollar annual bonus in a recession with an unemployment rate rising over eight percent.

They wouldn't have said a word about it had the Democrats not taken over the White House. They wouldn't have dared to raise a hand when everyone's good fortune was riding on the wings of national security. The military's interest had long been piqued by Case's mind-control research, and indeed they had used it in the field with a high degree of effectiveness. But secret defense department funding would no longer escape scrutiny in a Democrat-controlled Senate, and Case's new renderings of microwave delivery systems could be first on the list of cuts.

Thank God for Alixador, he thought. Case knew what impact Alixador would have on Case and Kimble's bottom line next year. Alixador was going to be the biggest thing to hit the market since aspirin, and all it required was the FDA's approval.

A phenomenon of cellular research, Alixador was designed to trick the brain into believing the stomach was full. Alixador, touting well-established trials of men and women under sixty, boasted a seventy percent success rate in non-narcotic weight loss trials. It was the weight-loss miracle of the twenty-first century and it was going to fly off the shelves.

Case knew how badly he needed that FDA approval. It had been years since they'd had a mega drug on any market, and if the government pulled their defense contract, they were at the mercy of any new legal disaster that might come their way. Alixador was going to hit the market just in time to save him.

Case had personally handled settlements in more than thirty percent of Case and Kimble's legal cases over the past five years, doing everything in his power to keep Case and Kimble's name clean until their new diet phenomenon hit the market.

Just one more year, he thought, one more home run, and he would cash in options and bonuses and quietly slip away.

The engine of a John Deere tractor was popping on a distant hill. The sweet smell of cut hay lay heavy on the morning air. Ed Case watched steam rise on the dew-covered lawn behind his Lancaster, Pennsylvania, estate. The sun was large and pink and not an hour above the horizon.

He toggled his wheelchair in a half circle, making his way through a maze of ornate statues and urns. A servant was setting china on the patio for morning coffee. A young blond woman was doing laps in the pool.

Case's eyes searched fields of clover; he looked deep in thought, as if he were thinking about another time, another place.

"What's with this kid and the Regeral research?" Case coughed into a handkerchief balled in his left hand.

"First-year law student at Boston College," the young blond man walking next to him said. "He wants to get out in front of the game. Skip the hard work and get rich quick."

"Is he anybody?"

"Does he have connections, do you mean?"

"The kind of connections that matter," the old man said emphatically. "Family, friends, mentors, anyone? Anyone that could make a stink?"

"His father is an attorney in Boston. Corporate law. Divorced for the last ten years."

"How does he get his clients?"

"Teen websites, and hundreds of them. He leaves posts on blogs to suggest kids could get money if they took Regeral as children for attention deficit disorder and suffered side effects."

"Side effects," Case said flatly.

"Self-harm, loss of memory, failure to achieve, difficulty with authority, you know. The kind of stuff every kid suffers from. You can imagine the responses he's getting."

"How did we get onto him?"

"He sent a letter to our attorneys on his father's stationery. Quite an old partnership, State Street in Boston, you know the type. It was enough to concern one of them, but it took me all of an hour to figure out who sent it."

"Kids." The doctor snorted. "So it was blackmail?" He looked up at the younger man.

"His version, but rather pathetic."

"Who else knows about the letter?"

"Charles in legal. No one else."

Case stopped the wheelchair short of the patio, watching the woman climb from the pool. A servant met her with a bath towel that she slowly wrapped around her bikini.

"You'll have no problem getting next to him."

"Like taking candy from a baby."

"I want the records first," Case said abruptly.

"Understood."

Case looked up at the man next to him. Troy Weir was thirty-two, handsome, charismatic, brilliant, sociopathic. Case's only stepson from his marriage to Marlo Weir, a soap opera star who managed to traverse almost five decades before dying of alcoholism at age forty-six, Troy had been a troubled youth, in and out of jails and treatment centers since he was fourteen years old.

It had started out as fistfights at school, but then there was a sexual assault charge and then another, and soon Troy faced rape charges in the California juvenile system. Frankly, Case's stepson had all the common traits of a sociopath; chameleon-like, manipulative, charming, inwardly hostile with a sense of entitlement. Case could see the boy's earliest manifestation of the social disorder, as he stood before the judge, remorseful, meek, breaking down only when he mentioned his mother's alcoholism. The judge released him to the custody of his stepfather and recommended counseling.

A year later the girl who had accused him disappeared. Try as they might, no one could ever connect Troy to a crime. She simply vanished. And then the other girl's parents moved to another country.

In college there had been an accusation of date rape, but victims rarely remember the hours after they ingest Rohypnol. Rarely can they say how they had been given the drug. Prosecutors refused to present it.

Case was sure the stories were true, but by then Marlo's drinking was spiraling out of control and Case had been meeting with old friends about a new defense contract coming on line. Case was far too busy researching his way toward becoming a pharmaceutical magnate. He had no time for either of them.

After graduation, Troy escaped to New York City, and Case hadn't seen him until he showed up in Amagansett for his mother's funeral in 2001. What the boy did or didn't do during his time alone in the city, buffered by a substantial allowance, he didn't want to know. But it was there, at the funeral, that Case saw a change in the boy. He was only twenty-six, undoubtedly unchanged, but he had lost all the rough edges. He had learned to present himself properly in front of others. Whatever rage he bore was suppressed, and he spoke with a degree of class and refinement. Perhaps, the old man thought, he had acquired his mother's acting ability along with all that motherly hate.

Troy stepped onto the patio and nodded to the blonde. Wendy had been a model in her teens, yet became more beautiful with each year that passed. Case had surprised her on her twenty-seventh birthday—last month—with a trip to Cannes and a movie contract. Troy knew what that woman and her contract had cost his stepfather. Case had been courting her since his wife's death, and while the papers made much ado over the young woman's intentions with a decrepit old scientist, he was indeed widowed and entitled to see whomever he wished.

Troy knew she was loyal. Loyal like Troy's mother was loyal, because with Ed Case, there was no other choice. Loyalty was rewarded in the Case mansion and treachery was grounds for unspeakable retribution.

As a teenager he had only considered his mother's self-hatred and her low self-esteem, how she projected her extreme dislike of herself onto him and caused him to act out. She had had the opportunity to protect him, but chose instead to retreat into bottles and the beds of strange men.

Nothing had really changed over the years, only the way he reacted to her now. He still saw her in every dark bar and behind every sloppy smile and lipstick-smeared glass. He still reviled the weakness that made her vulnerable to all who'd chosen to use her. But now he understood why his father had refused to let her go. She was his first lady, and first ladies were never permitted to divorce midterm.

Edward Case had managed to become one of the world's most successful CEOs because he kept his house in strict order. There were no scandals for the tabloids. He was legendary for establishing a foundation that patronized the needs of America's war veterans. He was loyal to his wife and her son no matter what their personal excesses, and who in these times could hold the father to blame for the sins of the son or even his mother? When you were as clean as Ed Case you could hold hands in every White House, be it Democratic or Republican. And you could continue a sixty-year legacy of providing American's most secret weapons.

Wendy brushed past Troy and leaned to kiss Case on the cheek. Her towel came open, water beads falling from her breasts, blotting the arm of his Dolce & Gabbana shirt. "Are you joining us?" she asked, looking into Troy's eyes.

He shook his head. "Just leaving."

She pulled the towel from her shoulders and tossed it on the grass and sat at the table as the servant poured coffee.

Troy bowed courteously and left.

5

Attached to Sherry's head were a profusion of colorful electrodes, each connected to tubes that snaked their way into somber-looking machines. The gurney was stainless steel and felt cold through her flimsy gown. She had the sense she was in a station, about to depart on some futuristic trip. A trip she would be taking alone.

She remembered their last afternoon together. They had made love for an hour and then sat in the sunroom, taking in the last rays of the day. Brian had told her he was sorry that he wouldn't be around for her tests, that he couldn't postpone his deployment. Sherry had said she understood. That she knew it could be weeks before she heard from him again. What she didn't say was what she feared most. That the tests would find something and that she wouldn't be the same person when he returned.

Sherry grieved now that he was gone, but the time apart would do them both good. She couldn't risk becoming a burden on him. He would be hurt now, but in the end, she knew, it was what was best for him.

• • •

The light flashes from the migraines had been getting worse, not better. She was also beginning to see colors, bright purples, reds, and orange. Ophthalmic migraines were common, Dr. Salix told her, and many people reported shapes and colors similar to what she was seeing. It was caused by blood vessel spasms behind the eye. People who suffered cortical or cerebral blindness, as Sherry did, might still be candidates for migraines, because it was whole-brain injury, not just damage to the occipital lobes, that prevented her from seeing. In other words, it takes all components of the brain to see, and whole-brain changes that might have altered the order of delicate nerve systems might also permit vision behind the cornea.

Sherry was convinced she was reacting to the radiation she'd absorbed. The only question for her right now was whether or not she was the same person she had been before New Mexico. What effect did this radiation have on an EEG of her brain and thus her ability to read memories of the dead?

"We want to perform some tests before we get started," Dr. Salix said, looking down at her.

Getting started meant bringing in the cadavers.

"You remember the strobe? You've done this before. We're going to move the machine over you and see how your brain perceives the light."

Sherry nodded.

"If you sense something, if you feel anything—pain, nausea—I want you to signal me by raising a hand. Otherwise, lie still and I'll let you know when we're done. Are you ready?"

She nodded and wheels squeaked as a machine was rolled into place.

Something snapped in the hollow-sounding room—a switch, she thought. She felt a vibration and then it was as if there was pressure against her eyes, but she saw no light.

She heard a metallic noise behind her; someone was moving to her left.

"It's on?" she asked, but was quickly countered with a *shhhhh*.

"Just your hand, Sherry. Look, don't listen."

She wanted so badly to see something, a glimmer of light, anything. She needed an answer for what was happening to her. And if she couldn't give them an explanation by seeing lights, she just wanted to return to the state she had been in all these years. Blind.

The switch snapped off and the machine was wheeled away.

She could feel warm tears streaking down the sides of her cheeks. "I didn't see anything."

Someone laid a hand on her shoulder. "Which is not important," Salix said. "We're bringing in the first of the bodies now. Once we get her alongside you, I'll need your right hand. Are you doing okay?"

Sherry nodded.

Someone dabbed her cheeks until they were dry.

This part was familiar. More than two decades familiar. Her very first experience with a corpse had been as a child. A roommate in the orphanage in Philadelphia had swallowed a lethal dose of rat poison. It took years to understand what she had seen in that moment holding the dead girl's hand. Years more to accept that it was going to happen every time she touched the dead. That it was now a part of herself.

She wasn't the only skeptic during those early years and she certainly wouldn't be the last. How did you accept that you are a freak of nature? Or, as Mr. Brigham, her best friend and neighbor, liked to say, a very special human being?

Well, there was special and there was *special*. Could someone, much less she—a blind woman who had retrograde amnesia due to a childhood head injury—really exhibit aptitude for reading people's minds? In time it became impossible for the medical community to ignore what she appeared to be doing. They wanted to have their own look at this freak from Philadelphia. Then came the psychologists and neurologists, and on it went until a young biologist from the University of Calgary in Alberta suggested she wasn't clairvoyant at all. He believed instead that electrical anomalies in her damaged brain somehow enabled her to connect with the dead person's central nervous system through the profusion of skin cell receptors in the human hand. Her brain then used the deceased person's neurological wiring to reach their short-term memory located in the frontal cortex. She was actually seeing the last visually encoded memories of what the deceased person had been thinking about in their final seconds of life.

Once she got past the macabre sensation of holding hands with the dead, Sherry found fulfillment in what she was doing. Helping murder victims find their killer. Setting straight someone's last moments in life. Locating missing persons. Helping find artifacts that might have been lost to antiquity. She had seen images that would lead investigators to crime scenes. She had a purpose in life—perhaps even a responsibility.

But it wasn't always easy.

Sherry's mind recorded the collage of human memories that assailed her when she was touching a hand, including countless seemingly mundane events in a person's life, not important to anyone else, but special enough for them to remember in those precious few seconds before death. Residual memory, Sherry called it. Everything that happened before the power went off and the brain recorded its last thought. They had become her memories now as well, those remnants of a life: a particularly beautiful sunrise, a smile on an old woman's face, a child's teddy bear, a grandfather's cane. Memories were both God's gift and God's punishment, it seemed. You didn't want to live with them and you didn't want to live without them.

The gurneys were pushed together. Sherry's hand was lifted

and laid next to the cadaver. She found the fingers quickly, a small hand, delicate. There wasn't anything to be done after that. Sometimes the response was immediate; sometimes she drifted into it like a dream. It had never taken more than a few seconds and even now she saw . . . *the lights in a child's bedroom, no, it was a ward, some kind of a hospital ward, and it had bright colors and murals painted on the walls.*

Parents were sitting with their children on the floor. Shelves and boxes and baskets in the corners were filled with plush toys and games and books and videos. Nurses wore pink and blue and yellow scrubs with a hodgepodge of prints that included stars and moons and nursery rhyme characters. There was an ice cream cart in the hall outside the door. There was a girl in the bed next to her and her head was shaved and she was playing a video game in her lap.

She saw a nurse leaning to pick up a Popsicle stick next to her bed and she reached out to touch her, but her arm was too short, her fingers too weak to stretch. She opened her mouth but no sound came out. She felt as if she were trapped inside her body, capable of understanding but not of getting anyone's attention.

She wanted that girl in the bed next to her to turn and look at her, to see that something was wrong. She moved her eyes toward the ceiling, and then the wall and the window and to the bathroom door before going back to the girl.

Right there, just a foot away, the red button on the call harness. She only had to mash it with her thumb and nurses would come running.

She felt odd, as if someone had hold of her arms and legs and now they were pulling her inside of herself, folding her up like a piece of luggage, and with every minute that passed she was recessing deeper and deeper within, until the clown lamp began to dim and the girl in the bed next door faded to black.

Sherry let the hand go and sighed.

"You had an event?"

Sherry nodded, a tear streaking the corner of one eye.

She hated the labels people tossed around so casually over the years. Yes, she'd had an "event." *Is everybody happy with that? Just another dead girl, yeah. Just another event.*

"Did you see anything different?" Salix asked her. "Vision, quality of vision, anything we haven't talked about before?"

Sherry shook her head. "What about you?" she retorted.

Salix grunted loudly and moved to Sherry's shoulder. "You know I won't look at the EEGs for a few more days, Sherry. I want to compare your brain's activity against some of your earliest base examples. This is really important."

Salix had been working with Sherry for years. He knew not to treat her like a patient, but then again he didn't know what else to do but study her tests.

"We're looking for velocity changes, Sherry. Changes in the speed at which your cells release neurotransmitters. Perhaps even chemical changes in the hippocampus; I can't determine much until I have it all in front of me. We'll know more later."

"What if the results are different from before?"

He laughed softly. "I can't really say it will tell us anything new," he said. "You know that, but be patient." He patted her hand. "Let me do my job and be patient. We'll do one more cadaver today and talk about where to go from here."

She nodded grimly. It was all just a crapshoot, she knew. They didn't know what they were looking for, and even if they found something, they wouldn't know what to do about it. And she couldn't blame them. She was no different from the twelve thousand epileptics in Philadelphia who, for reasons beyond the ken of science, had electrical storms in their brains. It wasn't a matter of matching up the color-coded wires and then everything was all right again. No one had an owner's manual for the brain.

A few minutes later, a second gurney was wheeled into the room. She heard the wheels pivot into position and then it was pushed alongside hers. There was a moment of activity as the nurses and assistants reset something on the equipment wired to Sherry's brain. Then someone pulled back the sheet over the cadaver and she got a whiff of decay.

She thought about that machine in New Mexico just then. How stupid those people had been to steal a radiological machine and start prying apart interior canisters. Stupid or just woefully ignorant. She could imagine that poor child, now in the morgue, eating bread from a table dusted with radioactive powder. Breathing it into her lungs as she lay in her filthy bed. She'd heard they found the mother and father inside the trailer, both dead in the living room. The son was found in the desert, miles away, behind the wheel of his pickup truck. There was an X burnt into the skin of his forearm.

And then there were two Indians who had been at the table. They'd carried a capful of the blue powder back to the reservation and showed it to the children. Twelve more—some in the public school—came down with the flu in a week. Everyone who touched the men's clothing was infected.

In the end the incident claimed fourteen lives. Twenty-eight others survived with undetermined prognoses.

Salix took her hand and quickly bridged it to the next gurney, placed it gently across the cadaver's hand.

It was a man's hand, the skin was slack—*did the room temperature suddenly rise?* He was an older man, she thought, seventies, perhaps eighties. The fingers were long but the hand itself was narrow, infirm as if the muscles had atrophied. Whoever he was, his hands had not been active for some time.

She closed her own hand around it and then her eyelids, aware of the wire harnesses pressing against her shoulder. . . .

She was in a room with white walls, a projector behind a hole in a wall was showing a grainy video of a child running naked between two thatch-covered huts; three dark-skinned women wearing cone straw hats were sitting nearby under the shade of a palm tree.

One of them was stirring something in a bowl. Another's hands appeared to be flailing in animated conversation.

Suddenly the child stopped and pointed at the sky. A moment later there was a blinding white light. The child stood in perfect silence, as if the world had suddenly come to a halt. The women and the child turned black against the white background, as if you were looking at a negative of the image. Then a hurricane-like wind obliterated everything with sand and debris. When the wind was gone there was no village, no child, no women, no tree, nothing but flames that licked the bare earth.

He was sitting at the end of a long wooden table. There was a gun in front of him within reach. He looked at the door and then at the dusty light coming from the projector through the hole. He turned and saw a dirt road on the wall. He was looking over the hood of an open-top jeep. There was a woman on the road in front of him, young, she was wearing a khaki-green uniform with Red Cross patches on the sleeves. Her shoes were missing. Her legs were spread wide and staked open, her arms held out from her sides as if on a cross. A hand grenade was pinched between her teeth, a string tied to the handle and the handle to the neck of a water buffalo standing over her. The jeep stopped, the buffalo stepped away, and she could see hands waving in front of the lens, gesturing for the animal to stay still. The buffalo shook its big head and snorted, went down on its front knees as if to pray, and then sprang sideways, leaping into a gallop. The string came taut and a red mist replaced the medical corps woman's face.

A bead of perspiration ran down Sherry's cheek; she could feel sweat forming on her scalp, itching under the hair. *God, it's warm.*

There was a metal box at the far end of the table, slits for air vents on top and a round white gauge at left front. There was black mesh cloth covering two cones facing him. They appeared at times to be vibrating. He turned his head to look at the door. "Can't . . . on, can't . . . on." Sherry started to say it out loud, "Can't . . . on, can't . . . on . . ." *Someone was looking at him through a glass ob-*

servation window in the door, a man with a white hat, and there was smoke rising around his face, distorting his features. He was smoking a pipe.

"Help me," he called to the man behind the door.

Sherry's lips continued to move; can't . . . on, can't . . . on, can't . . . on . . .

He looked down at the gun in front of him. His hand moved toward it as his eyes darted back to the white dial. "Can't . . . on, can't . . . on . . ."

He saw a man in a fishing boat with an open cabin. There were rectangular wire cages in the stern tied to dozens of battered cork buoys. He saw the man kneel and reach into the hold and come up with a rifle and start shooting at him.

There was a grinning soldier, American, sitting at a crude wooden table in a room. There were enemy soldiers all around him. A rifle pointed at his head. There was a gun on the table in front of him, just like the gun on the table in this room. He picked it up and put it to his head and pulled the trigger and his head jerked sideways and he fell to the floor and the soldiers were smiling at the camera and laughing.

Five, ten, fifteen, twenty, twenty-five, thirty, twenty-five, twenty, fifteen, ten . . .

There was a dirigible floating just above his head—it was massive—approaching a tall steel tower. There was lightning and the dirigible caught fire and exploded in a ball of flame. People were falling from everywhere, charred black people, and the people on the ground were catching on fire as the debris fell.

He looked away from the wall and tried not to watch, but voices kept telling him not to turn away, voices not from the cone-shaped objects or the hole in the door but from in his head, his own head, and they would not let him look away.

There was a young girl. She was wearing a sailor's cap and red lipstick. She was wearing a white shirt tied above her stomach and red pedal pushers. She was smiling at him and waving and a friend, another brunette, ran up next to her and was pushing an elbow in her side.

He forced his eyes down. Something was burning his skin on the arm of the chair. The gun on the table had a cylinder and he could see the ends of the shiny brass cartridges in the chambers. It was a six-shot revolver, double action, it had no safety, required no effort but to point the barrel and pull the trigger.

Thirty, twenty-five, twenty, fifteen, ten . . . there were wet spots on the table next to the revolver, beads of perspiration that had fallen from his cheeks. He didn't want to watch the girls on the wall, he didn't want to know what the shadows coming up behind them were.

There were marks on the table by the gun, grooves cut into the wood, the scars from someone's thumbnail that had been carved into the wood. He put his thumbnail in one and rocked it back and forth. His fingers were only inches from the revolver, it was shiny and he wanted to pick it up, pick it up and end it all . . . ten, five, zero, thirty, twenty-five, can't . . . on, can't . . . on.

It was dawn and he was awakening from sleep. He was covered with mud and lying on his side on the ground. There was an open-bed truck with the rear end facing him. It was full of corpses and next to the rear tire soldier helmets had been stacked. Next to the helmets were web belts and canteens and gas masks. A man wearing rank and chaplain corps insignia was putting his hands on each of the bodies. He rolled to look away, then he looked down, pulling a green leather-bound journal closer to his body.

Can't . . . on, can't . . . on, can't . . . on, can't . . . on, can't . . .

"Sherry?" Dr. Salix shook her shoulders roughly. "Sherry!"

Her eyes fluttered, but remained shut. Sherry could hear words, but they were far, far away. Suddenly she saw something pink, blue orbs floating in space, dark caverns that oddly reminded her of a nose and she felt as if she were falling through a soft warm light and the light would protect her. She was aware of the old man's hand. She could still feel the energy coursing between them. It wasn't over.

There is a riddle, she thinks, something she must solve. "Can't . . . on, can't . . . on," she repeated, thinking it would be dangerous to say anything else, to say the wrong thing.

"Sherry, it's Dr. Salix."

"Monahan," she said suddenly. "Thomas J., private first class, serial number 7613779 . . ."

"Sherry! Sherry Moore, I want you to focus on my voice. I want you to concentrate on the date. Tell me what day it is?"

"Can't . . . on, can't . . . on . . ."

"Sherry," he said sternly. "Tell me what day it is. Think about the day."

"Thanksgiving." She began to falter. "Can't . . . on, can't . . . on . . ."

"Sherry, you're in a hospital. You are in Philadelphia. Do you remember Philadelphia? That I'm Dr. Salix?"

She shook her head no, distrustful.

"Sherry!" he said, turning and pointing toward the ceiling. "Somebody, give me some light!" he yelled and one of the technicians turned on the overhead surgical lights.

He thumbed open one of Sherry's eyelids and she let out a bloodcurdling scream.

6

Garland Brigham sat in his favorite rocking chair in front of Sherry's gas fireplace. His work boots lay by the door with his old U.S. Navy peacoat. He had propped his wool socks on the hearth to warm. Sherry reposed on a couch.

He sipped coffee and watched her reaction to the front page of the newspaper he'd brought. He had been working in his yard most of the morning, organizing the woodpile and raking last winter's leaves from beneath the rhododendrons.

"The fire feels good," she said, turning toward Brigham. She tried to dry her cheeks with the fingers of both hands.

It was June, but the unseasonably cold nights held a chill within the heavy stone walls of Sherry's house on the Delaware.

He stood and leaned toward the coffee table, pushing the tissue box a few inches closer. She pulled one out and dabbed her face.

"Hurt?"

"Still tearing a lot. The light hurts."

"So don't overdo it, Sherry. Put your glasses back on."

She made a face and did, feeling remotely silly. The glasses were as big as ski goggles and wrapped around the sides of her face.

"Better?"

She nodded.

Sherry turned to face him. The room was blurred and smoky gray. She knew now that the small mark on the breast pocket of Brigham's plaid shirt was a polo pony. He had also explained the anchor carved on the buttons of his peacoat and the tiny scar that split one of his eyebrows. She couldn't see things clearly for any length of time, but Dr. Salix warned that her eyes were still weak and would take time to gain strength.

She closed her eyes and waited for the headache to recede. Then she squinted to watch the flames, more shadow than light as they danced beyond the lenses, never the same way twice, and she found them mesmerizing. How amazing, she thought, to put an image to the sounds and sensations around her.

"I can go outside." She studied Brigham for his reaction.

He nodded. "I know."

"Will you show me your house soon?"

Brigham shrugged. "Sure. When are you going to answer Brian Metcalf's calls?"

"You have photo albums, wedding pictures. I want to see what you looked like when you were young."

He made a face. She kept steering away from the subject.

"Mr. Brigham," she said sternly. "Let me worry about Brian and you show me the photographs."

"If you insist." He yawned and reached to test the toes of his socks and found them dry. "But not today. Maybe this weekend."

"You don't seem very happy about it."

"I'm never happy when you strong-arm me. What did you think of your picture in the paper?"

Sherry reached for the coffee table and picked up the *Inquirer*, tossing it irritably next to the tissues.

"It doesn't look like me."

"Pictures never do. Get used to it."

Sherry scratched a fingernail across the fabric of the sofa, watching the lighter image of her hand as it moved beneath the dark glasses on her face. "I'm sorry, Mr. Brigham, but I have to find out who he was. I want to meet his family."

"They don't give out that kind of information, Sherry."

"They certainly could. I don't want his Social Security number, for crying out loud. I want to call his wife, his children, anyone."

"You know what you saw on that table wasn't all that pleasant. You said it yourself. Something was very wrong about the man before he died."

"And yet it changed me, Mr. Brigham. I let go of his hand and I opened my eyes to see for the first time in thirty-two years! What in the heck do you do with that? How do you move on without acknowledging the miracle?"

"The man was preoccupied with death and still thinking about it fifty years after the fact. That's a little nuts, Sherry."

She shook her head firmly. "We don't know that. He was in a vegetative state. Maybe it's all he ever remembered about anything."

"All right, we'll ask Dr. Salix on Tuesday—will that satisfy you?"

"His nurse called to change the appointment. It's Monday at four, but don't change your plans. I want to go there myself."

"Sherry," Brigham said sternly.

"Really," she said. "I mean it."

Brigham looked at her, nodding, thinking she was even more pigheaded with sight.

"Where are we going for dinner?" she said happily, hoping to lighten the mood.

"Do you still feel up to it?"

"I've got to get out of this house."

"Well, it depends on what you want to eat."

"Something red," she said.

"Spaghetti?"

She shook her head, whipping her hair from side to side.

"Lobster?"

She clapped her hands. "Yes!"

"You've got to stop grinning like that!" Brigham said. "People will think you're daft."

"I'll be good, I swear," she said. "I won't stare, I won't ask questions, and I promise not to look surprised by anything."

Brigham rolled his eyes. "Promise to wear your glasses."

"Not these," she said. "One of my other pairs."

"Fine. We'll wait till dark, but you must wear something."

"Can we watch a movie when we get home? Please, please?"

"I've inherited a five-year-old," Brigham grumbled, getting to his feet. "I'll be back for you in a couple of hours. Why don't you close your eyes and go to sleep?"

Sherry reached for his hand and he took it and squeezed before continuing on to the door.

"Did you know my bathroom soap is green?" She giggled.

Sherry knew she had to take it slow. The doctor wanted her to wear eye patches five hours a day—to force her eyes to rest. She was down to two hours, and Brigham was sure she was pushing the envelope, as always. He was worried about her. She was worried that whatever radiation she had been exposed to in New Mexico would affect the already tenuous wiring of her brain.

Sherry wasn't sure what to think of the miracle of sight.

The experience, for better or worse, was a little disconcerting after thirty-two years. There was more to seeing again than just strengthening fibrous muscles that navigated the eyeballs around a crowded street or room. Sherry had to learn how not to be blind, how to abandon the instincts she had so long ago developed and honed and come to trust. She needed time to get her equilibrium under control. Suddenly she was relying on an entirely new means of navigation and she was tripping and bumping into things that she normally would have avoided. She also needed to practice being skeptical, she'd told herself, not to rely entirely on the presentation of things, on the world as it seemed.

Dr. Salix had never come right out and said it, but he didn't have to. It was possible that she would regain her vision in its entirety. It was equally possible, however, that one day she might be drying her hair and look up to find she was no longer in the mirror. There were no guarantees that she would continue to see. There were no guarantees that she would be alive in the morning either. Who knew better than she how quickly things could be taken from you in this world?

So she didn't yet dare to accept its permanency. Not yet and perhaps not for some time. It had been thirty-two years, after all, since she'd last seen a thing.

And that was okay, she told herself. Part of living practically was having the knowledge that whatever happened today was good enough. She would plan for the best and she would be positive, but only by tempering her elations daily. There were no more long-term plans for Sherry Moore.

Suddenly she thought of the empty shelves in her library. She must get books for that room. She must fill the empty shelves with colorful old books and then she would try to read as many as she could before her eyes went dark or she died.

She tapped the key on the computer, the screen came to life, and she spoke her name and the date.

A list came up and she listened to the choices, stopping at last with a video from MSNBC. She was in the news again. Front page of the *Philadelphia Inquirer* and headline cable news.

"They were calling it a minor miracle in Philadelphia last week. Blind celebrity psychic Sherry Moore is said to have regained full sight during a routine neurological test at Nazareth Hospital last Tuesday. In a prepared statement given just minutes after she was photographed leaving the hospital, Dr. William Salix confirmed that Moore has been totally blind for the past thirty-two years. Salix said that Moore's condition was the result of head trauma received as a child, a condition known as cerebral blindness. While there are no statistics to support that Moore is truly a miracle case, Salix says he knows of no other patient who has recovered sight after such a long period of time. Cerebral blindness, according to Salix, results from trauma to the occipital cortex. Victims of cerebral blindness are left without sight, but their pupils appear normal and actually fluctuate in varying degrees of light. Moore received national attention in 2006, when . . ."

Sherry turned the volume down and swiveled her chair to face the windows. The boughs of tall cedars bounced lightly in the breeze. There was a tugboat on the river and it was pulling a barge well behind it. She had heard the mournful moan of its horn dozens, perhaps hundreds, of times before. But now she was actually seeing the water ripple around its bow, right down to the pale green froth of its wake.

She turned back to the computer and touched another key. There was just one other nagging uncertainty that had come with her "minor miracle," and it had been bothering her since the moment she had opened her eyes. From the moment she had seen the blurred face of Dr. Salix in the operating room and screamed. Had sight come at the sacrifice of her longtime friend?

Did she still have the gift of second sight?

"Adult literacy," she said to the screen. "Private tutors, Philadelphia."

She scrolled through a dozen listings and listened to each description. After fifteen minutes she stopped and spoke a phone number that the computer dialed.

She thought about the cadaver on the table once more—his

hand, the texture of his skin, the terrible feeling she had watching those images. She thought it unusual that his last memories were trapped in the last century. She might not have been surprised if he had had no memories at all. He was in a coma, after all. Time might have cleansed the slate of short-term memory. She had a feeling from the images she had seen, the wind and flames, the woman staked in the road, that they had been played and replayed until they were frozen in his mind. His thoughts had ended in that room some fifty-odd years ago. She could still see that man behind the door, the box on the table, the gun by his hand. It was sad that he'd never thought of his parents, his siblings, or a wife when he died. It was rare that life parted from the body before retrieving some millisecond of someone loved. Only the boy in the trenches by the truck, the heaps of dead bodies, the chaplain, the helmets, and canteens seemed real. He had been there, she was sure. He was that boy with the green book.

She wondered too about the strange words she had spoken during her test. There was no image to go with them. They had bored into his mind, but from where? The words *can't* and *on* meant nothing out of context, so what was he trying to say? Can't *go* on? Can't *live* on? And the name she repeated. Monahan, Thomas J. Was it his? There was just no way to know.

"Jonathan David," the voice answered.

"Yes, Mr. David, I noticed your ad for literacy services. Private tutoring? Is that correct?"

"It is," the man said stiffly.

"I was impressed with your qualifications. Are you taking on new clients?"

"I have two days open a week."

"You're in Philadelphia."

"The city," he said, ruling out suburbs, which he must have found offensive.

"Perhaps we could meet. I'm a member of the Athenaeum," she said. "I could meet you there for an interview."

"The Athenaeum," he repeated. "It would have to be on Tuesdays and Fridays, both at three o'clock." He coughed. "If things work out I am to be paid on the date of each session, only before, not afterward."

Sherry had to remind herself she was looking for a qualified tutor, not a friendly chat over tea.

"Tuesday it is," she said. "Three o'clock."

They exchanged descriptions and settled on a location. She laid down the receiver and felt as if her world was about to take a new turn.

She had been given a wake-up call. And with it a window of the world she lived in.

From now on, she solemnly vowed, she would live in the here and now.

For Sherry Moore there were no more tomorrows.

7

Terry Simpson opened the door to his rented room, tossed his backpack on the floor, and kicked off dirty Nikes. One of them landed on a threadbare recliner, the other scattered flies from an open pizza box on the floor.

A roach ran across a radiator. A pay phone rang in the hall. He picked up an envelope that had been pushed under the door and threw it on a stack of *Playboy* magazines and campus newsletters.

He crossed the room and opened the refrigerator, snapped a Budweiser from a six-pack, and grabbed a half-eaten stick of pepperoni.

There was a note on a stained carton of Chinese food that read JAMIE'S KEEP OUT!

He slammed the door and walked to the window. He probably wouldn't remember much of Boston at all. A couple of girls—Jenny Stewart was really hot—but then Jenny was a second-year and interning at a city clinic on weekends, and who had time for all that crap?

He wiped pepperoni grease on his jeans and crossed the room to a frameless single bed with stained yellowed sheets. He peeled off his socks and let them fall by a keg tap snaking under the box spring. There were copies of opened letters and new schoolbooks under the bed.

He snatched a glossy brochure for a BMW from the desk by his side and rolled on his back, studying the interior of a roadster. Next week? Next month? Soon, he was sure. Soon his plan and all the hard work he had done would come to fruition. Two more weeks of fall semester partying and then one day the phone would ring and he would suddenly be a millionaire. What could any school possibly teach someone like him?

He tossed the brochure and pressed Power on the remote.

He flicked through channels to MTV and arched his back, unzipping his jeans and yanking them off to join the dirty laundry on the floor.

He lay in his boxers and chugged down more of the beer. Was it the third or fourth of the morning? Who cared? He'd rather nap here in his bed than in Connie Collins's constitutional law class.

The noon bells chimed from St. Mary's. He wondered how much a diamond stud earring like Randy Moss's would cost. He wondered what his classmates would say the day he parked his new convertible in front of the dorm and scribbled a check in the name of Elmer Fudd for the creepy fuck of a landlord who lived in the basement.

He reached for a sheet of paper on his desktop and held it up in front of him. *Simpson, Washburn and Shonik* was embossed across the top with an address on State Street. That would have gotten their attention, he knew. And if it didn't, the enclosed Excel spreadsheet would. It was but a fraction of the 709 names he'd collected, along with dates and symptoms of side effects of Regeral taken by teens for attention deficit disorder. There were even some names and dates of deaths that he had read about online. He didn't need to prove a case. Not even one. He didn't need any courtroom experience. Real lawyers didn't go to court. They settled.

All he needed was one legitimate complaint, even the fear of there being one legitimate complaint, and with his vast collection of potential plaintiffs the pharmaceutical giant Case and Kimble would be groveling at his feet, doing whatever they could to quell a class action suit.

He had suggested in the letter that his firm wanted no part of a protracted battle over the drug Regeral, but that it had an obligation to its client. If only there were some common ground between them, they might be able to put the matter to rest. The time and expense of researching similar cases could be forgotten, the documents destroyed. If his client could be compensated for a life in which he would never live up to his potential, things might be different. A low seven-figure number should be satisfactory, he wrote audaciously. My client wants only to get on with his life.

He snickered and tossed the empty beer can at the trash and missed. He put his feet up on the wall and looked at the cracked green ceiling, a daddy longlegs, a pencil someone had stuck through the drywall. How unbelievably simple life was, he thought. All you needed was some imagination and the balls to do something about it. He wasn't going to lick envelopes for some ass-wipe judge as a law clerk and he certainly wasn't going to take the bar only to wait in line for shit ambulance cases as a public defender. No, that was how his father had begun his life. He was going to have his BMW now. He was going to start out where his old man was finishing off.

He closed his eyes and rocked his head to the beat of the music, swiping at something annoying his ear, feeling good, feeling warm, feeling like the beer buzz was coming on fast.

Oh, God, that Jenny Stewart was so hot. No one came close to getting into her pants last year, or at least that was the word around the campus. Terry had walked up and talked to her a few times, but she wasn't interested. She kept to herself, dressed fashionably, though a little more conservatively than the other girls, and, unlike the other girls, looked like a million dollars without trying. You just knew she was going to be driving a hot car one day and have homes in the Hamptons and the Grand Cayman Islands. He'd like to see the look on her face when he made his first million dollars. Like to wipe a C note on his crotch and stick it down the front of her snobby bitch blouse. He'd like to see her end up like the blonde in the horror movie he watched last summer. Parents' house burning to the ground, family inside and dying, she lying half naked in a puddle in the street as water rained down from a broken fire hydrant. And then the utility pole snapped and crackling power lines started to fall down on her.

Sweat began to bead on the back of his neck. He wiped it and then felt the tickle in his ear again. Why did he suddenly think of that movie? He'd told everyone how lame and juvenile it was and now he couldn't get it out of his mind.

He sat up feeling lightheaded. He stared at his dirty toenails. Next to them the marks in the carpet where the pedestals of his computer tower had once sat. Had someone moved it while he was out?

He leaned over to take a look.

No one cleaned the room for him and his roommate had his own computer in the bedroom. It couldn't have been him. The thing had sat here since his parents had dropped him off in August and he sure as hell hadn't moved it himself.

He thought about a file of porn he kept on the desktop and then he remembered the list of supposed Regeral victims.

"Jesus, no way," he whispered. He got down on his knees and looked around the back side of the computer. The back plate was gone and the hard drive was missing!

Could Case and Kimble have sent someone to steal it? Sure, his computer required a password to get in, but that would be little more than a nuisance to Case and Kimble.

Or maybe it wasn't Case and Kimble themselves that broke into his room. Maybe they only figured out who he was and complained to the school? Would the school have come into his room and taken his hard drive? No, he thought not. Not even the cops could come into his room without a warrant.

Oh Jesus, Lord, he thought. What in the fuck is happening here? What in the fuck have I gotten myself into?

He ran to the stack of magazines by the door and ripped open the letter that he'd found on the floor. It was nothing. Just the landlord's fucking bill; he crumpled it in a ball and tossed it aside.

He walked to the window slowly, noticing the curtain had been pulled back and was hooked behind the speaker wire he had running to a corner of the ceiling. Had he done that?

He could see the apartment building across the street and the blank panes of glass over a dozen windows. He could see a shadow sitting behind the wheel of a black van in the Methodist Church parking lot.

He shook his head. This was too weird for words. Was someone fucking with him?

He felt the tickle at his ear again and swiped it once more with the side of his hand, and this time when he withdrew his hand he saw blood on the pad of his thumb.

"Jesus." He started to stagger, sticking his finger in his ear, and it made a wet sucking sound when it came out.

His stomach constricted and his scalp began to tingle. He looked at the blood on his finger and slowly turned toward the kitchen.

Now, as the room began to move, he put a hand out to steady himself and fell against the computer monitor, driving a corner into the old drywall and cutting a hole in it. He righted himself, took a step sideways, and a drop of blood smacked his toes. Then another hit the carpet and another his left foot. He felt the wet stream on his upper lip and tasted the coppery blood when he opened his mouth. Blood was pouring from his nose.

The bathroom mirror, he thought, staggering ahead through the kitchen. He needed to get to the bathroom mirror and see what was wrong. One foot, then another—the beer couldn't have done this! Halfway across the living room floor a wave of nausea doubled him over. What about the pepperoni? Had he been poisoned?

"Wow," he thought, brushing sweat from the back of his neck. Maybe he'd just had too much to drink. Maybe he'd fallen and hit his head last night and not remembered?

A horn honked and he heard laughing—kids on their way to the campus—and then there was nothing. The world went completely silent to his ears.

He stood up and the pain in his stomach was gone. Everything seemed so clear after that, as if a door had opened and all the world's knowledge were there for the taking. And when he could hear again, the voices were as clear as if they'd come straight from his own head.

He walked to the kitchen and took a screwdriver from the junk drawer. In the pantry, he slowly removed the gray safety plate from around the circuit breaker panel.

He went to his roommate's bedroom and kicked away the dirty jeans and underwear until he could pry open the closet door, then grabbed a metal ski pole that he grasped at both ends and brought down hard against his knee, snapping it in two.

Then he carried the broken pole back to the pantry and shoved the metal pole into a mass of bare wires in the circuit breaker box.

The bulb under the coach light at the front entrance exploded, spraying two pedestrians on the sidewalk with glass. The sound of a vacuum cleaner upstairs went silent. Every light in the building went dark.

Someone cursed and pounded a wall in the room directly

above, but Terry couldn't hear anymore. He was kneeling head down, in front of the electrical panel, still holding the metal pole as 220 volts of electricity surged into his body.

His hair began to smolder, then smoke. He had fouled himself. His skin was literally beginning to crisp by the time he teetered and crashed to the ground.

Somewhere a battery-powered smoke detector began to chirp.

8

PHILADELPHIA

"I don't quite know what to say, Sherry." Dr. Salix crooked his neck and squinted into his ophthalmoscope. He swept it across the retinas of her eyes. Finally he laid it down and shook his head. "I still can't explain it."

"And that's it? That's all you can say." Sherry laughed.

"I say let's just not question it anymore."

Sherry looked at him, blinking away the thick drops he had put in her eyes, dabbing at the corners with tissues.

"Yeah, easy for you to say."

"Your eyes are healthy, Sherry. They always have been. Call it what you like, but your vision is coming back and I think nicely. In two or three weeks you should be able to stop wearing the dark glasses completely." He shrugged and knocked on his desk twice. "What else can I say?"

"Okay, I have two other questions."

"Shoot," he said.

"Radiation? Is there any possibility my sight has something to do with what happened with the radiation?"

He shook his head. "Not a chance, I would see it in the corneas of the eyes. If anything the exposure would have caused cataracts. Look, Sherry, it sounds to me like your exposure was minimal. They got iodine in you in time. The Prussian blue is sure to cleanse your soft tissues. Who knows, maybe there's been no damage. Maybe you'll do better than hoped with your bone marrow, too."

Sherry nodded and looked at her hands. "One other thing."

The doctor nodded.

"The donor I touched. I want to know something about him."

"They only put ID numbers on the cadavers." Salix shook his head and put his records away. "Even I don't know his name."

"But you can find out where he came from?"

"I'm afraid not, Sherry. Anonymity is the underpinning of any donor program."

"Doctor." She waited until his eyes met hers. "I've been persuaded for fifteen years to let people poke around my mind when I would rather have said no."

Salix, of course, must be sure that she was speaking of him. That she'd made herself available for countless tests against donors whose corpses were also unknown.

"I understood when scientific questions seemed to outweigh my desire of privacy, so now I am simply asking the reverse. My interest is harmless. I only want to know his name and where he came from. You said yourself that radiation wasn't the reason I can see. So this man, I have to believe, is somehow responsible, Dr. Salix."

Salix raised a hand to protest the suggestion, but Sherry would have none of it.

"I know you don't believe it started on that examination table. I know that you think I was having eye migraines because my sight was returning, but I know myself better than that. What happened in there happened while I was on that table. It happened because I touched that man's hand."

She placed her hands on her knees.

"Dr. Salix, we aren't talking about a transplant here. I'm not walking around with this man's eyes or heart in my body. I just want to know who his family is. I just want to know something about him."

Salix pulled the tie free from his collar, undoing the top button of his shirt.

"Is this about your eyes, Sherry, or is this about the stress you are under?"

Sherry looked at him.

"I understand there is a new man in your life. A serious relationship."

Damn, Brigham, Sherry thought. She had left him alone with Brigham in the waiting room.

"You're trying to diagnose yourself, trying to find answers that aren't there. I know what's going through your mind, Sherry. You're worried about the gamma ray tests. Will you have cancer five years from now or not? Will you be able to see five years from now or not? Give it a rest, Sherry. None of us get answers."

"No more rest," Sherry said determinedly.

"I'm sorry." Salix looked at her curiously.

"No more rest," Sherry said flatly. "I'm just trying to come to terms with all of it. Believe me, I'm not angry, I'm not depressed, I'm not even sad. I'm happy with my life and how it turned out and I'm thankful for whatever time I have with these eyes. My goal in life now is to appreciate each day and what it gives back. I intend to be happy with that alone, Doctor. That and nothing else."

"Sherry—"

"And I never want to hurt anyone, including your body donor, Doctor Salix. Please just let me thank the family."

He looked at his watch and scanned a list of phone extensions taped to the blotter.

He punched a button on the phone and a moment later a woman answered.

"Con, it's Bill, you got a moment for me?"

Sherry watched his face.

"Yeah, it's about a donor"—he flipped through some manila folders on his desk—"one-eight-seven-seven-six. Is there any chance he had an EEG on record? I'm trying to rule out something here."

A moment later he looked at Sherry and cupped a hand over the receiver. "I get the name, you make the call."

"Deal," Sherry said.

Salix uncapped the phone, but then a quizzical look came over his face. "There has to be a history," he said to the person on the other end of the line. "What did they intend to do without it?"

He sat on the edge of his desk and looked down at his shoes swinging in the air. "All right, who is he and where did he come from?"

Salix listened, then rolled his eyes. "Yes, I know the rules, humor me."

A moment later Salix started scribbling across a prescription pad.

He hung up the phone and tore a sheet off, handing it to her. "That should explain it," he said.

"Explain what."

"T is for Thomas J. Monahan, the name you called out on the table, was a resident of the New York State Psychiatric Hospital from 1950 until last week. Any more questions about the strange things you saw?"

Salix took a prescription pad from his pocket and scribbled something. "I want you to put drops in your eyes twice a day and I want to see you back here in a week."

"Not a problem," Sherry said. "I appreciate it."

Salix looked at her. "Listen to what I told you. He was in a mental ward, Sherry. You know what I mean? Don't go getting yourself worked up over nothing."

"I don't care about that. I still want to talk to his family and I'll tread lightly. I just feel like I owe them something."

"You are a stubborn, stubborn woman," Salix said.

"What day?"

"Make it Tuesday afternoon. Same time, but you have to come to the hospital, not my office. I'll squeeze you in between patients."

"I'll be there," Sherry said.

Sherry stopped at McDonald's for a cheeseburger and milkshake. Afterward she took a cab to Rittenhouse Square and sat on a park bench, wondering why people ate fast food.

The sun broke through the clouds and shadows danced across the sidewalk. New buds clung to the trees. She closed her eyes and heard sirens a few blocks away, seagulls over the river.

New York State Psychiatric Hospital. He was in a mental institution. And the only memories he had were of his youth. Which meant what? That he'd been comatose for fifty-eight years? Was that even possible? And was he mentally ill or not? Maybe he had some brain injury from the war?

She looked up at the trees and closed one eye, waiting until the edges of the uppermost branches became clear. Then she pressed 411 on her cell phone; it took two rings to be connected.

A moment later an operator connected her with the New York State Psychiatric Hospital.

A woman answered. "Please hold."

A car with blacked-out windows cruised by slowly, speakers thumping at full volume. She felt the vibrations recede as it turned a corner, faint now like distant cannons, and then all was lost in the cacophony of evening rush hour.

"How may I help you?"

"My name is Sherry Moore, and I'm trying to locate one of your patients, Mr. Thomas Monahan."

"Please hold."

Sherry had no idea what she might learn from the call. A man who had been standing off to one side was watching her, she noticed. Trying to make eye contact. Trying to make up his mind whether or not to approach her.

She stood and casually walked away, leaned against a tree, before he started heading for her park bench.

Before she'd regained her sight, she was frequently approached by men on the street. Then there was always that awkward moment when they realized she was blind. Perhaps she played it up at times, using her walking stick as a prop when she was not interested in the conversation.

In any event, it was helpful, she realized, to be able to see it coming for a change.

There was an electronic click, then a bar of soft music, before another click, then a man said, "Hello. How may I help you?"

"I was trying to locate a patient of yours, Monahan. Thomas Monahan."

"You are?"

"Sherry Moore."

"Are you a relative of Mr. Monahan's?" the man wanted to know.

"An acquaintance. I was hoping to write his family."

"I'm afraid Mr. Monahan has passed away."

Sherry hesitated. "Yes, I know. Can you please help me get in touch with the family? I'm trying to deliver my condolences."

"We are not permitted to release patient information," the man said firmly.

"I don't need any patient information," she said lightly. "Just a number or address for the family. Enough to call or send them a card."

"I'm sorry, but that also falls within the privilege, Miss Moore. Is there anything else I can help you with?"

"No, no thanks," Sherry closed the phone and replaced it in her purse. She looked around. The man by the bench was gone. He must have taken the hint.

She started for the bus stop at the corner thinking there was but one thing left to do. Brigham had already promised on the day she came home from the hospital that he would take her for a drive in the country. That he would show her things she had only ever heard of before. He said they could go at her earliest convenience.

Sherry knew she wanted to go before the gamma ray tests at month's end. She wanted to see the country and look at the sky before there was anything weightier on her mind.

"The Catskills?" he repeated.

"It's only a four-hour drive. We can have dinner and spend the night."

"I'm not opposed to going to the Catskills," he assured her. "It's a beautiful drive. I'm just wondering what you're up to."

"Why do I have to be up to something?"

"Because you are always up to something. This wouldn't have anything to do with your body donor, Sherry?"

"Mr. Brigham." She humphed.

"Oh cut it out." He stood and uncorked a bottle of port.

"All right, I got the name from Dr. Salix."

"And?"

"His name was Thomas Monahan. The name I called out in the examination room."

"Good Irish lad," Brigham said flatly.

"He was in a mental hospital."

Brigham turned and looked at her, raised an eyebrow.

"The fact that he was in a psychiatric facility doesn't really mean anything. All kinds of people end up in those places."

"So I've read." Brigham rolled his eyes.

"It's where he's been for the last fifty-eight years."

Brigham sighed and took a sip from his glass. "Wow, that's a surprise."

"Oh, don't make fun of it. It would be a pleasant drive," Sherry said. "I've found some things online that we could see while we're there."

"Have you now?" Brigham replied. "You know, you had me going there. I thought you might actually want to do something for no other reason than doing it. Have you ever done that? Something spontaneous, just for the fun of it, you know? No strings attached? You might find it different. Maybe even fun."

"I intend to do lots of that in the future, but right now I only want to see where he came from, Mr. Brigham. I'll run in, ask a couple of questions, and we'll be back on the road in no time."

"Why don't you just call them?"

"They won't talk to me on the phone." She began to adjust the pillows on the sofa.

He looked at her curiously. "I wouldn't imagine they would," he said seriously. "What makes you think they'll talk to you in person?"

She shrugged. There really wasn't a reason she could think of. "My charming nature?"

"So how long have you known about this body donor?"

"Just today," she said. "You know I tell you everything."

"Where was he?"

"New York State Psychiatric Hospital, Mount Tamathy."

"Sounds gruesome."

"Someone there should be willing to talk to us. Once they see us in person, they won't be disinclined."

"Yes, so you say. I'm off Tuesday through the weekend. Pick your days." He finished the port and headed for the kitchen.

"Will you teach me how to drive while we're in the country?"

"In a Land Rover with sixteen hundred miles on the odometer?" He stopped at the kitchen door and looked at her like she was crazy.

"That's a bad idea, then?"

"What day?" he asked again.

"Friday. I'll make breakfast and we'll leave after morning rush hour. We can go shopping while we're there. There are all kinds of little boutique towns along the Hudson."

"I'm not sure I can stand all the excitement." Brigham walked to the sink and rinsed out his glass. "Do you have any more interest in your fan mail or are we calling it a night?"

"Let's go to the video store. I want to rent a *Rocky* movie."

Brigham groaned audibly.

"Come on"—she balled her hands in two fists—"there's only two more to go!"

They left the interstate at Kingston and took back roads toward Mount Tamathy, finding every mile west of the Hudson a virtual time line back into history. Modest residences interspersed through the trees included shacks of the most unusual shapes and colors, belonging to the artisans of one kind or another who had come to Woodstock in 1969 and never quite found their way home.

Beyond the foothills the mountains rose to Sullivan County, home to the hundreds of resorts that were so famous in the post–World War II years. Many had spawned television's earliest comedians and singers. Now it was a graveyard of weathered billboards, most of them blank, some sprouting wood-frame cocktail glasses or marquees framed in rusting iron. Shells of nightclubs and retreats, hay-covered lawns where bocce was once played. Where the finest diamonds adorned the cleavages of blue-haired ladies from New Rochelle and Great Neck. It all would have been a dalliance, however; the moss-covered pergolas must have shadowed many an interesting conversation about the conundrums of finance and war and politics and communism.

Leaving Ulster County for Sullivan was like leaving Manhattan for Queens. The homes were less imaginative and sturdy, built with handsaws and axes like the post-and-rail fences surrounding small barns. Crude signs offered jams, honey, turkeys, and maple syrup. Stone chimneys stood where houses had long ago burned. Covered bridges gapped the creekbeds between single stone-walled lanes.

Gates, doors, and timber garages were festooned with yellowing animal skulls, antlers as broad as tall. Cattle-soiled patches of boulder-strewn barnyards and muddy horses ringed the round wooden troughs. Everything down to the rooflines was practical, built for the environment, not aesthetics.

Mount Tamathy towered above the range, a dozen miles beyond the Village of Stockton.

"Half an hour," Sherry said. "According to MapQuest. You hungry?"

"Starved." He shook his head. "Does Brian know what he's getting into when he gets back, all the talk show hosts and television producers that have been calling?" He snorted. "All the movies and television you've been watching, for that matter."

Brigham knew that Sherry's mail had been piling up and that her PR agency had been told to put all contacts on hold. Sherry wanted nothing to do with it anymore. She wanted to get through the month and the gamma ray tests. After that not even Brigham was sure what her plans were. Maybe she'd had enough of her past. Maybe she was thinking about retiring into seclusion and anonymity. She didn't seem unhappy, that wasn't Sherry's style, but he knew she'd changed after New Mexico and there was a certain sadness about her that only he could see. It was almost as if she'd reached a crossroad in life and was deciding on which direction to take.

Sherry looked out the window and drew a circle in the condensation with her finger.

"I was a bitch before he left."

"Sherry, you're dramatizing. You don't even know how to be a bitch."

"Well, I wasn't very responsive."

"To what?"

"You know what."

"So you were worried. We all knew that. He didn't expect you to propose to him while you were in the hospital."

Sherry was silent.

"You've never been a pessimist before."

"I've never had to deal with a long-term relationship before. Or the possibility of cancer."

Sherry put dots in the circle for eyes and drew a mouth. "Everything seems different when you throw another person into the equation. I guess it was Brian and the way everything went with his family over Memorial Day. It just seemed too good to be true."

"You've never felt sorry for yourself either."

Sherry turned in her seat and looked at him.

"Is that what you think I'm doing, Mr. Brigham?"

"You tell me. Over Memorial Day you were blind and now you're not. Don't you think that's something to be thankful for?"

"And who's to say I'm not thankful? But what if the cesium lodged a tumor in my spine? I don't want to be a burden to anyone else for the rest of my life."

"You know, I don't get you. You love Brian. I know you do. You've gotten your sight back! Good things are happening." Brigham looked at her oddly. "I think you're underestimating Brian Metcalf. That you're cheating him of a chance to make his own decision about you."

"Right now, this minute, today, I'm focusing on Thomas J. Monahan. I want to know what happened to me in the hospital when I took his hand. I need to know why it happened."

"Why does it matter so much?"

"I can see because of Tom Monahan," she said emphatically. "I can see because he suffered some cerebral malady of his own. Because something put him in that mental hospital and I picked it up in the transfer of information from his brain to my own. Can't you see that's a possibility? I mean, look how I acted in that room, the strange words I was uttering. It was just different, Mr. Brigham."

"Sherry, you've been hearing for years that your eyes and memory could suddenly be restored. And you were seeing lights and shadows long before you took that test."

"Lights, not sight, and you and Dr. Salix don't seem to appreciate that I know the difference. It was an optical migraine, like the doctor's said before, nothing else. Nothing significant was happening to me before Monahan's corpse came along."

Sherry shifted in her seat. She felt frustrated, but it wasn't clear at whom.

"Yes, the doctors have been warning me something could change since I was five. The slightest head injury, a sinus infection, almost anything could affect my brain, they said. I was told I could lose the remainder of my memory or maybe instead I'd regain everything I'd lost before the accident. Truth be told, it's easy to say all that stuff when you don't have a clue what's going to happen. It's like weather people and psychics—if you throw enough predictions out there, sooner or later one of them has to come true. I've been through a lot of emotional trauma in my life, not as much as some, to be sure, but enough to know my own mind. To know that I regained my sight because I was lying on that table next to Thomas J. Monahan."

He cracked his window an inch, mostly because he didn't know what else to do.

"It just seems important now," Sherry said. "To find out what happened in that examination room."

"And not to communicate with Brian."

"Did you know Brian was engaged once before?" Sherry sat upright, looking straight out the windshield.

Brigham turned to look at her and shook his head. "No, I'm sorry, I didn't."

"They were living together in Norfolk. She was the daughter of his first commanding officer. The wedding was to take place a month after his discharge from the navy."

"What happened?" Brigham asked.

"Pancreatic cancer. She was twenty-six and died eighty-one days after she was diagnosed."

Brigham didn't say anything.

"I was happy at the Metcalfs' home in Boston. You remember Allison, his sister, who was caught in that storm on Mount McKinley last year. The one we helped save?"

He nodded.

"We ended up talking a lot after Brian and I started dating. We were getting so close she was beginning to feel like a sister to me. By the time we met again at the family reunion, she said her father and mother were already whispering about a fall wedding, my wedding, Mr. Brigham. We shared a lot about our lives. She told me all about Brian and how he had turned down a lucrative job with the State Department after his fiancée died. How he had his father pull strings to get him reinstated in the navy, and that he chose to be stationed in the Middle East for another four years."

Sherry turned and looked at Brigham. "Do you understand now?"

He nodded. "All I know is, he's a good guy."

"Yes, he is, and that's my point. What if my health doesn't last?"

"You think Brian Metcalf will leave you? You think he's that shallow? He still thinks you're blind, Sherry, and he's already willing to take the leap."

"He didn't discourage me when I told him I was going to New Mexico, but I know he didn't approve. And I wouldn't have liked it if it were the other way around, either. I would have wanted to have a conversation about it before he did anything like that. I knew about his fiancée then. I knew he'd lost someone before and I still got on that plane. I know he does the same thing every day, but I also know he would change his life if I only asked him to. I didn't give him that chance. And now he has to be thinking what I'm thinking, that I might have cancer in a year or five or ten." She wiped a tear from her eye. "Maybe I just wasn't meant to be in a relationship. Maybe I should just wait and see how this works out. Just wait awhile."

"And see how far you can stretch Mr. Metcalf's patience, so he gives up and you can blame it on providence. Blame it on him, even."

Sherry turned back away in her seat and looked out the window. Brigham kept his eyes on the road and his hands firmly on the wheel.

Two signs announced the Village of Stockton. One said its name, the other its elevation of 3,300 feet. It was an old town built mainly in the Federalist style—lots of straight-line homes and commercial buildings, an abundance of brick and white columns.

The streets were clean and lined with antique shops. There were numerous bed-and-breakfasts, a small franchise hotel, and dozens of boutique shops.

"There's a diner," Brigham pointed, nosing the Land Rover into an angled parking space between two New York State police cars.

Sherry saw what appeared to be a dozen sepia-colored photographs in the diner's front window.

"Look, Mr. Brigham," she said. "The asylum."

They were dated and portrayed people wearing a diversity of nineteenth- and twentieth-century fashions. Staff members stood unsmiling in front of a massive brick building with an arch labeled NYS HOSPITAL FOR THE INSANE. The oldest of the pictures showed patients in starched uniforms, some looking down at their knees, others with chins jutting proudly toward the sky as nurses in large white caps and oval eyeglasses stood rigidly in ankle-length dresses.

Brigham studied the pictures. "Civil War veterans, see, here?"

He scanned others, ending up with a color photo of the entrance. The date on it was 1966. "Here, see the sign out front, that's when it must have changed names."

"And Monahan was really here for almost sixty years?" she said in awe.

Brigham shrugged. "No reason he couldn't have been, I guess."

He put his finger to the glass. Veterans of the World Wars had gathered for a photograph. It was the Fourth of July, 1947. Brigham pointed out the distinctive uniforms. "This would have been before there was a veterans hospital in New York. Maybe Monahan was in World War Two, or more likely Korea, because of his age, and they cared for him here."

Brigham stepped to the door and pulled it open to the tinkle of a bell.

The walls of the diner were canary yellow, the booths dark wood, old and smoothed by the touch of hundreds of thousands of hands. Hundreds more photos of the asylum and its residents and staff adorned the walls.

"Coffee?" a pretty silver-haired woman asked as she leaned against the end of their booth.

"Please," they said, pushing their cups toward her.

"Looks like your town grew up around the asylum?" Brigham's eyes wandered along the walls.

"Some people get the Taj Mahal, we get a loony bin." The waitress shrugged. She was a very fit-looking woman in her mid-sixties, Sherry thought. She was wearing khaki shorts and running shoes, an apron over a cantaloupe orange polo shirt.

"I take it you're not from around here." She winked at Brigham.

Brigham shook his head and smiled. "Philadelphia."

Sherry looked at Brigham. Smiling! Is he flirting? she thought, astonished. The idea made her nearly giddy. Yes, he is, she thought. He really is flirting!

Brigham's wife had passed away many years ago, even before Sherry had moved to the house next door on the river. She'd never had an inkling that he thought about the opposite sex, but was that only because she was blind?

"How many people actually live here?" Brigham asked.

"Six hundred and seventy-eight as of this morning's obituary." She touched his arm. "I'm only kidding, but it's something like that."

"And everyone works at the asylum." Brigham nodded his head toward the pictures on the walls.

"If they don't now, they did at one time or another."

She smiled with her hand on her hip. "If you like breakfast, you'll love our pancakes. We serve them all day."

"Betsy?" a voice called from across the room.

"Whoops, be right back, dears." She patted Brigham's arm again and rushed away, scribbling numbers on a pad.

"Dears?" Sherry repeated slowly.

Brigham kept his eyes on his coffee. "Busy place," he said without inflection.

Sherry cocked her head. "Oh, let's not stray off the subject." She squinted at Brigham, with the slightest crook of a smile.

Brigham was every bit as elegant and handsome as she'd imagined him before she could see. He was the man in the room who you knew had stature and history. She loved that, in spite of his military background, he let his white hair do a flip over his back collar.

Brigham picked up a fork and began to turn it over in his fingers. "Subject?" he repeated.

"Mr. Brigham," Sherry said teasingly. "There is a whole other side of you." She tried to look away, but her grin kept growing bigger. "Who knew?" she erupted at last.

"That's quite enough." He leaned across the table, trying to keep his voice above a whisper. "She's just a nice lady." He shrugged with emphasis. "I like nice people, so what?"

"You're embarrassed," she said, still grinning. "How cute." The color of Brigham's neck was rich and red as the port he liked to drink. "Okay, okay"—she held up her hand—"I'm done." She wiped a tear from her eye. "So what are you having?"

"Pancakes," he growled, peeling off his reading glasses and stuffing them into his jacket pocket.

"Me, too, then," she said firmly.

She took a deep breath and folded her hands. Looked around the room.

"Let's leave it alone for a while, all that other stuff about Brian, okay? Let's just have fun today and tomorrow and see what life brings? Please?"

Brigham looked into her eyes and nodded.

"So what's all the pink and blue stuff about?" Sherry picked up a container of sweeteners.

"Don't use them," Brigham said sternly. "They just taste like sugar."

"She's actually pretty cute," Sherry said, nodding toward the waitress. "Seriously."

Brigham looked at her, waiting for a smirk and, when he saw none, nodded. "I guess."

"Maybe she worked there too." Sherry's mind was at work again. "The asylum."

Brigham shrugged. "Ask her."

"If you wish," she said with a straight face.

The woman rushed back to the booths, dropped change on

one, a check on another. Then she returned to them. "One more hour and it'll be dead until supper. You two know what you want?"

"Pancakes," Sherry said.

Brigham nodded. "Same."

"You here to visit a relative?"

"Just an acquaintance," Sherry said.

"I'm Betsy." The waitress stuck out her hand to Sherry. When Brigham took it he nodded and said, "Garland."

"Great name," Betsy said. "Juice, sausage, potatoes?"

"No thanks, just water."

"You've worked at the asylum too?" Sherry asked.

"Years ago, honey."

"Betsy!" someone yelled.

"I'll be back with more coffee in a minute." She dashed to a customer at the door and then down the corridor to the open kitchen door.

Betsy gave them directions to the hospital—hardly necessary with all the state's new green luminescent signage. She'd suggested they drive to the summit of Mount Tamathy afterward. The state had carved out a road to the top of the mountain and made a lookout at the pinnacle. There were telescopes there and park benches to picnic on. One could see both Pennsylvania and the Delaware River Gorge from it. She also suggested they return for dinner. Friday night was the Stockton Diner's catfish special.

Directions included a right at an intersection, past an Orvis store, a roadhouse called Grant's Tavern, a tobacconist, a candle store, and several more B&Bs. Whole-timber summer cottages followed the road out of town. Dozens more were clustered on side streets amid some older moss-covered homes. A grassy park by a stream included a statue of a Union soldier and a World War II antiaircraft gun.

"Are we going to come right out and ask about him or what?" Brigham wanted to know.

"I don't think they'll let us stroll the grounds and question patients, but who knows? Maybe it's not as bad as it sounds," Sherry said. "We'll just think of it as a country hospital and play it by ear."

The main entrance was set between two enormous brick columns and a polished marble sign that read NEW YORK STATE PSYCHIATRIC HOSPITAL. The road was short and the lawn on either side was groomed and lined with red flowers.

Sherry made a noise, an involuntary exclamation at the beauty of the flowers and tree buds exploding into new leaves. Brigham heard it almost every day from her now. She was literally awestruck by the world and all that was in it.

A hillside rose to meet formidable walls that disappeared into dense trees. The compound was like an old fort, ivy blotting out the brick and hundreds of feet of walls spiked with iron. The windows of four-story buildings behind it were barred, dark, and foreboding.

"Scary enough?" Sherry ducked to look up over the dash as they approached the iron gates. "I can't imagine going in here and knowing you're not coming back out."

Brigham rolled down his window.

A uniformed guard stepped from the sentry house. "Afternoon."

"Good afternoon, Officer. Hoping to visit a friend."

The officer handed Brigham two green passes on lanyards. "Stay on the road with green dots, keep your doors locked at all times, park only in visitor spaces in the lot in front of the main building. Leave cell phones, valuables, and cash in your car. Bags will be searched upon entering the facility."

Brigham pulled away, noticing people on the grounds. Some were obviously patients. They occupied park benches or sat on blankets on the ground. Staff wore orange polo shirts and khaki pants.

"Doesn't look too scary right here," Sherry said.

"I'm sure this is minimum security," Brigham answered.

There were large green circles painted on the road. Side roads were marked well with DO NOT ENTER and large red circles painted every thirty or forty feet. Buildings sat farther back and they had interior security fencing around them; the fencing was topped with razor wire.

"Doesn't look like we'll get to play it by ear very long," Sherry said.

"I'm thinking we won't either." Brigham pointed to a guard tower on one of the walls. There was a man sitting in it.

They parked and emptied their pockets into the glove box between the seats.

The entrance and parking area were separated from the rest of the grounds. Cameras followed their approach to the wide concrete steps.

Doors opened automatically to the smell of disinfectant. There was a uniformed guard by a metal detector they had to pass; bags were not permitted.

On the opposite side of the entrance was a long narrow sunroom filled with wicker rockers and potted plants, where white-haired men and women leaned to sleep or talk to their neighbors. Beyond the sunroom was a rotunda with plush chairs and ornate couches, potted trees that reached for the domed ceiling. A receptionist behind an exposed antique desk stood to greet them while a nicely dressed elderly couple said tearful good-byes to a young, expressionless woman. She was being admitted, Sherry thought.

"We're hoping to speak with someone who knew one of your residents," Sherry said with unrehearsed honesty.

"You're a family member?" The woman smiled.

Sherry shook her head. "I'm afraid I only became acquainted with your patient after he died."

The woman looked at Sherry oddly.

"In the hospital," Sherry stammered slightly. "In Phila-delphia."

The woman continued to smile, appraising her.

"He was transferred from here to a hospital. That's where I met him." Sherry held out the palms of her hands as she tried not to explain that he was dead before he got there. She continued to hold eye contact with the woman, whose smile never seemed to fatigue.

"His name was Monahan, Thomas Joseph Monahan. He was in his late seventies."

Sherry watched the receptionist's curious eyes, wondering what was so interesting about her that made the woman stare at her face.

"Until a week ago," she continued. "That's when he was sent to Nazareth Hospital in Philadelphia."

"You're that Sherry Moore woman," the receptionist said, head nodding cockily to the side. She moved her jaw sideways.

"I thought so at first, but then you don't expect someone you know from magazines to just walk in and sit down in front of you. It's just never the same as seeing someone in person, but I guess you've heard that before. Oh, my God!" Her hands flew to cover her mouth. "You just got your sight back. I read all about it. That is so cool."

Sherry nodded.

The woman reached out and touched the back of her wrist. "You really were blind, right? I mean, you couldn't see all that time?"

Sherry heard Brigham let out a sigh as she shook her head no.

"Would it be rude to ask for your autograph? My mother reads everything she can about you. She's a psychic too. She channels through a monk who died in the thirteenth century."

"Of course I'll give you an autograph," Sherry said, "while you check on the patient for me."

"Oh, of course, I'm sorry." The receptionist patted the

desk with the tips of her polished fingernails. "You're here about old T.J."

"I'd just like to have his relatives' names and addresses to send condolences."

The woman shrugged. "Sounds easy enough to me."

She pushed back her chair and got to her feet, leaned down, and whispered to Sherry, "Probably, if you wanted, you could just get the police to ask for it." She winked. "I know you have friends in high places."

Then she walked to the door behind her and swiped a scanner with a bar code card hanging from her belt. The door opened and she was gone.

"Holy shit," Sherry said.

Brigham turned to look at Sherry. "What kind of talk is that?"

She shrugged and looked contrite. "Too many movies?"

He shook his head in wonder and looked at his watch. "Maybe she's really one of the patients and pretends to work here."

"Either way, this is going to be easy," she said with confidence.

Sherry looked up at the gilded cornices, a fresco of sun rays parting clouds on a sky-blue dome. Dark oil portraits with small brass labels beneath them adorned the walls.

"Administrators?" she suggested, rising to walk toward them.

"That would be my guess." Brigham stood and joined her at one.

They started in 1868; all were men until 1982. The oldest were spectacled and wore white beards. Their suits modernized as they progressed around the rotunda until the last one, of Dr. Evelyn J. Canelli, and with the sound of a door being opened, they turned to see her in person, marching as if she were the military advancing upon them.

Dr. Canelli was anything but pleasant looking. Matronly and devoid of cheer, she appeared to have had an ill effect on the receptionist, who now trailed behind.

"Dr. Canelli," the woman pronounced loudly, her voice reverberating in the domed room. She stopped a few feet from Sherry and did not offer her hand. "How may I help you?"

"Sherry Moore." Sherry smiled. "I was hoping to get in touch with the family of one of your patients. Mr. Thomas J. Monahan," she said. "He died here about a week ago."

"We are not permitted to give out information regarding our patients, Miss Moore."

"Oh, I understand that," Sherry said quickly. "I am not interested in any information concerning Mr. Monahan himself. I just want to reach his family. To offer my condolences."

"No information means no information, Miss Moore," the doctor said sternly.

Brigham grunted and shifted his weight between his feet.

The receptionist who had originally greeted them was holding a writing pad in front of her skirt, kneading the paper into wrinkles with two nervous thumbs.

Sherry shook her head. "Perhaps I should have mentioned I am representing a neurologist from Nazareth Hospital in Philadelphia, Dr. Salix. Dr. Salix signed for Mr. Monahan's body last week and there was no paperwork to accompany the body. He has questions about Mr. Monahan's medical history for the family."

Dr. Canelli was unmoved. "When physicians have questions about our patients they do not send representatives, Miss Moore. Is there anything else I can do for you?"

Sherry shook her head.

"Then we must return to our business." Canelli spun on her heels.

The receptionist stood frozen by the side of her desk.

Brigham led Sherry to the exit.

"Whoa!" Sherry said as they went down the front steps.

"You gave it a try," Brigham said soothingly.

"For all the good it did. What is up with her?"

"You know as well as I do, Sherry. Lawyers. They're worried about lawyers."

"Dr. Salix will just have to get it out of them."

Brigham shrugged. "Want to see the overlook while we're here?"

"Only if we can stop for catfish afterward." She was serious, but teasing, of course.

"We can do that." Brigham smiled.

9

It was dark when they got back to Stockton, the storefront windows all black. A light rain drizzled on the asphalt, glistening pink under a capsule of red light on the wall of a brick firehouse. They parked on the curb and watched pedestrians exiting Grant's Tavern. It was a merry-looking place with colorful wreaths and white twinkling lights strung through shrubberies and trees. The building was old and painted white with black shutters. The brochure—Sherry had taken one from the diner earlier—said there were nineteen guest rooms, a pub, confectionary, and restaurant.

"We could get drinks and see if they have rooms for the night?"

"Suits me," he said.

They quickly secured rooms, dropped their bags on tall quilted sleigh beds, and met in the pub for cocktails.

Grant's had been a roadhouse since 1846, the walls of the pub adorned with nineteenth-century horse tack. An antique guest register on display was open to the signature of Ulysses S. Grant, 1868, with notations for a room and a stable for his horse.

The bar featured several microbrewed beers, and Sherry ordered the Devil's Hoof while Brigham ordered port and oysters on the half-shell.

The bartender was in his early thirties, Sherry thought. He wore a goatee and his head was shaved clean. There was a tattoo of the state of Texas on his forearm and there were hoop earrings in both ears.

"You're from Texas?"

"Nope." He shook his head. "Rhode Island."

Sherry nodded. "Have you been here long?"

"Three years." His accent was Scottish, making his origin all the more confusing.

"I work at the asylum, that's my paying job," he said.

Sherry laughed. "And this is for fun?"

"You've seen the nightlife in this town?" He raised his eyebrows.

She shook her head.

"I'm it, so I might as well be getting paid at the same time." He put a bowl of peanuts in front of them.

"Must be an interesting place to work, the asylum," she said. "Lots of history."

"You've got that right," he agreed. "You like the beer?"

Sherry nodded. "A little hoppy, but yes."

"We've got a great selection of pale ales if you'd rather have a bottle."

"No, no." Sherry shook her head. "I'll finish this first. You ever hear of a patient at the hospital called T.J. Monahan? Older man, maybe seventy-something, they called him T.J."

The bartender shook his head. "I'm a dietician, so I'm always in the kitchen. I only get to know the names of patients with allergies. Not quite what I went to school for, but the skiing's good in the winter."

A young woman brought out oysters on ice from the kitchen and then returned.

"I'm Sherry," she said to the bartender. "This is my friend Garland Brigham."

"Mike." The young man leaned across to shake their hands. "Nice to meet you both. How long's your friend T.J. been up there?"

"Since 1950," she said.

"Jesus, what a life. You know they're pretty uptight about confidentiality there. I think they've got a lot of old ghosts in their closets."

"Yeah, we noticed," Brigham said. "And that was at the front door."

The bartender laughed. "You meet Dr. Canelli?"

"We did." Sherry smiled.

"She's hell on wheels, but if you really want to find anything out around here you just ask the locals. They know more about that place than half the people working there."

A family of five entered in wet windbreakers and took a table in the corner.

"Excuse me." He grabbed a handful of menus and silverware and headed for the dining room.

"Your guest room okay?" Brigham asked.

"Lovely," Sherry said. "Yours?"

"Bed might be a bit soft, but all in all I'd say it's great for the middle of nowhere. You're being suitably nosy, I see."

"I just thought he might know our man."

"You see the pictures of General Grant in the lobby when we came in?"

Sherry nodded. "Must have been on the campaign trail visiting old battlefield friends and getting his name in the paper."

"I can't even fathom what that place must have looked like after the Civil War."

"Forget what it looked like. Imagine the smell," Brigham said gravely.

Sherry knew that Brigham was speaking from experience.

"Okay, what's next?" Sherry reached for an oyster.

"Fried catfish," Brigham said.

"Uh-huh." Sherry attempted a twang. "Why, we'd love to come back for some catfish, Miss Betsy."

Brigham picked up a peanut and tossed it at her sideways. "Actually, I think it is you who should want to see her most. I mean, who would know more about the patients than the hospital's former director of intake and admissions?"

"Says who?"

"Her picture's on the wall at the entrance to the confectionary. Just above the brochure rack. She's a lot younger, but you'll recognize her. She's posing with Yul Brynner."

Sherry slid from her stool. "Who's Yul Brynner?"

Brigham shook his head in dismay. "He's the bald guy. You won't miss it."

Sherry was back in five minutes. "I'm liking your friend Betsy more and more," she said.

A baby began to scream at the corner table. Brigham downed his port and laid a twenty on the check. "Ready for catfish?"

"I'm ready for anything but screaming," Sherry said. "And I'll bet Miss Betsy will be willing to tell you anything you want to know."

The diner was starting to empty by 8 p.m. The rain had picked up, and slick umbrellas were stacked in the corner by the door.

They took a booth at the front window and watched dogwood blossoms fly from the trees, plastering themselves to park benches and hoods of cars and the shimmering pools of light along the dark street.

"It's downright cold out there," Sherry rubbed her arms and shivered.

"We're in the mountains," Brigham said. "Two hundred miles from Montreal."

A gum-chewing girl came toward the booth, but then Betsy yelled from across the room. "Hey, Adel, I got it, go on home when you finish your tables."

A minute later Betsy arrived with water and silverware.

"You came back." She smiled, hand on her hip, blew the silver bangs off her forehead.

"And we're staying," Sherry said, pointing toward the back wall. "Grant's Tavern."

"Excellent choice," she said, "It's the town hub for us forty and older crowd. The kids won't pay five bucks for a beer, which is the way we like it. So is it the catfish or you want menus?"

"Catfish times two," Sherry said. "We saw your picture in the lobby over there."

Betsy nodded. "Yul Brynner, 1980. It was a charity event and I was a little blonder then." She lifted the hair off her shoulder with the backs of her fingers and let it drop.

"You must have known everyone in the hospital," Sherry said.

"Just about." Betsy leaned over to place the silverware. "Salad or coleslaw?"

"Coleslaw," Sherry said. Brigham ordered a salad.

"Tea or soda?"

Sherry and Brigham both shook their heads, asked for water, and in an instant Betsy was gone.

They noticed the nicely dressed couple they'd seen earlier at the hospital, the ones saying good-bye to the young woman. The rest of the clientele were dressed comfortably enough to be locals.

"How many years were you there?" Sherry asked Betsy as she dropped off the coleslaw.

"Seventeen, but the town was growing and the diner was getting to be a handful. I had to quit and come run it full-time."

"You own this?" Sherry asked, surprised.

The woman nodded. "Used to be I could find someone to run it for me. People aren't like that anymore. Not that I've found,

102

anyhow. And staff. That's a whole other story. All the kids want to be managers and nobody wants to do the work. I'll be right back with your dinners."

The catfish was good. The crowd was gone by nine.

Sherry took the check and walked it to the cash register. "You wouldn't want to join us for a drink at the tavern, would you?" she said.

Betsy was stacking plates for the dishwasher. "That actually sounds good," she said. "My niece is opening for me in the morning, so I can run up to Kingston and pick up my new eyeglasses, which means I can sleep in until eight. I'll need another twenty minutes to get out of here."

"We'll be at the bar." Sherry laid money on the check.

"You like chocolate?"

"Mmmmmm." Sherry smiled.

"Tell Mike to make a blender of Mississippi Mud, and mention my name. If you don't like it, I'll finish what you don't drink."

10

LANCASTER, PENNSYLVANIA

A phone rang in the spa room at Case's Lancaster farm.

"It's Troy."

"Is it done?" Case cradled the receiver against his ear. He was pouring scotch over tumblers of ice. He let the towel fall from his waist and opened the door to the sauna. Wendy was sitting cross-legged on the bench, naked, her body beaded with perspiration.

"It's done. I have the kid's hard drive," Troy said.

"Good, good. Destroy it." He leaned forward in his wheelchair and handed the young woman her drink.

"There's something else."

"What?" Case asked impatiently.

"Veterans Affairs received a call from a psychiatric hospital in upstate New York. They said the caller wanted to speak with you personally. At your request."

"What request?" Case pushed the glass against his forehead. "I didn't request to speak with anyone," he growled.

"All they said was that a patient named Monahan died and they had instructions to call the foundation."

Case leaned against the door frame. "Say that again."

"Monahan—he was a patient there and he died. Does that mean anything to you?"

There was a long moment of silence. Case leaned back in his wheelchair and shut the door to the sauna.

"How did he die? Did they say?"

"Aortal aneurysm."

Case bent forward, elbows on knees, head cradled in his hands.

It had been years since he'd thought of Thomas Monahan. Even now the memory was indistinct. A boy of twenty or so, heavily bandaged and lying on a hospital gurney.

"That's it? They didn't say anything else?"

"That's all."

It had all happened in another lifetime, when Case was a very young man himself. When doctors fresh out of medical school were putting to practice theories that had only ever before been hypothesized on blackboards in the bowels of Cornell or Harvard or Yale. It was a new generation of knowledge. The world was there for the taking. And take it he did. He looked through the glass door at the young woman in his sauna, studying the curve of her hip and the purple polish on ten perfect toes.

Yes, he took, and long before the *Carpe Diem* T-shirt was in vogue. To take advantage of that small window in time when the world cared more about science than human lives. More about a future for all than about the rights of privacy and informed consent.

He had accomplished in two decades what would have required those so-called geniuses a lifetime. He had circumvented generations of clinical lab work by taking his drugs directly to the field. What better or faster way to know how humans might react to certain combinations of chemicals than to test them on human beings from the beginning?

Society might not agree with that approach today, but from the 1950s to the 1970s it helped launch the ideas of two men to become an industry that would stand for centuries.

Case had no regrets for the lives sacrificed to his theories. How many more people had been saved? In fact, his only lament was the truth behind the adage that youth was wasted on the young. Oh, for just twenty more years, he thought.

The news about Monahan was a relief, but Lord, that man had taken his good old time to die. All those brilliant doctors in the room in 1950 and none had given the boy more than a decade to live. He would never walk again, they were all so sure. His lungs would not be able to keep up with his heart. He would be dead before he was thirty.

It was just another example of how little doctors knew about the human body in 1950. Monahan had outlived all of them, save Case.

"Thanks," he said. "I'll see you in the morning," and he hung up the phone.

He opened the sauna door again and pulled himself out of the wheelchair and pivoted onto the bench next to Wendy, one finger tracing a line from her knee to her hip. He lifted his drink and raised it to his lips and felt her hand on him.

"Did you take your meds?" she whispered, looking up at him.

"The one that counts." He brushed the sweat from her forehead and tucked her hair behind her ear.

Troy Weir should have had a long jump start on life. He was handsome, athletic, and certainly gifted, but Troy lacked something fundamental inside. He was emotionally void.

When he finally came to ask his stepfather for a job at Case and Kimble, he was aware that his life was spinning out of control. That he needed to rein in his hostilities. He considered re-search monotonous, but it offered solitude and a way to anchor himself for at least part of the day. He had already seen three of his West Coast friends dead by age eighteen. His classmates at Franklin University in New York were all on Wall Street now, but corporations required far too much contact with cohorts and clients. He could never pull off so much sincerity in the light of day.

His stepfather was skeptical but assigned him to a research and development facility near Reading, Pennsylvania. Then an opening appeared in Lancaster for a clerk at Case and Kimble's PR darling, the Global Responsibility Lab, or GRL "girl" lab, confined to research of cures for the world's hot-list diseases, such as AIDS, *E. coli,* and West Nile virus.

Terry Hopping, in charge of the lab, was typical for a GRL group leader. Beautiful, photogenic, racially diverse (part Irish, part Cherokee Indian), pedigreed (cellular pathologist from the University of North Carolina, Chapel Hill School of Medicine), and quirky (she appeared to be as fascinated by sex as she was by homeostasis). In other words, she was window dressing for Case and Kimble's much touted and purely self-serving philanthropic contribution to humanity around the world.

Hopping's team worked on public relation cases, donating time, equipment, and manpower wherever news cameras ap-peared. In reality they were underfunded and overworked, and Hopping had also been demoted from the mainstream C&K ca-reer ladder for numerous complaints of sexual harassment.

She was all but ecstatic when Troy Weir ended up in her group. It was innocent enough at first, brushing against him in the confines of the small office, lewd intimations in conversation, displaying her underwear at any opportunity that presented it-self—she found plenty of reasons to sit across from him or to bend over to give him a good view of her thong.

She had another act, which included stripping down to her

bra and panties to step into her yellow protective suit that she wore in the biocontainment chamber. This she did in full view of a glass vacuum-sealed door, and Troy gave her what he considered her humiliation, the proper attention she sought.

Then came the day they were alone and a breach alarm sounded in the chamber. Troy ran into the lab to see what was wrong and noticed that the warning patch on the breast of her suit was flashing red. Hopping was holding a glass slide smeared with blood and there was a half-inch tear in the finger of her glove.

She looked up as he ran to the observation window. Her eyes went wide when he punched the emergency bar locking the chamber, and though it emitted a piercing shriek to alert staff there was a breach, there was no one to hear it that day but him. Hopping dropped the slide and screamed in silent rage as she ran to the window, pressed her mask against the glass, teeth bared, lips demanding, then begging Troy to unlock the door. Her demands diminished to whimpers by the time the first blotches of black and red appeared on her face, and fifteen minutes later she slipped to the floor, where she died of convulsions.

The lab was heavily criticized for allowing a clerk into the unit, even though he was the owner's stepson. You couldn't blame the death of a scientist on a clerk, and you couldn't blame the clerk for understaffing the lab. It looked like what it was, a bad management decision. Even police were unsure how to proceed until Case himself got involved.

In the end Troy was exonerated, an internal board fired an administrator, and sixteen single-spaced pages were added to the organization's general operating procedures. And a bronze plaque bearing a likeness of Terry Hopping was placed in an obscure hallway near the GRL lab.

Edward Case, however, was suddenly more interested in the young man who so coldly watched a scientist die rather than open the door and put himself others at risk. It took a special kind of person to do that, a man very much like himself at that age. Even the best trained in the business had a tendency to let their hearts and emotions interfere with their minds.

The company's board of directors would make noise about employing Troy again, but not where Ed Case needed him most. In Ed Case's world there were places for a man like Troy.

11

"Remember a patient named T.J. Monahan? Thomas J. Monahan?" Sherry asked.

Betsy nodded, sipping from her straw. She touched her lips with a napkin.

"Absolutely," she said. "I haven't thought of him in years, but, yes, he came with the asylum."

They were just starting their second pitcher of Mississippi Muds, a concoction of ice cream, Kahlúa, and Southern Comfort. Sherry, enjoying the moment, was beginning to wonder if she hadn't been a bore all these years. It wasn't like her to deviate from the serious beers she favored toward candy-like drinks she'd always considered frivolous. The wonder of sight seemed to have brought about a sea change in Sherry's approach to life.

Sherry nodded. "Any family?"

"None," Betsy said. "Never had a visitor in my seventeen years."

"You said he came with the asylum?"

"Nineteen fifty, as I recall. He's probably in his late seventies now. He outlived anyone that was there when he was admitted."

Brigham shook his head. "He died."

Betsy turned abruptly. "Monahan's dead?" she said softly. "He was like the saddest thing you ever saw. He was there in a way and yet not. We could move him around, stand him on his own two feet, but there was no one inside. He'd just stare at the walls, year after year; sometimes he'd move his lips, but never said an intelligible word. We brought him to every holiday celebration, gave him a birthday and baked him cakes; he was like our mascot." She smiled. "We always kidded about how he was the best patient in the ward. We didn't mean anything by it. We really loved him."

"Do you know how he got there?" Brigham asked.

Betsy shook her head. "Security brought him in one day, we were told. He took a fall off the rocks on Mount Tamathy, up at the overlook where you guys went today. The road wasn't there back then, and the guardrails, the fencing before you get to the rocks, were all open. There wasn't much in the records, but he was with the army base that used to be up here, one of those high-security areas, secret Cold War stuff. I guess he didn't have any family and since he was brain-dead, they just left him at the asylum. Nowadays there's a VA hospital in Syracuse, but . . ." She shrugged and sipped her drink.

"An army base?" Sherry repeated, thinking of the images she had seen in Monahan's memories.

"That base was the talk of the town when I was kid. When it finally closed the boys used to go up and root around the rubble they left behind. Some people came around now and then and wrote articles on it; I think it was Discovery or one of the science-fiction channels that did a documentary of it. They were supposed to have been doing some kind of top-secret research there, very sensitive stuff. Of course now, like everything else, it's supposed to be haunted."

"When did the army abandon it?"

"Early seventies. One day they just came in with trucks and hauled everything away. You remember when the CIA was in front of Congress over refusing to release old records? The old administration destroyed thousands of documents; it was"—she shook a finger—"it's on the tip of my tongue. . . ."

"Richard Helms," Brigham said. "He ordered that their secret research projects be destroyed."

"What about Monahan's hospital records? Don't they say what happened to him?" Sherry asked.

Betsy topped off her drink and turned on her stool, knee pressed tightly against the side of Brigham's thigh. Her eyes were a very dark, perhaps a Scandinavian, blue, he thought.

"So how are you related to T.J.?" she asked.

"We're not," Brigham said.

Betsy withdrew her knee and looked at Brigham, then at Sherry.

"I'm beginning to think you aren't as interested in my pancakes and catfish as what goes on in that asylum. Are you two lawyers or something? You know, you could have just asked me some questions at the diner if that's what you're here for."

"Please don't be offended. I'm really enjoying your company," Brigham said with extraordinary sincerity. "No, we're not lawyers and it's certainly not what you're thinking."

"It's about me," Sherry said. "And it's kind of difficult to explain."

Brigham put up his hand. "Have you ever heard of a woman who can take the hand of a dead person and see their last memories before they died?"

Betsy looked at him like he was crazy. She shook her head no and looked at her drink.

"I have a story to tell you, then," he said. "It's a little long, but worth hearing, I assure you. Will you give me a few minutes?"

Betsy nodded her head slowly, but uncertainly.

Thirty minutes later her knee was back against Brigham's thigh. She was on her fourth Mississippi Mud.

"You know, I heard there was a statistic floating around about our hospital having the highest cancer rate for patients across the country."

"What about Monahan's medical history when he came in?"

"There wasn't a single document in his file about his admission," Betsy said. "The only thing we ever had was an authorization to continue care and send bills to the Veterans Administration in Washington, D.C. The staff tried to find family through the army for years, we called half the Monahans in the country just out of curiosity, but no one ever found a next of kin and the army refused to talk about him."

"Normally a vet would rate funeral arrangements," Brigham said.

She shook her head. "Whole body donor. It was marked in his jacket from day one. I'm really sorry to hear he's gone."

"You said security brought him into the hospital, not the army?"

Betsy nodded. "Jack McCullough was the asylum security chief back then. His widow, sweet lady, still lives here, just up the street. It was on a Thanksgiving, I remember, because she talked about how they waited for him all day. She said he got called out early in the morning for an inmate that was supposed to have escaped. When he finally got home he had blood all over his shirt and said they found one of the army boys that jumped from the rocks on Mount Tamathy. The story sticks with everyone so well, because Jack shot himself a few weeks later. December twenty-sixth. The state police did an investigation because no one that knew him believed he could do that to himself, but in the end, he was alone in his office and the door was locked."

"His office? You mean his office up at the asylum?"

"Uh-huh."

"And you know her well you said? The widow?"

Betsy nodded. "Her name's Corcoran now. Carla Corcoran. Her new husband owns a golf course off the Ashokan Reservoir."

"Do you think she'd talk with us?"

Betsy shrugged. "She talks to everyone. She's just a nice lady, like I said."

Betsy put her hand on Brigham's arm. "Did you know there is a wine bar in Kingston that features port tastings?"

Brigham studied the woman carefully.

"You don't say?" He smiled.

12

Dr. Canelli sat rigid in her leather chair, flipping through cards in an old metal Rolodex. She found the name Case and Kimble and dialed a number in Pennsylvania. The phone rang once and was answered with "Executive offices."

"I need to speak with Dr. Case's assistant, please," she said.

"Just a moment," the operator said, and a moment later she was transferred to a gentleman who took her message and put her on hold.

The directive lying on the desk in front of her and regarding Thomas J. Monahan had been passed from one administrator to another since 1950. It was the only standing directive at the State Hospital and it had survived more than half a century of cultural and intellectual evolution. Simply put it required the bearer to notify the Case Foundation in the event patient 108953, one Thomas J. Monahan, received out of house inquiries, visitors, public mention, or if there were any significant changes to his health or if he were to expire.

Dr. Canelli, the first administrator ever to have to act on the directive, was now doing it for the second time in as many weeks.

She, like all her predecessors, had wondered what connection there could be between the hospital's longest-tenured patient and the foundation of a pharmaceutical Goliath. Case's name was all over early research at the hospital, but then all the renowned physicians of the day came there. Psychiatry was in vogue in the fifties. The public was obsessed with psychological analysis. One family in three was admitting a member to some kind of mental facility for extreme behaviors.

But Case was known less for his research of psychiatric disorders than for amassing a fortune with nuclear medicine. While MRIs and CAT scans were relegated to identifying anatomical anomalies in the body, sophisticated nuclear diagnostic machines like SPECT could show the body's very organs at work. And nothing makes money like more money. Case was able to fund research, monopolizing advances in aspirin-free pain medications, birth control, antidepressants, and erectile dysfunction elixirs.

His critics had but one thing to say of him. It was rumored that the government, in their zeal to protect soldiers in a nuclear age, had knowingly supplied him with hundreds if not thousands of unwitting test subjects to experiment on. Who could predict the effects of radium dosages and interactions of experimental drugs when you were a decade ahead of the world in trials? It was an outrage, they charged, but it was never an outrage they could prove.

Dr. Canelli was hardly stupid. Dr. Case might have made countless contributions in the field of mental health, but he would have had quite the toy chest of lab rats in the asylum of seven thousand people. How hard would it have been with an army base next door and, what's more, an army base that had failed to publish a single printed word of its activities in a dozen years?

"I'm connecting your call," the voice said.

"May I help you?"

"Dr. Case?"

"Troy Weir. I am the doctor's representative to the Case Foundation."

"Of course, we spoke last week. Dr. Canelli from the state psychiatric hospital in New York."

"Yes, Dr. Canelli."

"Thomas Monahan. His name has come up again, I'm afraid."

"In what context, Doctor?"

"He had visitors today. Not for him exactly, but two people wanted to know if he had family they could contact. One of them was Sherry Moore."

"Sherry Moore?" Weir repeated.

"The psychic from Philadelphia. She . . . "

"I know who she is. The other?"

"An older gentleman. I didn't get his name."

"What did you tell them?"

"As I said, they already knew of Monahan's death. Miss Moore mentioned a physician in Philadelphia, a neurosurgeon by the name of Salix. She claimed to represent him and said there were questions about his records. I told her that the hospital's files were confidential. End of story."

"Thank you, Dr. Canelli."

"Do you wish me to contact Dr. Salix?"

"No. Do nothing," Weir said, perhaps too abruptly. "You have been troubled enough. We are most grateful."

Troy replaced the receiver, scanned his contacts directory, made himself a drink, and dialed a number at Nazareth Hospital in Philadelphia.

It rang, clicked, transferred to another number and rang again.

"General counsel," a woman said unenthusiastically.

"Jean? It's Troy Weir."

"Troy," she said, surprised. "To what do I owe the plea-sure?"

"Know a Dr. Salix?" he said, touching the ice in his glass with his tongue.

"William Salix?"

"He's a neurosurgeon?"

"We only have one," the attorney said tiredly.

"I need to know why he pulled a donor from the New York Psych Institute, a whole-body donor?"

"Is this another IOU?" Her voice was full of sarcasm, husky like a heavy smoker's.

"You know what Case gives to Nazareth each year," he said blandly.

"I know—don't ask, don't tell?" she snorted. "I'll see what I can find out."

"That's my girl."

"So when are you taking me out on that date, Troy? You said you had tricks to show me."

"Oh, Jean." He laughed. "I have tricks you wouldn't believe."

13

Sherry Moore arrived early for her appointment. She was wearing headphones as she often did in public to avoid conversation. Today she was listening to Bon Jovi's "Lost Highway" as an alternative to competing televisions and staff members calling out names over tinny loudspeakers.

"Beatrice Specter to billing station two." A particularly gravelly voice repeated the name a moment later. "Dr. Mark Cairns, pick up line one . . ."

The waiting room was a new experience to her as an adult. She had always met Dr. Salix in his Newbury office at the end of his day, always when other patients were gone. She had to admit, guiltily, that she resented having to be here. Shuffling, one of the many, like sheep through the chutes of a registration process, sitting for hours to be seen for five minutes, waiting for the billing department to assess and release you, the cure seeming worse than the disease.

It was much like the childhood she recalled, the litany of second-rate—and sometimes lecherous—doctors who visited the orphanage. The children were defenseless, made to strip while standing in lines and then paraded past everyone from journey-men to janitors. Who knew who owned the hands that squeezed or pinched or spread this or that—certainly not a blind girl.

She marveled constantly at how little attention they'd paid her back then. No one was interested in her health or education, not until it was evident that she was seeing things she shouldn't be seeing and then all of a sudden the professionals were coming out of the woodwork. Everyone was throwing themselves at her feet.

She was twenty when it first happened in public. A man in the throes of a heart attack had grabbed her hand on a busy Philadelphia street corner and pulled her to the sidewalk. She remembered the moment that life slipped from his body, his hand still clamped around hers feeling somehow different, and then the din of traffic and screaming pedestrians faded into si-lence and she saw a vision of a man being cast off a bridge into a dark river.

She felt ridiculous sharing her story with a detective that evening, and undoubtedly he did as well. But Sherry's descrip-tion of the bridge was so specific that police divers located it and recovered the body of a teamster boss who had gone missing hours before he was to give testimony to a secret grand jury. Then a clerk in the organized crime division of the U.S. Attor-ney's Office leaked to the press that it was a blind woman who led investigators to the body.

Weeks later Sherry received a request from the widow of a car rental tycoon to help locate her husband in the Canadian wil-derness. When she did, the media besieged her, and then the medical community as well, wanting to know about the blind girl's gift. They wanted to study her brain. They wanted to test her sight. To this day she received invitations from optometrists, ophthalmologists, and neurologists galore for free treatments.

It was sad, she realized, looking around the waiting room, that the people who most need help are the ones who never get it.

The minutes went by, faces staring blankly at the floor, teenagers in wheelchairs swaying to some unfathomable cadence, the weary-looking mothers and fathers with fixed smiles. Neurology departments in city hospitals were fermenting stews of suffering and sadness.

"Sherry Moore," a voice yelled mechanically from a hole in a glass partition.

Sherry walked to the counter, smiling politely at the handsome young man in the seat by the door. What tragedy had brought such a good-looking young man to this place? she wondered. Perhaps it was a relative. Perhaps he suffered some invisible malady like epilepsy.

The clerk pushed a paper in front of Sherry and told her to sign it.

Sherry looked for the blank line she had so infrequently signed in a life without sight and scribbled an indecipherable signature she had adopted over the years, triggering a tirade from the woman who snatched the form and replaced it with another, drawing an X by the correct line and jabbing her finger at it. "There! Write it there! See where it says *patient's* signature?"

Sherry signed it and turned for the corridor to Dr. Salix's office, noticing that the young man by the door had left. She had to acknowledge that being blind was even more limiting than she had come to think over the years. Certainly she had missed all kinds of interesting people around her, the wonders of nature and miracles of man. Eyes were truly remarkable things, she realized, and again she was reminded of her fear of losing them.

"Sherry"—the doctor smiled—"you look awesome."

"Thank you." She sat. "I feel good."

He picked up the ophthalmoscope and pulled up her eyelids as he checked both eyes. "No spots or shadows?"

"None."

"No blurriness?"

She shook her head.

"Light sensitive?"

"Huh-uh."

"What about the light showers?"

"Gone."

"Completely gone?"

She shrugged. "Mostly gone."

He laid the scope down and shook his head. "What color are the lights?"

"White," she said. "Sparkles of white light."

Salix took a seat behind his desk. "Sherry, do you have any, um, unusual electronic equipment around your house? High-tech alarm systems, something with an electromagnetic field?"

She shook her head no. "I have an alarm, but it's been there for years. Why do you ask?"

"There's a phenomenon called phosphene. It is the experience of seeing light without light entering the eye. Phosphenes can be triggered by electrical or magnetic stimulation of the visual cortex, sometimes the random firing of ocular cells."

"Meaning?"

"Your eyes may be particularly sensitive to the electronic clutter in the air. Radio and microwave transmissions, cell phone signals; God knows what's out there."

"Will it hurt me?"

"No, and if you can find the source of the energy, you could actually make it go away."

"So all is good then," she said.

"It's good." He held out his open hands.

She smiled.

"Sherry, what do you know about the ECoG?"

"You're not going to ruin this by cutting into my skull." Sherry recalled hearing a discussion about cranially implanting a pulse generator to stimulate an electrocorticogram's targets.

"It's just a suggestion. Food for future thought."

"You think this is temporary?"

"What if it is, Sherry?"

"Then it's temporary. I know how to be blind, Dr. Salix. I can do blind just fine again."

The doctor shook his head.

"Let's just take it a month at a time. If anything seems out of the ordinary, call me back. If not, we'll wait three months and do another EEG. If that's the same we'll go back to our annual checkups. Deal?"

Sherry nodded.

"When is your gamma ray test in Boston?"

"The thirty-first," she said.

He wrote something down.

"Dr. Salix. The man I tested with, Thomas Monahan. I went to the hospital up in Stockton. They told me he had been there almost all his life, but there are no records about his admission. Nothing about his family."

Salix sat and leaned forward toward her, his forearms on his knees, hands folded.

"What do you want me to do, Sherry? Whole-body donors aren't specifically categorized. Not unless there's a specific condition under study. The cadavers brought to Nazareth would have ended up in pathology. Nazareth is a teaching hospital." He shrugged. "I just pulled two at random from the lineup."

"Something about his brain, the way it worked, might have been responsible for my regaining sight. I think there was some kind of response from his memories—you said yourself I was talking out loud in the lab. I have never done that before. Whatever came back to me from him was more than just memory."

"Sherry, that's hardly probable."

"Yeah, well, so are my abilities, and this guy was in a psychiatric institute."

"I'll say it again. What do you want me to do?"

"I want you to find his records and compare them with mine. They had to have given him an EEG in sixty years!"

"Sherry . . ." He sighed, holding up his outstretched hands. She gave him a look and he nodded.

"Okay, okay, you're right, I'm sorry. I'll give it one more try. I'll have my assistant call the hospital in a day or two. They're working on month's-end books right now, but maybe Thursday. We'll get a doctor on the phone and we'll see what was going on with him before he died."

"Thanks," Sherry said. "That's all I want."

14

CASE ESTATE
LANCASTER, PENNSYLVANIA

"Do you know of her, then?"

"What I read in the papers," Case said impatiently. "What about her?"

"She was having tests done at Nazareth, simple electroencephalogram. Dr. Salix is her neurologist, has been for fifteen years."

"I know the fucking miracle story if that's what you're getting to," Case said.

"Salix brought in two cadavers and used them in his tests. One of them was Monahan."

"Jesus fucking Christ."

"I thought you'd want to know."

"Is there a recording?"

"My source says there was."

"Of what exactly?"

"Well, it still hasn't been transcribed, but whatever was said

in that room during the procedure. Dr. Salix records all his procedures. It's all on tape."

"His notes. What did they say?"

"They haven't been transcribed either. His staff is doing a
month's end on the books."

"I want a fucking copy."

"It's done. I have people on the inside."

"What happened to Monahan?"

"He should have been returned to the pool for the students.
They use a Delaware crematory afterward."

"Don't tell me what should have been done. Make sure he
finds his way there."

"Yes." Weir hesitated. "May I ask just who this cadaver is?"

"A very old acquaintance." Case kneaded his forehead with
thumb and middle finger. Then he looked up and stretched his
neck. Monahan was the very tip of the iceberg, he thought. How
many Monahans were out there still waiting to surface? And all
it would take is one nosy bitch to get it started. One would set off
another and they would tumble like dominoes . . . no, more like
fallen tombstones in a long, winding path that would lead directly to Case and Kimble's door.

"Just find out what you can." Case's voice seemed to falter.

"Is there anything else I should know?"

"He's dead." Case shrugged. "But listen to me, Troy. I want
him to remain dead. No one can go snooping into his life. If this
woman Moore so much as utters his name I want her silenced.
You get those transcripts. I want to know what happened in
that room."

"Yes, Dr. Case."

Case stood and looked down, tapping his fingers on the
desk. There was nothing he hadn't done in this dog-eat-dog world
to get ahead. His work would still be unknown if it hadn't been
for the Monahans of the world. Thank God they had all given
their lives.

15

Troy Weir approached the mirror above the marble bathroom sink and studied his face in the bright light. He smoothed his eyebrows, plucked a stray hair, and brushed back his bangs with a trace of alcohol-free gel on his fingertips. Then he straightened the knot of his pearl silk tie and gave himself a nod of approval.

An hour later he parked his Porsche on Chestnut Street and took a corner stool at Christian's bar. The hostess gave him a smile as he walked by her podium and when he looked back she was still checking him out behind an armful of menus.

He ordered a Ketel One on the rocks and scanned the two-story room. Tables were occupied on both levels, the air filled with hundreds of voices, glassware clinking, silverware clattering, the harsh sound of busboys stacking plates. The dinner crowd would soon leave the room to night prowlers, and the mating dance would begin. A few were already planted at the immense bar in their preferred stools, some advantage gained by facing the ladies' room door or a mirror that doubled the view, or maybe it was just what they considered their lucky seat. Two very young women in short dresses giggled over lime margaritas. Another, a brunette some ten years older, was using her reflection in a martini shaker to get her bangs to lie right.

A man in his forties was looking up the skirts of ladies climbing the stairwell to the balcony tables. The bartender was juggling glasses while watching his own reflection in the mirror.

Troy stabbed an olive and thought about Sherry Moore. He'd seen her picture before he arrived at the neurology department yesterday afternoon. It was grainy and admittedly not a good one, a journalist's photo of her getting into a car outside Nazareth Hospital the day she was released. Still, he wouldn't have picked her out of the masses in the waiting room. She looked nothing at all like her picture. Nothing at all like what he'd expected. In fact, if the clerk at the Neurology Department hadn't called out her name at just the right moment, he might have walked back out thinking she had failed to show or that he had somehow missed her.

Not that he'd missed her. You couldn't miss Sherry Moore. He simply hadn't made the connection. He'd remembered thinking at the time that she must be a sales representative for some pharmaceutical company. Who knew better than Troy how sexed up the pharmaceutical sales rep business was? I mean, you didn't just send any old fuddy-duddy with a briefcase to attempt to interrupt a doctor's busy schedule. That took a very special and highly motivated individual. A very sexy individual.

The vodka felt warm on his throat. There was energy in the crowded room. He wondered if Sherry Moore had ever been to Christian's before. Perhaps he could bring her here and make her do tricks for him some night. That would be different. That would be fun.

If she ever had appeared to be blind, there was no longer a clue of it. In fact, she looked stunning in that waiting room with her earphones parting tangles of long chestnut hair. Composed, assured. It was impossible to tell if she was listening to NPR or Black Eyed Peas.

And once he saw her it changed everything. He wondered what he could do to move her. To make her look at him twice. Oh, sure, he could have turned the equipment on and had her doing cartwheels in front of the Lombard-South subway train, but this wasn't some trollop from Jamborees or Vespers or the Pennypack Club. Not some snot-nosed law student from Boston College who thought he could extort money from the Defense Department's number one psychological warfare contractor.

Sherry Moore deserved so much better. She deserved his personal attention and he intended that she should not be disappointed.

He'd been reading about Sherry Moore ever since his encounter. He had downloaded every piece of material he could find on Moore and devoured it in six long early-morning hours. She had never been married and had no children. She had not been able to see since the age of five, when she was found abandoned on the steps of Nazareth Hospital in an ice storm. She suffered retrograde amnesia in addition to loss of sight. She was unable to recall the events prior to her head injury at age five.

Sherry Moore had been written about in every major newspaper. She had the confidence of at least one state attorney general and half a dozen law enforcement entities. She had surfaced in hundreds of investigations, from missing persons to missing wills, treasure hunting, historical research, and archaeology. And now, after thirty-two years, she could see.

"Is this seat taken?" A woman with dyed red hair was at his shoulder, perfectly positioned to afford him an eye-level view of one barely covered breast.

He shook his head. "Be my guest."

She smiled slyly and removed her sweater. The man at the opposite side of the bar suddenly found posture and began fumbling with the cuffs of his sleeves. The bartender flipped two bottles, catching one behind his back.

He'd read there'd been a life-changing incident for Sherry

Moore, something about a case in Wildwood, New Jersey, that sparked a suicidal spiral into depression. One of the articles suggested there was more to Sherry's relationship with one of the detectives in Wildwood than met the eye. The article went on to quote her as saying that a favorite memory of the detective was when he surprised her on her birthday at an aquarium in Camden and the staff let her feed and pet the dolphins. Of course, there were always exposés and insinuations by overly enthusiastic journalists. Anyone could make an affair out of anything said, but there was no indication in recent print that Sherry was carrying on a relationship now. No boyfriends showed up at the hospital when she miraculously regained her sight. No girlfriends came to see her, if that was how she was inclined. That would have made news, for sure.

By all appearances she was single and had no one to share her newfound miracle with.

He wanted to see how she would react to him. How she felt after suddenly being able to see after thirty years. One would expect her to be overwhelmed, of course, and animated, curious about everything. She might also be scared of eye contact with the faces that had so long eluded her. He knew she had seen his face at the neurological department at Nazareth. He knew it would register with her again, but it would take more than a wink to get Sherry Moore's attention.

Two more men sat at the bar. The redhead to his right was whispering into a cell phone. The margarita girls had spun backward on their stools and were talking to two boys with U.S. Naval Academy sweaters. A group of four women, young, late twenties, took a high-top table twenty feet away. They were all stunning, a collage of bare legs and shoulders. One of them smiled at him and then quickly looked away.

But it was a table behind theirs that drew his attention, a family of three—father, wife, and toddler. They were money for sure. Oatmeal-colored sweaters lay across their shoulders. Her diamond was the size of a cocktail olive. All pretty and proper and pristine they were.

She was thirty-something and blond. Hair pulled back in a short ponytail. The kind you might see behind a black riding helmet in the Lancaster Rolex Classic each August. Her face was perfect without makeup. She wore a lemon-colored blouse buttoned to the neck, khaki slacks, and practical leather moccasins. She was drinking Perrier and he iced tea. They were indulging the child, he imagined, putting into service their parental obligations before handing off the infant to a nanny for bedtime stories and another week of freedom.

There were shopping bags piled at her feet. They would have an apartment in the city, he guessed. Either that or they would be staying at the Rittenhouse. Most likely a driver was waiting for them outside. The time was only 8 p.m. On Saturday night the stores were open until 10 p.m. She could say she forgot something. She could catch a taxi back to the apartment or hotel later. "Oh please, while we're here in the city," she might say. He wouldn't want the headache of an argument.

"Crowded, huh?" The redhead leaned close.

"It's springtime. Everyone's getting out of the house."

"Cat," she said, offering him a small hand.

"Cat?" He took it.

"Short for Cathy."

"Of course," he said, smiling. "Will you hold my seat while I go to the men's room, Cat?" He stood and abruptly walked away.

MIRA was no bigger than—and actually quite looked like— an oversized pen. It was developed and paid for by the Defense Advanced Research Projects Agency, a small but financially powerful arm of the Department of Defense and National Security Agency. DARPA's grant money was derived from a budget so black that knowledge of MIRA's existence was limited to DOD's upper echelon, NSA, CIA, and its creators at Case and Kimble.

No more than seven people in Case and Kimble, including Troy and his stepfather, were familiar with its capabilities, and only Troy or his stepfather could remove it from the laboratory. It was as secret as anything got to be in the twenty-first century.

Troy made his way to the second-floor balcony, found a wooden beam to lean against, and feigned a cell phone call, pretending to be writing as he aimed the pen until the blond woman's face appeared on the phone's screen. Then he pressed a preset code.

Things had changed a lot since 1950, when his stepfather bombarded his first test subject with low-frequency radio waves. Like the stimoceiver of an earlier day, the objective was to stimulate primitive areas of the brain, to program the desire to kill or even die.

Nearly sixty years later, the technology had changed more than dramatically. Electromagnetic energy could be used to draw upon the target's own short- and long-term memories. Subtle suggestions based on models of emotional signatures mapped on computer-enhanced EEGs were now stored in databases and later used to trigger similar emotions in other human beings, suggestions as precise as the desire to cheat on a husband or as subtle as the desire to sleep with the next man a woman saw wearing a pearl-colored tie. All he needed to do was to send the blonde a packet of brain waves.

It had been years since pilots had been given the capability to eye their targets and mentally release their payloads. Now it was possible to bond any number of minds together.

The blonde reached up and touched her ear, wiped away a spot of perspiration. She picked up her ice water and drank from it. Then she pulled the sweater from her shoulders and leaned over and said something to her husband.

He nodded.

She began to look around the room, first at the other diners, but then she swiveled to check out the bar, settled a moment on the man at one end, and wrestled herself out of her seat and marched toward the ladies' room.

Troy smiled and put the MIRA back in his jacket, walked down the steps and back to his seat at the bar. And waited.

A few minutes later the blonde emerged. She had pulled the band from her ponytail and brushed her hair across her shoulders.

Back at the table she drank more water and squirmed in her seat, throwing glances over her shoulder toward the bar until at last she met Troy's eyes and he smiled.

The waiter brought their check. The busboy began to remove their plates. She put a hand on her husband's arm and leaned close to speak.

The man listened to her a moment and shook his head, pointing at the child. He made a gesture with both hands—*What am I supposed to do*? Then she said something else, but it only irritated him more and he stood and threw bills on the check. Without another word, he gathered the packages and made his way to the door with the stroller.

The blond woman just sat there. She unrolled an unused set of silverware and began to blot the sweat from her cheeks and forehead. She looked unnatural, her shoulders rigid; she was clearly uncomfortable, but then slowly she turned her neck until her eyes caught Troy's at the bar and she held his gaze a long moment. The connection was palpable.

"Yes," Troy whispered. The dance had begun.

"Excuse me?" The redhead in the stool next to him turned completely around until the toes of her heels were rubbing against his shoes.

"I was just thinking out loud." He pointed at his shirt pocket. "Forgot an important call."

He took out his phone and turned away from her again and the redhead made a face, took her drink, and marched to the end of the bar to talk to someone else.

He opened the cell phone and the blonde's face was back on the screen, bangs and perfectly cropped ponytail the way he remembered from when he'd photographed her fifteen minutes before. He liked her like that. Without all the makeup and flesh sticking out. Not like these bar sluts, but superior looking. He wanted to see her that way again. And then he wanted to watch her disassemble before his eyes.

The first successful intracerebral radio stimulation was attributable to a Dr. José Manuel Rodriguez Delgado in the 1950s, he knew. Delgado, as impatient as Troy's stepfather, quickly grew tired of working on cats and monkeys and moved his stimoceiver into mental institutions to work on patients.

The stimoceiver, unlike today's MIRA, was invasive and required implants to be placed in the brain. Once the patient was ready, he or she was bombarded by radio waves, stimulating the amygdala and hippocampus and producing a wide variety of emotions and effects, some pleasant and some not so pleasant.

MIRA was to the stimoceiver what the space shuttle was to the Wright Brothers' plane. Troy had read everything there was to know on the subject of mind control. He understood that the key to manipulating another person's thoughts was not by subliminal suggestion. It was by giving them a preordained set of instructions from electroencephalograms of test subjects having the identical thought that was to be reproduced. If X was thinking about a white-haired woman wearing a mink hat and, upon seeing one, pushed her in front of an approaching train, the EEG blueprint of that thought imprinted into another person—with a boost from an on-site medium such as himself—would produce the identical result. Catalogue a few million scenarios of EEGs from test subjects and you had an arsenal of impersonal weapons that would never leave a trace.

MIRA was the brainchild of Ed Case. Troy knew that it could only have been developed through years of trials on human guinea pigs—there were no substitutes for brains when it came to humans; you couldn't ask rats and guinea pigs to commit mur-der—and he sensed a great opportunity when his stepfather chose him to liaise Case and Kimble's multibillion-dollar defense contract with the Defense Special Projects team of the National Security Agency.

The blond woman was calling the waiter back to the table. They came to some agreement and he pointed to the bar. Then she returned to the ladies' room.

This was the moment, Troy knew. The redhead seated next to him earlier was still talking to a woman at the end of the bar, but her Nissan key fob and lipstick case lay next to a used cocktail napkin. He gathered them quickly and nested them behind the rack of glasses at the service bar to his left. Then he cleaned the bar with a linen handkerchief and placed his own glass upon it.

The door to the ladies' room opened; he saw her in tripli-cate, reflected in mirrors dividing the coatroom, bar, and dining room. The redhead was still talking, hands all over the place, strategically arching her back to thrust her breasts out for any-one who cared to see them.

The blonde was coming toward him now, slowly, eyes fixed on the bartender as she passed a dozen seats. She feigned notic-ing the open stool next to Troy, and he deftly removed the drink before she could see it.

"Taken?" she asked.

He shook his head. "Just opened."

The blonde slid in next to him, trying to look more inter-ested in getting the bartender's attention than in him.

The last time Troy had done this was at Seneca's on Market Street, just before the Christmas holidays. MIRA wasn't some-thing you just stuck in your pocket and walked out of Case and Kimble's most secure laboratory with. Removing it required a password and key card that only he and his stepfather possessed. But, owner or not, DARPA and the NSA wanted to be certain their device never fell into enemy hands. The system required that both men be present and both passwords used, to prevent either one of them from being kidnapped and forced to release the MIRA unwillingly. But Troy knew more about his stepfather than the old man could ever have imagined. Troy knew the one secret that Edward Case believed was his and his alone.

In 1949, as the Allies turned Hungary over to the communists and the Hungarian Academy of Sciences became a socialist academy, the famous communist physicist Nicolao Somogyi begged young Case to help obtain a green card for his only daughter, Syuzanna. Four months later Case married sixteen-year-old Syuzanna Somogyi of Budapest. The marriage was then annulled in Ashland, New Hampshire, in 1950.

Troy Weir knew it because his mother found the parched original of the marriage certificate in the fireplace ashes of the Case family home in the Catskill Mountains on January 22, 1952, when she dated and placed it in a photo album sleeve. When Troy was twenty-two and she was on her deathbed, she told him where to locate the document. With Edward Case, one could never underestimate the value of holding a trump card. Case's marriage to a communist in 1950 would surely jeopardize his lasting legacy to democracy. Not to mention that America was still talking about the traitor scientists from the Manhattan Project who along with Klaus Fuchs sold A-bomb technology to the Soviet Reds in 1945.

The password *somogyi* opened all of Ed Case's locked doors. Even his numerical key codes had been formed from the alphabetical equivalents of *somogyi*. Case thought the secret was his and his alone.

It wasn't something you could do every day. Security still printed a readout of who came and went from the lab, and Troy was most certainly on it. But Troy was the director of the lab, and unless his stepfather was specifically looking, there was no one to know any different.

He had had quite the night with the woman at Seneca's. The famous sports club had been crowded that holiday weekend. Jean

Stark, a sideline announcer for one of the nation's largest sports channels, was having dinner with five of the National Football League's Hall of Famers in town for Sunday's Eagles halftime show. Suddenly she saw Troy standing by the door at the opposite end of the room. He still had MIRA in his hand and her face on the screen when she walked up to him and gave him her phone number. Six hours later she was found—drunk and naked, stumbling through the eighth-floor halls of an upscale city hotel—by a tabloid reporter who had been tipped about Stark's having an orgy in her room with the Hall of Famers.

Her picture made the headlines. The tabloid somehow got a copy of a credit card receipt signed by Stark to purchase the room and a cell phone photo of women's clothing scattered around an unmade bed. The hallway outside the room was filled with empty liquor bottles.

The former players vehemently denied having sex with Stark in the room, but the damage was already done. Stark was off the network before Sunday's kickoff.

"Do you know what time it is?" the blond woman asked nervously.

"Early," Troy said. "Hopefully it's early." He chuckled, raising his sleeve, and he told her it was a quarter to nine.

"Thank you." She tried to smile.

"In town for the weekend?"

She looked at him and found she couldn't stop. She nodded, her blue eyes locked innocently on his.

"Excuse me!"

Troy looked over his shoulder and found the redhead who had been sitting next to him earlier. The spell was broken momentarily as the blonde turned and looked at her, and for a moment he saw fear in her eyes. Fear that she would lose him?

"I don't suppose you remember what happened to my keys." The redhead reached roughly over the blonde's shoulder and moved a glass to look around the rail.

"I think the bartender put them over there," Troy said innocently, pointing toward the rack of clean glasses to his left.

"Yeah, right, and screw you too." The redhead pushed her way between Troy and the service bar and retrieved her things. "Real classy," she said, and walked away.

"People." Troy shook his head.

The blonde looked at him again. Looked as if he were some long-lost thing she had just found.

"Troy," he said, reaching for and taking her hand.

She nodded, hand limp, every bit his. "Courtney," she said.

"Courtney. What a beautiful name." He looked at her hand and turned it over and rubbed his thumb over the tan lines where a wedding ring had been.

"You're married," he said, enjoying the game.

She covered the hand as the bartender arrived to take her order.

"Martini," she said. "Vodka."

She drank it fast and ordered another. She looked like she wanted to bolt for the door, but she wasn't moving and Troy knew it.

After the second martini, she turned toward him. Her eyes looked glazed.

"Take me somewhere," she said earnestly. "Please."

Troy looked into her eyes and smiled.

"Pretty please works on me." His face was now deadly serious.

"Pretty please," she said sincerely.

"Don't forget those words," he told her. "You'll need them later."

The debasing of Courtney Logan took most of eight hours.

He first had her fix her ponytail in the restroom and wipe the lipstick from her face. He had her button her shirt to the neck and put her wedding ring back on. Then he had pretended to forget his wallet, had her pay the tab for both of their drinks with her credit card.

He unzipped his pants in the cab and had her perform fellatio on the way to a dive bar in Camden, New Jersey. At the bar, he had her raise her shirt and show her breasts to a dozen patrons with cell phone cameras.

She begged him to take her to a hotel, and he did—her credit card again. They had sex and then he told her he wanted to watch her perform on other men and he sent her to the hotel bar and she brought back two more before the night was over. He took dozens of pictures of her from the closet, close-ups of her face, and then he dropped her penniless and without her phone on a dark street corner at 4 a.m. And e-mailed her husband a hyperlink.

16

Sherry was on the phone when Brigham came through the door. He was carrying a leather folio and dropped his jacket on a chair on the way to the dining room. She waved and held up a finger to her ear.

"Yes, I'll hold, thank you," she said.

Brigham heard her plop into the leather recliner by the secretary.

"Dr. Salix, that was quick, thank you."

Sherry listened as Brigham walked to the window. A public utility truck was parked on the far side of the hedge, its yellow strobe light reflecting off the second-story windows of a distant neighbor's house. The sound of a chain saw rose and fell; a tree had come down on some power lines overnight.

"How can that be? Surely someone from Veterans Affairs would have had to have examined him in fifty-some years! The army would at least have sent someone from personnel to see him in all that time. They were paying out the money?"

She was on her feet again and pacing the floor.

"No records. You're telling me there are no records. That is unbelievable," she said.

Brigham walked into the dining room and took a seat at the table.

"I know you know and I'm sorry. So where is the body now?"

"All right, but do me one more favor. See that he is not cremated. Can you promise me that, Dr. Salix?"

She waited for his response.

"Heck, I don't know," she answered. "A day, two days, a week, give me a week. Can you do that?"

A moment later she nodded. "Thanks, Doctor," Sherry said, pushing the End button on the receiver.

"Maybe I'm overreacting," she said, as much to herself as to Brigham. She dropped the phone and grabbed a mug of coffee from the top of an antique secretary, spilling some on the hardwood floor on her way to the dining room.

"Maybe I'm complicating things. Maybe it's not all that sinister. Maybe it's just some stupid chain of coincidences." She slammed the mug down, spilling more coffee on the table.

Brigham was dumping the contents of his cracked leather folio across the table.

"What did you see that day, Sherry?"

"I don't know," she said tiredly, pulling out a chair and falling back into it. "You mean about Monahan, right?"

He nodded.

"I was sitting at the end of a long wooden table. There was a gun in front of me, a revolver; small frame; two-, maybe two-and-a-half-inch barrel. Blue steel, wooden grips, it looked like one of Detective Payne's backup guns, the Colt .38 Special. There was a metal box at the other end of the table facing me. It had switches on it and a dial. The dial was white with a black needle. There were cones facing out toward the corners of the room; they were covered in black fabric. The room was white—the walls, the ceiling, all white. There was a man at the door watching me, looking in at me through a glass window. I remember he was wearing a hat and smoking a pipe."

She closed her eyes and seemed to be drifting.

"Go on."

"My skin was burning at the wrist; the top of the table was warm to the touch. I remember I looked at the man at the door and called for him to open it, but he just kept on smoking."

Sherry squinted, eyes moving right and left; the corner of her mouth twitched.

"Tell me about the box," Brigham said. "What was the needle doing?"

She looked perplexed for a moment, then concentrated.

"It was moving, bouncing, sort of, up to number five and back. When the needle rested it was low to the left." She nodded, trying to recall it all. "It was numbered five through thirty in increments of five. There were grooves on top of the box, air vents maybe, like it had a fan. Maybe it generated some kind of heat from inside."

"Tubes," Brigham said.

"Tubes?"

"Glass vacuum tubes. They preceded transistors and they used to get hot as hell. What else?"

"I felt like the fabric over the cones was vibrating. As if I should be hearing music or something, and yet the room was silent."

She lifted her arm suddenly and looked at a spot behind her wrist. "His arm touched a bolt or rivet or something on the arm of the chair, and the metal burned a spot on his forearm.

"I looked at the man at the door once more, then I heard a voice telling me to pick up the gun. I remember trying to watch the man, but my eyes were torn away, torn back to the table and the gun. I remember looking across it, trying to focus on the white dial, on the numbers, but the voice was in my head and it kept repeating itself. 'Pick up the gun. Pick up the gun.'"

"Was the man at the door speaking?"

She shook her head no. "It was definitely in my head. I couldn't close my eyes, and I remember concentrating on that white dial, not the gun." Her voice was slightly elevated. "I studied everything about it—tiny digits too small to read, the tip of the needle was fashioned into an arrow, there were words—but then my concentration broke, my eyes went back to that gun. I remember thinking there were people dying, bombs going off, dead bodies piled in a truck. A woman's head exploded on a dirt roadway. I pulled my eyes back to the dial, but my hand was moving toward the gun and I picked it up and blood was running down my wrist as I put it to my head."

"Blood?"

"From . . ." She hesitated. "It was coming from my nose. I was having a nosebleed."

"Tell me about the people dying."

Sherry closed her eyes and tried to remember. She stood and paced the dining room and at last she left for the kitchen and returned with another mug of coffee. "They were in the room with me," she said, raising the coffee to her lips. "They were over my left shoulder."

"You could actually see them? Physically see them?" Brigham asked.

She shook her head. "On the wall."

"A movie, then."

"Yes," she agreed, "but always the same one, it played over and over; they were always there to see and sometimes I couldn't look away from them."

"Okay, so then what happened?"

Sherry drank another sip of coffee. "I picked up the gun and put it to my temple and pulled the trigger."

"That's it? That's all you remember?"

"That's it," she said. Her eyes were wet with tears.

She took a deep breath, picked up her mug, and set it back down. "Maybe he was crazy, huh? I mean, what kind of a last memory is that?"

"He didn't die from the gunshot to his head. We know that much, Sherry, so this was something else. Betsy said they found him at the bottom of a cliff. He jumped or fell or was pushed. Whatever you saw in that room must have preceded his escape. Maybe by minutes or hours or days, we cannot know."

"But how is that possible, Mr. Brigham? How can someone just omit the last dozen hours or so of their life? How could I not see him escaping, running through the trees, lying at the bottom of the rocks when he was found? How could I not remember something about the next fifty-eight years before he died?"

"I don't know exactly," Brigham said. "But I've collected some things and I have a theory."

He took a seat across from her. Pushed one of his documents toward her. "This is a birth certificate. It says Thomas J. Monahan, born October twenty-seventh, 1932, Ahoskie, North Carolina, to Roy and Elizabeth Monahan."

"How did you find him?" she asked, astonished.

"Friends," Brigham said obliquely.

"Who was he?"

"Well, whoever else he was, he joined the army as a teenager and was shipped to Korea in 1950, Seventh Division, Thirty-second Infantry. He was there within weeks of the Battle of Incheon."

"Why doesn't the army know about him and claim him?"

"Because he died in Korea. A letter was hand-delivered to his parents December twenty-seventh, 1950. It says he was killed in action on Hill 105, twenty-five miles west of Seoul. There is a copy in his jacket in Washington."

"So why do you think it's the same Monahan?"

"The letter in his file wasn't signed by the CO of the Seventh

Division. I checked. It came from a General Henry Keith attached to the office of the secretary of defense."

"That's unusual."

"That's unheard of."

"Still, it's possible?"

Brigham snorted. "The secretary of defense was also a retired general in 1950. George Marshall, chief of staff of the Army until 1945. Guess who Alpha Company reported to in 1950? The secretary of defense."

"All right, but then how did Monahan end up in New York when he was supposed to have died in Korea?"

"My guess is that the Defense Department pulled him off the front lines at Seoul and made him an offer he couldn't refuse. It would hardly have been noticed in the confusion of battle. Divisions and battalions were always getting mixed up on the front lines."

"You think he was offered a trip back home?"

"To act as a guinea pig in military experiments."

"Experiments?"

"Let's just say it happened. And I'm telling you right here and now that I know that it happened. In the U.S., in Norway, in England, certainly in every communist state in the world, everywhere."

"And that would be an easy choice for a soldier? To leave his buddies and return to the States to become a lab rat?"

Brigham nodded. "From where he was sitting in Korea it would have been a very easy choice."

"But why go to all the trouble of bringing back volunteers from Korea? Weren't there hundreds of recruits stateside who would have been happy not to ship out in the first place?"

"Because if they came back from a war zone, the Department of Defense could plausibly deny putting their hands on them. Change a single line on a battle order and who is to say Monahan didn't get killed or go missing in action in Korea? We lost seven thousand boys in Korea and I'm not talking about men killed in action. We actually lost and then left them behind."

Sherry finished her coffee. "Which would be of great advantage should something happen to one of their guinea pigs," she said. She looked at Brigham a long moment. "You know, I'm surprised I'm hearing this from you of all people. You've had nothing but respect for the military for as long as I have known you."

Brigham scratched at a thumbnail. "I still do. It was a very strange time in history, Sherry. It would still be wrong to judge anyone's decision in isolation."

"You can't believe what you describe was right!"

"And you can't appreciate how naïve we were in 1950." He leaned back and sighed. "No, I don't believe in using humans as guinea pigs, but I can empathize with the decision makers at the time. I know how little we understood about the science and physics we were employing in the field. Just sixty years before World War Two, Indians were slinging arrows at Wounded Knee. Suddenly we've split the atom and can obliterate whole cities. You've got to put yourself in the moment. We didn't grow up with laptops and calculators in our book bags. Hell, we didn't have ballpoint pens until 1945. Suddenly, in one generation, we'd gone from the Stone Age to the hydrogen bomb. Suddenly, after four billion years, man had figured out how to destroy life on earth. And it wasn't that it was suddenly just plausible, Sherry. We cope with that knowledge ourselves and we cope with it every day. It was the speed with which it came upon us, and Germany, Japan, and the Soviet Union were all racing to devise the next superweapon, all threatening to rule the world."

Brigham shrugged. "The practice of soldier volunteers went back to World War One, perhaps to the beginning of history. We didn't have time to run test trials on mice when the enemy was spraying mustard gas in our faces. Soldiers had to test the worthiness of their own gas masks, containment suits, malaria pills, venereal vaccines."

"Without their knowledge?"

"Usually with their knowledge. People really used to volunteer, even when we told them that we couldn't warn them of the actual risks. We didn't know the risks ourselves."

"And this is what Alpha Company was doing in the Catskills."

"All I can say is that Monahan, whoever he was, spent the better part of his life in an asylum next to an army base that the government still considers classified. Draw your own conclusions."

"What would they have been doing there when he was twenty years old? I mean, what kind of research would have been conducted at the time?"

"I can't emphasize it enough. The world was a ticking time bomb back then. Stalin wanted all of Europe and he spent every penny of the Soviet economy eclipsing what the Americans did in Japan. Based on what you've told me of his memories, I'd say they were subjecting him to radiation and radio or microwaves. Radar was brand-new technology in World War Two. One of the questions not known at the time was what would happen if different frequencies and strengths of radio waves were concentrated on human beings for any length of time. Hitler's scientists had a device called the rheotron, essentially an X-ray generator with a concave cathode they aimed at aircraft trying to destroy them. The Japanese made significant improvements by testing it on animals, proving it lethal by disrupting neurological systems. The Soviets' intention for the technology was twofold. Khrushchev, who would become the next Soviet premier, said publicly on television that the Soviets had developed a weapon capable of wiping out all life on earth. We know they wanted the death ray, but we also knew they were attempting to put voices in the enemy's head. The CIA was near frantic in the 1950s over a device the Soviets called the LIDA Machine. A spy in Moscow claimed there were pictures of an auditorium full of people who had been rendered unconscious by it. We know that Soviet inter-rogators in Korea used it during the war to interrogate U.S. pris-oners by beaming microwaves at them with metal plates fixed against the sides of their heads. The soldiers that had been through the experience said it put them in a dreamlike state in which they had no control over answers they gave to certain questions. Suddenly we were pouring millions into mind-control research under the code name Pandora's Box."

Sherry looked at the documents. "And we wanted the ma-chine."

Brigham nodded. "Goddamn right we wanted the ma-chine."

"You think they scrambled Monahan's brain?"

"I think it's possible." Brigham thumbed through the docu-ments on the table, pulled one toward him, and raised his chin to deploy his reading glasses.

"The tests were using extremely low frequency ranges. ELF waves, they call them. They can be felt but not heard."

"Felt. You mean physically felt?"

"Physically and emotionally. First there's a marked rise in body temperature, then nausea, nosebleeds, maybe disorienta-tion, and consciousness of a presence before the voices begin. Sound familiar?"

Brigham leaned back in his chair and threw a leg over the end of the table. "The Soviets were putting political and war prisoners on television to confess to crimes against the state. They looked for all the world like zombies to us. Their speech was mechanical, their enunciation emotionless, reflex-ive. The conclusion was that the Russian scientists had per-fected psychoacoustic technology to beam messages directly to the brain."

"Is that a possibility? I mean even today?"

"Are you asking me as your friend or as a former admiral of the navy?"

"Jesus," Sherry said.

"Sherry, you can't imagine what technology is out there today."

Brigham shifted in his chair and held up his hand, ending the line of inquiry.

But Sherry wasn't listening anymore. She pushed her chair from the table and walked to the window.

"If Monahan was subjected to radio waves that altered his neurological system, isn't it possible that when I tapped into his mind I altered my own? Maybe the contact between us changed the cerebral partitioning of my optical nerves?" Sherry looked at Brigham.

Brigham shrugged. "I'm actually beginning to believe it myself."

"Did you find his parents?"

"Both dead. I asked a friend with contacts in the North Carolina State Bureau of Investigation to locate the family. There are none. No siblings, no aunts, no uncles."

"So that's it. End of story."

"What Alpha Company did in the Catskills during the Cold War will long be protected by the National Security Act. This I can assure you."

"After all this time?" Sherry looked skeptical.

Brigham laughed. "The CIA is still protecting invisible ink formulas from 1917." He picked up his coffee. "Look it up."

"Okay, so what isn't classified?"

"All the conjecture."

"Great."

"No, wait, it's better than you think. There are dozens of tell-all books about the Cold War. Someone is always willing to talk."

"Summary?"

"Area Seventeen was rumored to be a secret weapons lab. Their proximity to the asylum would have made it one of the better locations to test radiation, and radiation testing in other places in the country has been well documented during the period Monahan would have been there."

"The radiation testing itself? The government admitted to doing it?"

"Absolutely. The government's settled out of court on a number of cases already, but it was hardly more than a token. The thing to remember is that, in spite of what we admitted to in the past, many of the projects that they were working on then continue even today. That's the reason the records remain sensitive and secret."

"God. . . . What else?" Sherry wanted to know more.

"There are always civilians involved. Scientists, doctors, people who if still living would not want the world to associate them with what they had done in Area 17."

"Meaning?"

"Meaning, if you start making noises about any of the people still alive, you're liable to ruffle some feathers. There are still secrets to protect."

"So you're saying leave it alone. That there's no one left or willing to tell us anything about this man."

"I'm saying that the more you know before you go around asking questions in public, the better chance you won't be stopped by some spook in a trench coat. The better chance that more records won't disappear. You know there's always that security chief that found Monahan's body at the bottom of the rocks. Betsy said she could introduce us to his widow—maybe there's something there to learn. She said the lady would talk to you."

Sherry's eyes dropped to the table, roaming across the papers that Brigham had laid in front of her. She let out a deep sigh, met eyes with him, and rubbed her knees with the palms of her hands.

She nodded. "We have to go back there."

"Well, I'm in for now, but just for a while," Brigham said. "Don't go nuts on me, like you're prone to do."

"Nuts!"

"Remember your solemn promise of atonement in the hospital? For all the worry you've put me through?"

"All right, you're right, I promise I won't go crazy." She put up both hands as if to surrender. "If there's nothing to learn from the widow, it's over."

"That's very reasonable, Sherry," Brigham said admiringly.

"I have a surprise," Sherry said out of context.

Brigham cringed. "Oh, Lord."

"Oh, don't get all excited. I'm taking a literacy course. That's all."

Brigham looked at her, surprised. "So soon?"

"Why wait? If my sight stays, it stays, and I'll be ahead of the game. If it goes away again I'll have lost nothing but a little time. Right?"

He nodded.

"My first class is on Tuesday at three, in the city. Could we go to Stockton on Wednesday?"

He nodded. "I'll call Betsy and find out if McCullough's widow will be there and talk to us."

Sherry smiled.

"Stop smiling like that," Brigham said.

17

Weir could have appealed to the Department of Defense for a more sophisticated means of tracking Sherry Moore. The government shared its technology liberally when it came to protecting MIRA. But Weir didn't want DOD to know about Sherry Moore. Not if there was a chance she would have to go missing. And they had already seen each other in the hospital waiting room. He only needed one opportunity to introduce himself into her life.

Weir parked his car on the busy side street that paralleled Sherry's riverfront home. It didn't take long. On Tuesday just before 2 p.m. a city cab pulled into the half-circle portico and Sherry left the house alone. Forty-five minutes later, Troy and his quarry were in the city, on Walnut and approaching South Sixth Street, when the cab put on its turn signal, bent the corner, and pulled to the curb. Troy passed hurriedly, parking in a handicapped zone for the American Philosophical Society, where he left a government ID on the dash. Then he grabbed two books from the trunk and ran down South Sixth to where he'd last seen the cab. Sherry was on foot and just turning the corner at St.

James. At a quarter to three he caught up to her. She was climbing the steps of the Athenaeum.

Troy passed the security guard and walked down the dimly lit hall. Sherry was in a room to his right, talking to the receptionist, a pretty black woman. He pretended to be interested in exhibits in the hall and repositioned himself when she left the desk, seeing her take a seat at a table in the corner of the room. Five minutes later a man with thick gray hair approached the door and walked to the information desk. The receptionist pointed toward Sherry, who stood, waiting to shake his hand. A moment later they sat and began to talk.

At five minutes after four, Sherry exited the Athenaeum and was walking down the steps when she heard someone yell, "Excuse me," and she turned to see a handsome young gentleman getting to his feet. He had been sitting on the steps with books in his hand.

"I know you." He grinned with a look of boyish enthusiasm.

"The hospital," Sherry said. "You were in the neurology department last week. Right?"

He nodded and rolled his eyes. "Sorry, I just couldn't let you get by"—he pointed toward the sidewalk—"the city is so big it keeps reminding me I'm so small. I'm quite new to Philadelphia." He waved a hand and shook his head. "It just struck me that I actually recognized one face in all of the masses." He put out a hand, palm facing Sherry. "I'm sorry; you must think I'm very silly."

"Don't count on it," Sherry said, sizing him up. "Odd place to meet someone who doesn't know the city well. The neurology department of a city hospital."

"Yeah, well, then there's that," he said, scratching an ear with the cuff of his sleeve. "Can't go anywhere without checking in with those buggers."

She didn't say anything.

"Fibromyalgia. I need therapy for pain. It messes with my sleep big-time. Bad genes, I guess, what can I say."

GEORGE D. SHUMAN

"Old head injury." Sherry touched her scalp to explain her own visit to the unit. "They like to get their money's worth out of you."

He laughed. "I'm Troy—" He tried to shift the books to his left hand to shake her hand, but he lost his grip and they fell clattering to the concrete. They stooped together to retrieve them and Sherry saw the open covers. One appeared to be a history book. There were men in powdered wigs in front of a flag-draped cannon. The other had only a black-and-white photograph of an old dilapidated building.

"Sherry," she said, taking his hand, but her mind was fully on the building. Sherry had never seen it before, but she was certain she knew what it was.

"That book?" she said, pointing.

"Halley House Orphanage." He shrugged, tucking the books back under his arm. "I'm not really into ghost stories, but I was picking up stuff on Philadelphia's history and there it was."

"I didn't know there was a book," Sherry said softly, trying to keep her composure.

"You know the place, then. Yeah, they closed it in 1994. Supposed to be one of the oldest surviving orphanages from the 1800s."

"They started sending the residents to foster homes in the 1980s," Sherry said absently. "Subsidized apartments. The projects," she added more distastefully.

"So you're a historian?" The young man smiled.

"No, I knew someone who grew up in there." She had to force her eyes away from the picture. "And now they say it's haunted." She laughed nervously, wondering if she looked as stunned as she felt.

"Everything's haunted these days," he said. "Helps the economy, I guess. More bad TV and ghost tours."

"Where do you live?" they both asked at the same time, and laughed.

"South, near the river," she said ambiguously.

"Price Towers," he said. "One bedroom takes three weeks' salary every month. Could I buy you a coffee or a beer or something?"

Sherry laughed again. "I like beer," she said, thinking it so strange that he was carrying a book about her childhood.

He looked around and shrugged. "Where's a good place around here?" He looked lost.

"Come on," she said. "Follow me, and don't drop your books."

Jamborees was getting the first few arrivals for happy hour. They took one of the high-back wooden booths opposite a brass and marble bar, ordered Guinness, and cracked open peanuts from galvanized buckets that advertised Corona.

"You're studying?" He looked at the books she had laid on her seat.

"A secret," she said mysteriously, pushing the cloth bag with *Visual Dictionary and Phonemics Awareness* behind her back.

"Really?" He pretended to look concerned.

"Really," she said. "If I told you, you wouldn't believe me. What about you?"

"History," he said, "but only for my fun reading, and Philadelphia history in particular because I've recently taken up residence here. Never hurts to know something about where you live. I like history. It's so much better when I already know the outcome of a story."

"I'd be better off that way with relationships too," she joked, and could not afterward fathom why.

He nodded. "I sense we have some common ground there." He was pretending to be gravely serious, except that nothing was serious about him. He was fun. He was just fun, she thought.

And if he got up this moment and walked away it wouldn't matter in the least to her, except that she could say she had had a good time.

"You're an academic?"

"God no." She laughed. Then she thought about the books by her side and really started to laugh, having to cover her face with a napkin.

"Me neither." He smiled, getting caught up in her mirth. "I am the last person you might find in a classroom."

"But you like history."

"I like sticking my feet in the mud too. Frankly, I'm terrified of classrooms. I can't deal with the sight of a lectern or podium."

"So what do you do?"

"I'm a biologist. Molecular."

"Get out."

"No, seriously. Trait genetics is my specialty. Do you want to know where that nose of yours came from?"

"Actually I would, but another time." Sherry studied his face for a clue that he was joking. There was none.

"And you?"

"I do private readings."

"Stop it," he said, mocking, raising his beer and leaving his lip covered in foam.

A waiter came by offering menus. They ordered appetizers and another round of beer.

"It's complicated," she said. "But let's leave that for another time, okay?"

"Okay," he said. "We'll just keep it light, then."

He stuck out his hand and she took it and shook. They had made a pact and she thought that his hand felt good. A good, strong hand.

"May I look through your book, the orphanage book?" she asked.

"Of course," he said, pushing it toward her.

"You said you're from a small town. Where?" she asked, opening the cover.

"Tall Timbers, Maryland."

She shook her head. "Never heard of it," she said, flipping through the pages and looking for pictures.

"Tip of southern Maryland in the Chesapeake Bay."

"You grew up on the water." She turned a page and the black-and-white photo showed a ward of white metal beds pushed up, one against another. There were shoes at the ends and white night dresses folded and stacked on the pillows. Two ancient crones in black aprons and wearing black pinafores and tented hats stood rigidly in the background. Sherry knew the room, though she'd never seen it with her own two eyes, the arched ceiling with small dirty panes of barred glass, the cracked columns down the center. Her childhood flooded back to her, drowning her in waves of profound melancholy.

"I grew up in a dump, but with plenty of water around it," Troy said. "And lots of little critters swimming around in it."

"Hence your major," Sherry managed to say. She closed the book and pushed it back across the table. This wasn't the time to relive Halley House. This wasn't the place.

"Hence my major," he repeated, raising his mug to toast, and they touched glass as new beers arrived.

"Are you divorced or is that too personal?" Troy asked.

"Never married," Sherry said, wondering what she would make of this conversation, this man, if she didn't have eyes to see with. Did the eyes take the edge off other senses? Well, of course, she knew that to be true in a dozen different ways, but the question was more about making judgments. Did the eyes favor beauty over insight? Did they automatically adjust or compensate for traits you could not see?

He was interesting, to say the least. How many people did you bump into in the middle of a city carrying a book about your childhood origin?

"I can't even respond to that," he said. His face registered surprise.

"That I wasn't married?"

He nodded. "You're not . . . ?"

She smiled and shook her head. "I don't think I'm whatever it is you're asking. If that's what you're asking."

He leaned forward with a most serious look on his face. "You realize you're gorgeous, right? I mean, not pretty, but downright gorgeous."

Sherry looked down at the table.

"No, you must know that." He looked around the room. "Every guy in this place envies me. Every guy that passed us on the street envies me."

"That's a little dramatic, wouldn't you say?" Sherry put her mug to her lips, thankful that the booths were high-backed and very few people could get a look at her. She wasn't recognized often out in public, but then she hadn't spent a lot of time in public. When she did, she did her best to downplay her distinctive hair and the fact that she was blind. But who knew how many people had pointed at her over the years and hadn't had the nerve to approach?

Troy shook his head in wonder. "You really don't know, do you?"

"Where do you study genetic traits?" she asked, changing the subject.

Troy laughed. "I'm sorry, really I am. Um, have you heard of the Case-Kimble Foundation, Fairmount Park, near Roxborough Hospital?"

"The pharmaceutical labs," Sherry said. "I've never seen the buildings, but I know the park."

He nodded. "I have an office there. A lab."

"Nice place to work?" she asked, impressed.

"It's amazing," he said. "They really treat us well. It's like a city inside a city. Barber shop, spa, convenience store, there's even a museum. Company history, of course. Stuffy things."

"And a four-story black marble mortar and pestle surrounded by fountains. The artist was Janssen from Estonia."

"They can afford to be extravagant."

"I'm sure they can," Sherry said.

"So you know Fairmount Park."

"The stables. I've been out to ride once or twice."

"Horses. That fits you," he said. "One day you will have to
see the foundation with me. I'll give you the insider's tour. If you
wish, of course."

Sherry turned the glass in her fingers. "Sure," she said.
"Someday."

Two beers turned into three and then four, and at seven thirty
they'd run out of things to say, but by then they'd begun to brush
against each other's shoes and fingers across the table. Now there
was an unspoken bond and it was at times awkward and at others tantalizing. The night would end with a comma, not a period,
she thought.

She knew it was wrong. That she was disrespecting Brian
Metcalf. But, unlike Brian, this man held no power over her. He
was handsome and charming and, above all, disposable. If she
went blind and never saw him again it would hurt neither one of
them. If she died of cancer in five years, he wouldn't even know
it. He was safe. And she knew she would give him her phone
number.

18

It was odd, Sherry thought, how the same drive to some distant place never seemed as long the second time around. They reached Stockton in less than four hours, which included a three-mile stretch of construction on I-87 with hundreds of orange cones and not a single highway worker.

Once they left the interstate she saw tulips beginning to bloom. They had long been out of Philadelphia and Sherry was surprised once more at the cool temperature and the number of chimney fires and the smell of burnt wood in the air.

"Betsy working today?"

Brigham shook his head.

"Well, are you ever going to tell me what she is doing?"

"She said she'd meet us at the tavern at two."

"You know, I'm so glad I have eyes to witness this one re-markable event in my life."

"Oh, stop being so dramatic."

"We'll make it there by then?" she asked.

He nodded.

Sherry reached to touch her Braille watch and smiled inwardly at the gaffe—for what, the thousandth time, was it? She glanced down and judged they were less than twenty minutes away. She pulled the visor down and checked herself in the mirror. She couldn't say if it was because she cared what she saw or if she was only making up for all the times she hadn't been able to do it before.

"Did you date a lot before you met your wife, Mr. Brigham?" Sherry asked.

"I dated a few women," he said, not committing to a number.

"How did you know Lynn was the one?"

Brigham looked at her, then back at the road.

"You just know," he said. "It isn't about any one thing."

"Did you ever have regrets?"

"None that mattered," he said.

"Did you ever wonder if she had regrets?"

Brigham was silent for a while, but Sherry sensed he was mulling it over.

"I think I could have spent more time with her," he said at last.

"Because you were in the navy?"

"Because of that, because of the committees I was on, because I thought I was indispensable to the government."

"She was happy, though. You two were happy?"

"She never said different."

"I'm sorry," she said. "I didn't mean to put it that—"

"There were never any bad anythings," Brigham said grouchily. "We were apart a lot, is all. I don't think either of us would have chosen differently if we had a second time around."

Stockton was all but deserted on a Wednesday afternoon. A wind was coming out of the north and whipping new buds on the trees. A stop sign wobbled on its post and the single flashing traffic signal in town was swinging on its cable.

"Looks like an *X-Files* episode," Sherry said. "Where is everybody?"

Brigham turned to look at her. "Is that what you do all night long? Watch TV?"

"Just rounding myself out," she said defensively.

The parking lot of Grant's was empty but for a red Saab; likewise the small public parking lot across the street, where someone had chained an old bicycle.

Brigham held Sherry's arm as they pushed through the gusting wind to the door.

The lobby smelled like old leather and sawdust; the hallway to the dining room hinted of delicious smoked food from the grill.

"Now I'm hungry," she said. "For red meat."

"We can do that." Brigham removed his sports jacket and pulled Sherry's sweater from her shoulders.

Betsy was in a corner of the dining room, next to a woman with completely white hair. There was an old album on the table between coffee cups and empty soup bowls. Betsy stood and offered them hugs rather than handshakes, a gesture that might only reflect small-town friendliness or perhaps was calculated to beguile Mr. Brigham.

Betsy introduced them. "Carla McCullough Corcoran, Sherry Moore"—they shook hands—"and Mr. Garland Brigham."

"Pleased, Mrs. Corcoran," he said.

Brigham and Sherry took seats opposite the women.

"I can't believe that someone has mentioned my Jack's name after all these years." Mrs. Corcoran reached out and cupped both of her hands over Sherry's and then Brigham's.

Carla had a soft face and beautiful blue eyes. Sherry noticed that her nails were filed and polished, her hair was smart and short, and she wore a lamb's wool sweater with a pair of designer stonewashed jeans.

"We can't thank you enough for seeing us, Mrs. Corcoran."

"Oh, pooh." She took her hands away and waved them over the table. "But it's not exactly Jack you're interested in?" Carla had a knack for using her eyes, centering on you, making you feel as if you were the object of her attention, and the only object. Betsy had mentioned that Carla was a retired schoolteacher, and Sherry was sure she had used the technique to effect in many a classroom over the years.

"I met a man in Philadelphia," Sherry started to say. "Not really met, but he was . . ."

"I know who you are, Miss Moore," Carla said kindly. "I think you mean to say you met a dead man."

Sherry laughed with embarrassment, determined not to underestimate this woman.

"He was from the hospital here, Betsy told me."

"Yes, yes," the old woman said.

"Betsy said you knew about him too?"

"Of course I did." She laughed. "Everyone in town knew about him. The staff always joked how at least that poor boy was getting his money's worth out of Uncle Sam. After a while the townspeople began to ask about how he was doing every year, glad to hear he lived another one on the government's dime."

"The town doesn't much hold the government in esteem." Brigham didn't quite phrase it as a question.

"Oh, we've got nothing against the government. . . ." Carla shook her head slowly, eyes alive with light. Happy eyes, Brigham thought. "No different than any other town around the country. But there was a time here we were all part of something bigger. Back then a lot of strangers came through town, quiet people, maybe even scared people, we thought. They were from the military, of course."

Carla picked up a pack of soup crackers and worked at tearing them open. "You ever see anybody that looked like they were crumbling under the weight of their own knowledge?" The old woman turned her eyes on Sherry. "You ever felt like that yourself? Like you heard something that changed your life and you couldn't unhear it again?"

Sherry thought of New Mexico and nodded. "Yes. I think I know what you mean."

Sherry found that she very much liked the manner of Carla McCullough Corcoran.

"That's what they reminded me of. Some of them came to the hospital after my husband brought the boy there. There were a couple of high-ranking officers, he said, from that army base of theirs, and the asylum administrators let the army do pretty much as they pleased back then. When the staff began to ask about the boy's relatives, they sealed off the room and had their own doctors brought in. I heard all this much later, of course. After Jack was gone."

Betsy nodded, as if remembering the times she had heard the same story, over and over.

"A day after they found him at the foot of Mount Tamathy they concluded he was brain-dead." She glanced at Betsy. "They've got better words for that now, I'm sure, but it's all the same. Anyhow"—she looked back at Sherry—"they just left after that. Betsy knows more about the rest than I do. I heard the army's doctors spent some time with the asylum's administrator and the administrator later announced to the staff that Thomas Monahan had no living relatives and he was moved to the old E Annex, where they kept terminal patients back then."

"Your husband was in charge of security at the hospital."

"It really was an asylum," Carla smiled. "Still is. Asylum's not such a bad word. Means shelter from danger, refuge."

After a pause, Carla opened the photo album she had brought. "That's Jack," she said, her little finger poking at a tall man sitting at a dining room table.

"Handsome," Sherry said softly.

Carla nodded, never taking her eyes from the picture. Sherry watched her gaze drift ever so slightly, teeth catching her upper lip. She flipped pages. "He was the first one to find Monahan." She sighed, stopping at a page and turning the album to face Sherry and Brigham. "That's the only thing Jack ever said about the whole thing. That he found the boy. Oh, look here." She pointed. "This is what the asylum looked like back then. They've fixed it up quite a bit now." She scrunched her face. "Now that mental illness is respectable."

"Monahan was AWOL when your husband found him."

"Well, no one ever came out and said so, but he'd been running in the opposite direction from the base when he was seen that morning, so you can draw your own conclusions." Carla looked around the table. "Still in uniform. Jack said he'd jumped from the Tamathy summit."

"That's what he said? He used the word 'jumped'?"

She nodded. "That's what he said to me. I guess no one could prove it one way or another, 'cause the boy never came to consciousness again."

"They documented this, of course? Took a report of some kind?"

Carla nodded. "Jack kept a security log of all incidents on the property. He was very meticulous about things like that."

"But it wasn't there in the seventies when I was at the asylum," Betsy said. "Security looked for it, we all looked for it. Believe me when I tell you, it isn't in that building."

"So the army got to it?"

"All other records from the fifties and sixties are in archives in the basement." Betsy shrugged. "Besides, I've never heard a better explanation."

"What about the administrators?"

"You saw the portraits in the lobby," Betsy said. "They changed administrators like you change tires over the years. Who could doubt the government had one or more of their own people in charge in the last fifty years?"

"What else did your husband say about it?"

"Really nothing." Carla's eyes locked on Sherry's and she wagged a finger. "And that was unusual for Jack. I knew it had happened an hour or two after they got him to the emergency room. Jack came home tired. He'd been searching the mountain all day and now he had the boy's blood all over him. He said he just wanted to shower and change." She resumed slowly flipping through the album. "He was upset, I could tell. He'd just found this boy dying at the bottom of the rocks, and that's not easy, I don't think it matters how much bad stuff you've seen before. It can't get all that much easier."

Her eyes turned slightly to the right, but she wasn't so much looking at the rough wood wall as looking through it.

"You know, he mentioned the boy's eyes," Carla said discordantly. "They were bleeding from inside his head."

The memory must have taken her by surprise, Sherry thought.

"He said he'd never seen anything like that boy's eyes before. That's when he was walking out the door to go back to the asylum. It seemed to me then that there was something else he wanted to say, but I figured we'd talk it out later when he got home, that's the way he was. But he didn't talk it out later. Not ever. It was like it never happened after that day and the one time I prodded he had nothing at all to say."

"Which was strange?" Betsy nodded encouragingly at Carla.

Carla shook her head. "Which wasn't like him at all. We talked about everything that bothered him at work. Jack wasn't a man of many words. Not out in public, but we had a different relationship. He confided in me about everything and I confided in him. We took on life as a team. I don't know how these young working couples do it today. They go out to their own lives every day and meet for a few hectic hours in the middle, picking up or dropping off children, maybe even trading them for a night or a weekend, and they never talk. How anyone can take all the world has to throw at you alone is beyond me. I mean, you do what you've got to do, but it's a whole lot easier to share your problems with another person. Life was a lot less stressful when I had Jack. Colter, my current husband"—her eyes moved to Sherry, then Brigham—"he has friends of his own. He owns a golf course on the Ashokan, so he gets his stress out on the green, or more likely, in the clubhouse." She grinned. "We don't talk like Jack and I did, but then everyone is different."

Carla touched the album with a finger. "Jack had opinions about what went on up there at that army base. I know he did. But he didn't say a thing about it in front of me." She took a drink of water and dabbed her lip with a paper napkin.

"I talked to Emmet Fry at a company picnic years later. He was Jack's deputy at the time and became the chief of security after Jack died. Anyhow, Emmet asked me if Jack had ever talked to me about the incident with the Monahan boy. I told him what Jack had said about the boy jumping from the rocks and he looked surprised, like he'd never considered the idea that the boy committed suicide before. He said, Carla, are you sure Jack said the boy jumped? And I told him yes, I was sure. That was exactly the word Jack used. Then Emmet told me he and Jack had seen freshly dug graves inside the fence of Area 17, way around on the far side of the base. That was the last time he or I ever spoke of it."

Carla shook her head and looked around the room. Her eyes were getting watery and she was rubbing a finger back and forth across the table. She leaned toward her friend. "Emmet's been gone almost a dozen years now, wouldn't you say, Betsy?"

"About that, dear," Betsy answered.

"Jack wasn't right after that day." She began to draw figure eights on the tabletop with her finger. "I think he was afraid of something. I think he was afraid for both of us."

"Afraid of the army, you mean?" Sherry asked.

The old woman shrugged. "Who else?"

"Jack died right after the incident, Carla?" Sherry said.

The woman nodded. "Five weeks later."

"Nothing else was happening in his life at that time?"

She shook her head, still drawing figure eights. Her eyes had lost focus, as if she had left them all sitting there at the table and gone away for a time. Then she laughed all at once and sat back, folding her arms across her chest. "The time capsule." She smiled.

"Time capsule?"

"They were all the rage back then, ever since the World's Fair in 1939," Carla said. "They buried a big one that year in Manhattan that was to be opened in five thousand years. The thing weighed something like eight hundred pounds. Westing-house manufactured it, I remember, and it was filled with crop seeds and literature, threads and microscopes, newsreels, phone books, and on and on. After that a lot of schools started making their own time capsules and of course when students of one school heard about it they told others and pretty much every school ended up having to bury one of the darned things.

"For us it was sixth-grade English class in 1950, the subject I taught for thirty years at Stockton Middle School. The kids were determined to bury midyear essays with a class picture near the construction site for the new gym going in. The equipment was already there. It was no big deal to ask them to drill another hole in the ground.

"Of course, the list grew of things they wanted to put into the jar: Raggedy Anns, Buck Rogers water pistols, Cootie, Silly Putty, things like that. We were going to use this humongous candy jar and seal the lid with wax, but the kids brought in so much stuff, we ended up needing two of them. Then we printed a declaration of intent and had it read into town council minutes requiring the governing body of Stockton to unearth the jars and share our history with the sixth-grade class of 2050."

Everyone nodded, wondering where the story was going.

"Jack," she said, "was sitting in his rocking chair the night I was sealing the jars. I had a pan on the stove to melt wax. . . ." She stuck her tongue in the side of her mouth, remembering something from long ago. "And he did the strangest thing," she said at last. "He got up and left the room, and when he came back was holding a green leather book, a writing book, like a journal. He asked me if he could put it in one of the jars.

"I didn't say anything at first. I knew he made sketches of things he saw in the forest, he was quite a good artist, but I never knew him to keep a journal. Jack was spare with words, you understand, and there wasn't a frivolous bone in his body. He never did anything just for fun."

"So you put it in," Betsy said, excited.

Carla nodded. "And I sealed it in front of him. Jack knew me well. He knew I'd never pry. I respected him, and I respected his judgment, everyone did."

Sherry's cell phone buzzed on her hip and she reached to silence it. "The jars won't be opened for another forty-some years," she said without missing a beat.

Carla shrugged. "That was the plan. Might have worked, if the cable company hadn't come to Stockton. They managed to run their trencher right into them. I was retired by then, but the principal knew the story. The seal had broken on one of them and most of the contents were soaked and rotting. The other one's up in my attic. Glass is cracked. I kept meaning to ask someone to put it in a decent can and bury it again, but people just don't do things like that anymore. It hardly seemed worth the effort now."

"Your husband's journal?"

She smiled. "It was in the jar that survived. And out of respect I have been determined not to open it."

No one spoke for a minute.

"May I ask a personal question, Carla?" Sherry asked.

"Sure."

"Was your husband ill or depressed?"

Carla shook her head emphatically. "We had one doctor in town back in the day. Dick McKinley. He said Jack was the last person in the world he would expect to take his life."

"And he would have known if there was anything seriously wrong with him."

"They hunted together," Carla said. "He would have known."

"You know what I'm going to ask you?" Sherry leaned across the table in the old woman's direction.

"You'd like to see the journal, I'm sure." The eyes were alive again, piercing.

"I would promise to be discreet."

"I'm sure you would, Miss Moore, and I'm inclined to say yes to you. Would you give me a little time, though? It's not easy to explain, just a few days."

"I understand perfectly." Sherry held up a hand to stop her. "Have Betsy call me when you're ready."

Carla smiled and folded her hands in front of her.

Betsy stood. "I asked Mike to let us be for a while. You folks want drinks or menus?"

"Will you stay with us for lunch, Carla?" Brigham asked.

The old woman shook her head. "Nah. If you'll excuse me I'll be getting home now."

"May I walk you?" Brigham got to his feet.

She waved him off. "Oh, heck no, I'm just half a block from home."

Sherry got up as well. "It was very nice meeting you."

Everyone shook hands and Betsy excused herself to go to the ladies' room.

"What do you think?"

"I'm not sure," Sherry said.

"The journal sounds interesting."

"Can you believe she wouldn't open it after all that happened?"

"That's love." Brigham looked at her.

Sherry avoided his eyes. "And the old security records. Someone must have wanted to erase everything about Monahan's life."

Brigham nodded. "I have a feeling if the army had found Monahan before this guy McCullough, you would never have had the opportunity to meet him in a Philadelphia hospital some fifty years later."

"You think they would have killed him?" Sherry looked shocked.

"All I can say is, there was an emergency room full of witnesses that knew he survived. The only thing they could do by the time they found him was to make sure he never woke up or spoke again."

"According to Betsy, they most certainly accomplished that."

Betsy returned to the table and Sherry got up to check her phone and to give Betsy and Garland some time together. She saw that she had missed a call, and she sighed when she saw the number.

"Troy Weir," she whispered. "What in the hell am I supposed to do about you?"

19

"The transcripts aren't all that interesting." Weir handed an envelope to his stepfather, who glanced at it and then stuffed it into a leather sleeve at the side of his wheelchair.

They were on the Lancaster farm, and two young women in khaki slacks and uniform shirts were leading Thoroughbreds around a track. The horses were sleek, one chestnut, one black, and they cantered with knees high and hooves dropping in flawless repetition.

"It was interesting enough to give her sight again," Case said with a rare smile. He looked up to see the young man's reaction.

"You don't believe that, I take it?"

"Does it matter?"

Weir shrugged. "That's why she's so hot on figuring out this guy Monahan. Dr. Salix writes that she's convinced her contact with Monahan was responsible for restoring her sight."

"Which he thinks is ridiculous too, I'm sure."

"So is touching someone and seeing their last seconds of memory."

Case wheeled his chairthrough the stables, reaching up and rubbing the velvet noses of his Thoroughbreds along the way. "If that's what she does," he said with a sigh. "Ever been to Las Vegas and watched a magic show? Anyhow, she can't just disappear."

"No"—Weir scratched the back of his neck—"that would definitely be noticed."

Case cast him a glance. "So what's your plan?"

"She was hospitalized two years ago for depression."

Case turned to face the younger man. "She tried to kill herself?"

Weir shrugged. "Pills, I was told, although she denied it. She claimed the overdose was accidental."

"Well, that makes it a little easier."

"You want her to die?"

"I don't care what happens to her as long as I don't hear the name Thomas Monahan again."

Weir nodded. "It may be too early to panic. I think she'll drop the whole business once she gets used to her eyes. She's vulnerable now. You can see it on her face. She's overwhelmed by everything around her. She's still getting used to the world."

"What's she up to now?"

"I don't know. She wasn't home last night, said she was visiting a friend. I couldn't come right out and ask her where she was."

"Make her a priority until you're satisfied this is over. Don't let her out of your sight, and if you have to, push."

Case watched one of the horses do a lap.

Then he turned toward his stepson. "You're a smart man, Troy. I worried about you at first, I didn't think you'd make it to the big league, but you figured out the kind of stuff that mattered in time. The stuff most men never get."

He was talking about his favorite subject, Troy knew—Ed Case's law of probability and response. Case believed that mankind was disadvantaged by an inherent—and unwarranted—

173

concern for fellow human beings. He thought that society was its own greatest obstacle to progress. That it wasn't possible to properly evaluate an endeavor's true potential and respond to it appropriately unless consideration of its detrimental impact on the human race was eliminated. This was why so few people became giants in the world and why everyone else was piling up behind the great wall of mediocrity.

If you wanted to know how deep the water was, you had to ride out into the middle of it. A young Colonel Custer once demonstrated that point to a humiliated General McClellan, who had been riding up and down the riverbank asking the question of everyone. Likewise, if you wanted to know how far you could go with stem cell transplants following high-dose chemotherapy, you needed to try it out on a human. Period. To have that ability was to have limitless potential. To retain it required keeping it veiled from a squeamish public.

"What's your plan?"

"To show her something spectacular," Troy said.

Case started moving again. "And then what, she'll melt into your arms and tell you all her secrets?"

"Exactly," the younger man said, wondering if his stepfather was really ignorant of his misuse of the MIRA technology.

"Well, be quick about it. This should never have happened in the first place. Monahan should have been incinerated by now."

"It's all being taken care of," Weir assured him. "There is nothing more to learn in Stockton. There is nothing the government can tell them except what's in his file, and that has been reduced to nothing."

"And I'll accept that for now, but the moment you sense different, I want it handled. I never want to hear anything about Monahan, Area 17 or Alpha Company again."

"I'll find out what this friend of hers is all about and where she stayed last night. I have a date with her tomorrow afternoon."

"Good," Case said. "In fact, very good."

He stopped the wheelchair and spun to face Weir. "You did a fine job with that law-school kid in Springfield. I'll see you are properly rewarded."

"Thank you." Weir removed his rimless glasses to clean them. "It was fun."

20

Sherry was more nervous than she could recall ever being. She'd had two or three one-night flings in her past, but never one that had been born of circumstances so insubstantial. There didn't seem to be anything between her and this man but a chance meeting of a few hours and a physical attraction. He was fun to be with, yes. She wouldn't deny that, but something told her that nothing more would have happened between her and Troy but for the fact that she had seen him with her own two eyes. And, yes, she knew that eyes can only see, they have no ear for duplicity, no sieve for filtering out mistakes of intent. That any wife or husband or altarboy could be fooled by what looked like the sincerest of smiles and the kindest of eyes. She didn't have any gift more special than anyone else's, no innate way to recognize subterfuge in another human being. And yet she had always sensed and been told that her gift of second sight conferred on her an uncanny sense of intuition. Did she still have it?

Then there was Brian Metcalf. Perhaps all this worry over Troy Weir was because she felt guilty about Brian. Something was holding her back, preventing her from having an innocent and guilt-free relationship with Troy. What did she owe Brian to cause such consternation? They might have been serious, but they weren't engaged. There were no vows expressed. Of course, you knew when you were dating someone more seriously. You knew when faithfulness and a belief in someone else's loyalty were implied.

No, it wasn't the right thing to do to see Troy. Not if she allowed more to come of it than friendship. Not if she had thoughts of spending her life with Brian.

But a lot of things weren't right in life. How often did you end up holding a canister of radioactive cesium that could turn healthy cells into cancer? How often did you have to see loved ones torn away by a violent world? Brian was halfway around the world at this minute, and who knew if he was coming home? Nothing was certain in this world. It was pompous to plan for anything beyond the moment.

Sherry had never before been exposed to a level playing field. Didn't she deserve to find out what life was like? Wasn't spontaneity an element of happiness? Brigham himself had called her a wallflower. He'd once said she was God's little masterpiece trapped on the canvas. Brigham didn't do drama, and she could never imagine where he'd found those words, but during those dark months, after her best friend was murdered and preceding her spiral into depression, he had wanted her to get out of the house, to talk to someone, a therapist, her neurologist, hairdresser, client, stranger, anyone.

And now she was doing just that.

She heard a car in the drive and took a last look in the mirror. Then she set the alarm code and walked to the open door of a wine-colored Porsche. The top was down and she lowered herself into the leather seat.

"Nice car for a biologist who can barely afford his rent!"

"I had a small windfall last year. An aunt died in Oregon,

quite unexpectedly. I should have invested, but what the hell. I'm impulsive at times."

There were clouds in the sky and she marveled at their shapes. Clouds remained one of the few memories she'd retained from before her accident—clouds and ocean and sand and a smiling woman who smothered her in piles of rich dark hair. She wished she had a mother to talk to about all this, about life and men and happiness.

"Did you come straight to Case and Kimble from school or did you work somewhere else?" she asked.

"I bounced around schools for a while," he said cagily.

"And you last went to . . . I'm sorry, I forgot if you told me."

"George Mason."

"I have a friend on the Fairfax County police department. What years were you there?"

"Am I being grilled?" Troy laughed.

"No"—Sherry smiled and shook her head innocently—"just making conversation."

She asked where they were going, but he told her it was a surprise. They were city bound, however, the theater or a museum perhaps. She hadn't told him anything about herself yet. He would have been astounded to know she had grown up in the Halley House Orphanage that he had been reading about lately and that she'd had the use of her eyes for only three weeks; astounded to know she couldn't read a word of English and that she supported herself by interpreting the last memories of dead people.

"You get around pretty good for being new to the area."

"I have an instinctive sense of direction." He smiled and tapped the dash. "I studied the PCM earlier too."

"PCM?"

"Porsche Communication Management." He laughed. "It's a map, GPS technology, you know?"

Sherry laughed back, nodding, deciding to back off the questions for a while.

Suddenly they were following ramp signs to Camden, and Sherry wondered what in the world they could possibly find in New Jersey, until he parked outside the aquarium.

And she felt at that moment as if a ghost had laid a hand on her shoulder.

"This okay with you?" he asked.

How could he know, she wondered? How could he have imagined it was so important on the list of things she had ever seen or done? The last time she was here it was with her old friend John Payne. She remembered him holding her hand, reaching out, fingers entwined, as he laid it upon the back of a dolphin.

For two hours she tried to recall Payne's descriptions of all the fish and creatures as they walked by the tanks. But when they left the aquarium this time it wasn't Payne's hand she was holding. It was Troy Weir's. He had given her the gift of actually seeing an old and wonderful memory.

"Now where?" she said.

"Lobster Claw at the wharf?" Troy asked. "They have a great lobster salad sandwich."

"I don't think I could eat something I just saw walking around in a tank," Sherry said glumly.

"How about the Tuscan Grill?"

"You even know about Philadelphia culinary?"

"I looked up restaurants on the Internet to impress you. The ratings were good at both."

Sherry nodded. "Yeah, okay," she said, half smiling.

Troy punched buttons on his PCM and cracked his window an inch. He was losing her, he thought. He would need to give her some encouragement, synthetic or otherwise, and soon.

They found a table off to themselves. Sherry watched people come and go as Troy went to the restroom.

She thought about Brian Metcalf and decided she should return his messages soon. It wasn't certain he could be reached, but it was possible to leave a message where he could retrieve it. Troy Weir aside, she wanted to tell him about the miracle in Nazareth Hospital. She wanted to tell him she could see. Who knew, maybe next week, after the gamma ray test, she would have even better news to tell. Better news for the two of them?

Sherry stared into her iced tea and realized that she was having the first positive thought since leaving New Mexico. Maybe Brigham had been right all along. Maybe she'd just needed time to get through the stress of all that had been going on around her. Maybe the dazzle of being able to see had clouded her mind and her judgment.

After dinner they parked at Weir's apartment house on Society Hill and walked the three blocks to the Dark Horse Tavern. By dusk they were back on the sidewalk, weaving slightly, linked arm in arm.

The apartment was contemporary. She expected no less and guessed correctly that a designer had decorated it.

She couldn't say she had a plan. She just sat there and listened to music, drank wine, and tried with all her senses to summon her inner voice.

There was no cause to stop him when he kissed her. She had walked into his apartment under her own power. She had never suggested there was a significant other. She had allowed him to take her hand at the aquarium and she had held his arm on the way home. His hands moved, first around her neck, around her ears, lifting her hair and kissing the back of her neck. He pulled her into him. She felt his fingers brush across her back and the strap of her bra. He pulled her gently into him, managed to push his knee between her thighs as he rolled her toward him.

It was good, not great; wanted, not needed. But how long had it been? Oh, there was Brian. She had certainly slept with Brian. But Brian came with strings, like John Payne had come with strings. She could have loved either of them. She could have been happy with either one and for the rest of her life. Except that she had no control over the rest of her life. She was damaged goods, she thought. She could only bring someone pain.

Wow, that wine had hit her hard!

"Ladies' room?" she asked, and he gave her directions. She had to be careful not to stumble as she turned down the hall.

She looked at herself in the mirror and threw handfuls of water on her face. She used a towel to dry it and saw the slightest stain of blood that she traced to her nose. Her nose must have been bleeding, she realized, and she wiped it with a tissue and rinsed the blood from the towel. How odd.

She took a deep breath and then made her way back to the living room.

Perhaps she had held herself to too high a standard. Troy seemed like a wonderful young man. A couple of drinks, a few laughs, a little love, and they could go on their way. No harm, no foul. Right?

His fingers found her stomach where he'd separated the buttons. Deft hand was inside and flat across her ribs, thumb prying up the underwire of her bra. His lips moved down her neck, her throat; she felt his tongue flicker across the top of her breast.

"Troy."

"Yes," he whispered, thumb slipping up on her breast.

"No."

He retracted the thumb from under her bra.

"Not yet," she said, kissing the side of his neck. "Just not yet."

He nodded, his forehead damp, and turned to her with a smile. "You tell me when," he said politely. "I want it to be right."

"Thank you," she whispered hoarsely. "It's way late and I should really get home."

"I'll get the car," he said, rising.

"No," she said quickly. "I'll take a cab. You're already home."

"I don't mind."

"But I do," she said kissing him on the lips. "We'll do it again."

"Promise."

She nodded drunkenly. "Promise."

21

"I'm beginning to think we should move up to Stockton. Maybe we could get homes next to each other near the asylum."

"Oh, you love it, Mr. Brigham. You get to see Betsy every time we go."

Brigham didn't respond.

Carla had told Betsy they could come to get the journal; she was ready to give it up. Brigham asked Betsy if Carla had looked at it, and Betsy said she had not. Carla didn't want to know if there was anything painful inside. She wanted to remember her husband the way he was in her mind.

Betsy was taking Brigham sightseeing in Old Town Kingston on the Hudson this evening. It would be their first official date. Sherry would have the night—and the journal—to herself at a room in Grant's Tavern.

She didn't know what to expect. McCullough, according to his wife, was a woodsman through and through. He knew the trees of the forest and the sound of every bird. His friend Dick McKinley used to brag that he could track a snail to Schenectady.

And so she couldn't know if the pages were going to be filled with wild ramblings of a suicidal man or sketches of life in the Catskill Mountains. Clearly Carla also didn't know, or she would have opened it. Something scared her about the journal, about Jack's wanting it to be locked away until they were both long dead.

Betsy met them at Grant's Tavern once more. They had cocktails at the bar, where she turned over McCullough's strange book. "Carla said to keep it as long as you need to. Or destroy it if you have to. She said she'd trust your judgment to that. I peeked, of course." She smiled and stirred her drink with a straw.

"And?" Sherry asked.

Betsy shrugged. "I didn't know McCullough all that well, I mean, I was still a kid when he died, but I can tell you this. He didn't write that journal."

Sherry looked at Betsy questioningly.

"Oh, I didn't examine it at length, but it goes on about war. A kid in boot camp and then overseas in battle, reasonably intelligent stuff at first, he volunteered for some research and then it digresses into numbers and random words, I guess the kid really did lose it in the end."

"Monahan?"

"Well, there's blood all over the pages. Carla said Jack was covered with blood, but she never said anything about Jack being injured." Betsy shrugged.

Sherry squeezed it to her chest with one arm. "Jesus."

The bartender gave a thumbs-up. Suddenly Sherry felt weak and the sparkling lights came in and out of focus.

"You okay?" Brigham reached for her arm.

"I'm fine," she said, taking a breath and patting Betsy on the back. "You guys sit." After a moment she stood to go to the ladies' room. "I'll be right back."

Sherry went into the ladies' room and locked the door, wet a handful of paper towels, and sat on the toilet lid, pressing them to her face. "Please, please, please," she whispered. "Please don't take this away, God."

She thought about Brian just then. What would he think if they were in a restaurant one day and she went to the ladies' room and returned as blind as the day he met her?

When Sherry returned, Betsy had her forehead against Brigham's and they were laughing over something private.

Sherry felt a tinge of unexpected jealousy. She had never had to share her best friend with anyone before.

"You okay?" Brigham asked again.

Sherry gave him a nod as she slid onto her stool.

"You two off on an adventure, then?" Sherry asked.

"I have some favorite places on the eastern side of the Hudson. A little town called Rhinebeck, and then we'll come back to Old Town in Kingston and try a glass or two of port."

Sherry just sat there and grinned and Brigham turned his profile to her.

"All right, kids," she said, "I'm going upstairs to listen to a bedtime story. I'll see you in the morning for breakfast."

She put money on the bar and asked Mike the bartender how late he was serving in case she got restless.

But Sherry did not come back downstairs that evening, nor was she asleep when Brigham turned the lock in his door across the hall at nearly 3 a.m. A late night with Betsy, she thought smugly.

The optical scanner Sherry possessed was a year more advanced than any model available to the general public. It was able to convert handwritten text more accurately than all previous scanners on the market, because its computer was taught to make decisions based both on probability of character likeness and a nearly infallible formula for predicting—by context—what the author intended to convey. In other words, Sherry was able to listen to an electronic transcription of the journal to within ninety-two percent accuracy.

Betsy had been right about the text lapsing into seemingly random words and numbers, but what she didn't understand was what made those words and numbers significant.

All evening, Sherry had been listening to Monahan describing a dreary two months in boot camp.

Now he was deployed and about to land in Korea.

She laid in her bed looking up at the old tin ceiling, put the headphones back on and pressed her thumb against the track wheel on the scanner's remote.

August 26th, 1950

We arrived last week, rough seas under a full moon and puke all over the landing craft. None of us had slept the night before, anticipating what we'd heard about the fighting at Old Baldy and knowing we'd be there by the end of the week. Most of the battalion we were joining had only been in country six months before us, but they sure acted salty as hell. Our captain, Jim Merritts—he was in World War II in the Philippines—said it wouldn't take long to get our battle scars here and that the way commissioned officers were falling, battle promotions either. We thought he was being dramatic and laughed at the way they said he slept with a gun in his hand. Someone said he'd seen too many Tex Ritter movies. Then last night one of the guys went out to use the latrine and didn't come back. They found him barbwired to a tree along the perimeter the next morning, his tongue had been cut out. He kept shaking his head and making noises as they began to untangle him. When they were finally able to pull him from the tree a grenade blew two of them to pieces. His back had been holding the spoon down.

That was how it started for us.

We heard that the Koreans liked to sneak into the camps at night and use their knives on our soldiers. We never saw any thank God, but one night they bombed us from a glider and all these guys were set on fire. You didn't sleep much at first, you marched and you bedded down. That was it. And in between you waited for the enemy to come over the next rise and overrun you. After a few days the exhaustion set in. You didn't jump at the sound of a rifle shot anymore. You learned to put your head on your knees and go unconscious. We were already salty by the time we got to the 38th Parallel.

September 22nd, 1950

We are at the base of a prominence they call Hill 105, near railroad tracks that run into Seoul. I know the Marines have tried to get on top of it and they were pushed back down, but we're going back up there with them in thirty-six hours to do it all again.

I promised myself I would never say goodbye to you in any of my letters. I don't plan to break that promise, but I have to tell you all that I love you, Mom, Papa, Sophie and Sam. Never forget that.

Captain Merritts says we aren't to worry, that if anybody should be afraid it's them gooks in the 25th Infantry who are about to meet the Fighting 32nd. I'm wearing my cross, Mom, I know that makes you happy and tell Papa there is a Gunny Sergeant somewhere here in Seoul whose name is Theodore Roosevelt Monahan just like Grandpa. I haven't met him yet, but if I do, I'll tell him Grandpa was in the battle of Somme. I know that will impress him.

Well, I've got to go, Captain Merritts says we have to listen to some Washington armchair commando who's just arrived at the front. Probably bringing us news the Chinese have joined the war, as if we didn't already know. The Captain says the 7th Division has been seeing them for a year and if they ever do come in force we'll have hell to pay. They say you kill a hundred they'll send a thousand more. You kill a thousand they send ten thousand.

I'll write tomorrow if I get a chance. If not it may be a while till we get dug in again. Hopefully on top of that hill.

September 29th, 1950

We made it! It's hard to believe, but we really made it. We are here. Back in the good old US of A. You can't know this of course, not for another three months and I won't be able to tell you everything, but it will be around Christmas by then and I'll be home for good this time. Papa won't need to worry about his leg any longer. I'll be there for planting when spring comes around.

I am so glad now that I wasn't able to get mail out to you in Korea. I know now my last letter would have worried you terribly. You might have read something about the battle on Hill 105 and thought I was there.

I was last telling you about an officer from Washington coming to the front line. Well he came all right and he was a bird colonel at that. He was looking for volunteers for a special but dangerous assignment he told us, and there we are in our field jackets loaded down with ammo and grenades wondering what in the heck could be worse than going up that hill in the morning. Next thing I know Captain Merritts grabs Tim Pollock by the shoulder and pulls him out in front of us. Then he looks at me and grabs my web belt and pulls me out of line. "Talk to them two," he told the colonel and then growled, "Dismissed!" to the others. Last I saw was his sandy colored crew cut as he knelt by the phosphorous fire we'd built to keep warm.

The colonel took us to the CO's tent where no one could hear and asked us if we would be interested in returning to the States. He said that the army was conducting secret tests that might help us win the war and I know it sounds crazy, but we would get honorable discharges after just three months if we volunteered to act as guinea pigs.

I don't have to tell you with Hill 105 looming overhead what we said to him.

And here we are. Just like he said.

We've all been encouraged to write on pads they gave us, or in my case my diary, to help pass the time, even though we probably won't be allowed to keep them after we are discharged. Everything here is top secret they told us. They have civilians walking around and I've never seen so many medals on uniforms like these officers have.

There isn't much to do with our days, we read and play checkers and there is a ping-pong table in the mess. The tan I had from basic training is all but gone, Korea was cold as a Chesapeake shad, but here we live underground and it's a constant 66 degrees because of how deep it is, somewhere in the Northeast or by the Great Lakes from what we can put together from our collective experiences.

It may seem odd, all this work to write down our thoughts and then not be allowed to share them, but I find it helps get things out of my system. Things I'd rather not bring home when I'm discharged in December.

I admit that I sometimes feel guilty about leaving friends behind in Korea. I know the 32nd was going into battle while I was being driven back to the harbor at Inchon. After that we were launched to the carrier Valley Forge and were hustled into a Douglas Skyraider bound for Tokyo.

Maybe, as Mom says, the Lord decides our fate. I can only hope to do my country proud, as I would have tried to do in Korea.

Well it's suppertime and I best go. The meals are pretty good, we have a cook who is Italian and speaks no English. We pretty much have to make sign language to tell him we like his food. The table might be light again tonight. Two of the guys taking radiation shots got the flu. Now we're all worried 'cause some of us had been in the Orient, but the doctor here

said he's sure it's not the Asian flu. Whew. That's a relief. To-
morrow I'm going to try to hear radio waves in the R-lab. They
say they are like radar pulses only stronger.

Sherry laid the journal open across her stomach, closed her
eyes, and felt the tickle of cool air from the ceiling fan. A horn
honked outside the window, then a door opened and she heard a
car radio and loud, drunken voices before the door slammed and
the car drove away. Boys—maybe eighteen, maybe twenty, not
much younger than Thomas J. Monahan had been when he
penned these words.

She tried to appreciate the mind-set of the Cold War era.
Especially the early years, as Brigham had explained. She tried
to imagine the threat of a weapon capable of destroying the
United States in one blow. It was real to them, Brigham had said.
They knew that a hydrogen bomb had been tested in the Philippines in 1947—one thousand times more powerful than the
bombs dropped on Hiroshima and Nagasaki. Brigham said that
not long afterward, the Soviets detonated a bomb that eclipsed
all bombs dropped in World War II.

He had reminded her that the youth of 1950 had not
grown up in a nuclear world. They remembered Roy Rogers
and gangsters and tommy guns, not missiles, Al-Qaeda, and
dirty briefcases.

What could one make of it? Under the circumstances, how
many citizens would have cried out for a ban on testing weapons
of any kind? How many would have insisted on months, years,
even a decade of trials before new drugs were introduced in order
to save a soldier's life? Few, she thought. Few would quarrel with
the research and development of new weapons and the age-old
solution of using volunteers.

What, she wondered, had been done to that boy's brain to
silence him for half a century? She thought about the device on
the far side of that table she had seen. . . . "Can't . . . on, can't . . .

on," she whispered. Had she actually felt her temperature rising when she was holding his hand, or was it only a memory? And what was *can't . . . on?*

Had Monahan been brainwashed, controlled by some remote means, and could that neurological aberration have triggered a response in her own brain fifty-eight years later? Sherry had no idea how memories were conveyed to her mind, only that somehow they were, and that they must travel through a conduit between the deceased person's central nervous system and her own.

Her alarm went off far too soon the next morning. Sherry saw bags under her eyes in the mirror and wondered how many mornings of her life they had been there. They checked out at nine and headed out to the diner for breakfast.

"I'm having company for dinner tonight," Sherry told Brigham, sliding into a booth.

"Who?" he asked, unconcerned.

"A guy," she said, watching him.

"What guy?" he asked, now suspicious.

"Just a guy," Sherry said.

Brigham just looked at her. "What do you mean, just a guy?"

"You know, a guy."

"I know you're seeing Brian Metcalf. Since when is there just another guy in your life?"

Something was going on with her, Brigham thought. She was waging a war within herself. She was trying to hide from her own future. Trying to hide from the results of gamma ray tests that might show radioactivity in her bone marrow or lungs next week. Trying to hide from not knowing—or knowing—whether she would develop cancer, whether she would retain her sight.

It was rationalizing, in a way. Rationalizing that her life was at best uncertain, and what the hell, she'd make new friends, find new ways to forget about the future—except that Sherry understood the difference between right and wrong.

"He's nobody. Someone I bumped into. It's nothing, really, nothing at all."

"It's something if you're inviting him to dinner."

"What? Can't I have friends now?"

"What about Brian?"

"What about him?" Sherry said defensively.

"Does he know about your new friend? I thought you two had something going on."

"I only met him six months ago."

"And you went to meet his family three weeks ago."

"Coffee?" A young woman stood in front of the table with two pots, stifling any response.

"Please," Sherry said, and he pushed his cup forward as well.

Brigham continued to watch her face intently. "You haven't even told him yet, have you? Brian doesn't even know you can see."

"There hasn't been a good time."

"So you've talked," he said.

"He called," she said guiltily.

"And you've talked?" He didn't try to hide his concern.

"He left messages."

"Why didn't you answer them? Why didn't you tell him your sight came back?"

"I'm not ready," she said emphatically.

"Ready for what?"

"To talk about it. It's too early."

Sherry looked down at the table and turned the cup around on the saucer. "I'm sorry. I'm just not used to getting grilled by you."

"And I'm not used to strangers waltzing into your life."

"You worry too much about me."

He nodded. "And there you are probably right, young lady."

The waitress brought ice water and menus. "Need a minute?" she asked, and Sherry shook her head. "Pancakes for me."

He ordered an omelet and the waitress left them alone.

"It's none of my business, I suppose."

Sherry remained silent.

"Still, you should tell Brian. And if you're going to see someone else, maybe you should tell him that too," he said gruffly.

"It's none of your business, remember?"

"What does this guy do?"

"He's a scientist."

"A scientist," Brigham said dully.

"Case and Kimble."

Brigham nodded. "Big company."

"Huge," Sherry retorted.

"I'll be home all night."

"As in, you'll be home if I need you?" Sherry laughed.

He shrugged.

"I'll be perfectly all right, Mr. Brigham. Would you like me to call you when he's gone? You could come over afterward and we'll go over the journal again. You could read so I wouldn't have to use my machine."

"Not if it's after ten."

"I'll be in bed myself at ten. He's coming for dinner and then he's out the door. I'll call you the moment he leaves." She stopped suddenly and tried to focus as the room began to blur.

"You okay?"

She nodded, taking deep breaths. "I'm fine," she said. "It's the Prussian blue. It makes me nauseous."

"One more week, Sherry," he said. "Just one more week. You should remember that."

"Let's not rush it," she said. "This week at least I still have the luxury of not knowing what the test will show."

22

"Can we do two more entries?" Brigham asked.

Sherry nodded, trying to get herself together. "Two more," she said, "then I've got to shower."

Brigham flipped open the journal and pushed on his reading glasses.

October 27th, 1950

Something is wrong. One of the guys, Henry Wade, left last week. He was supposed to have been sent home. He was in C-lab where they take the radiation shots. The captain told us he completed his trials, but Sandy found his wristwatch last night. It was under his bunk and we all know he wouldn't have left it because his fiancée bought it for him before he shipped out to Korea. He was getting pretty sick, like he had the flu real bad. Sandy was in his group, three of them had it, but Henry was starting to lose his hair as well.

We don't know what to think. Tim Pollock—he's on tri-

als in the R-lab with me—wanted to give the watch to the commanding officer here.

I told them to give it to one of the doctors when they came back, but Sandy said we should keep it as evidence in case something happened to Henry.

We aren't supposed to talk to each other about what we're doing here, but that seems kind of silly now. Sandy's been bleeding in the toilet and the doctor gave him something to stop it, but he should be in a hospital.

I don't think that anyone will ever get to read this. They'll likely search us when we're discharged in sixty days. We've decided to meet near Baltimore after we get out. Baltimore is between where Tim and I live. We want to find out if Henry is all right before we come home. Don't worry about me. Tim and I were told to do some pretty weird things here, but at least we don't have to take the shots yet. Seems like an easy way out of the war, listening to voices in our heads, but the doctor here says its important work. Who are we to say it's not?

November 2, 1950

Sandy was taken to the hospital yesterday. He won't be coming back they say. The captain came by and picked up all his stuff. I don't know why he thought he'd have to wear gloves. It isn't like the rest of us are protected in any way.

Anyhow the Captain said that he contacted Henry and that Henry was home safe with his parents. Henry said that he'd left his watch behind and asked that we keep it for him. We don't know if it's true or not or if they can somehow overhear us talking.

It's confusing here. You can't tell by their expressions if they want you to do well on their tests or not. Sometimes they seem happy when you do and sometimes not.

All I know is fifty-some days and I'm coming home. We

were told they sent letters to all of you telling you we were all right. We'll be able to write our own letters home the week before we leave as well. I'm going to ask you for a special favor this year. I want you to hold Christmas when I get home. I know that's a bit selfish, but Sam and Sophie are old enough to wait for their presents. Anyhow, if you can't wait I'll understand. Just save me some giblets and gravy.

Brigham returned the journal and Sherry walked him to the door. He was upset, she could tell. Upset about what he was reading. Upset about her relationship with Brian Metcalf. Upset with her, for all she knew. He had really wanted Sherry and Brian to work out.

She turned the lock when he was out.

Well, she also had wanted it. That was life, wasn't it? If she lost her sight again tomorrow, well, that would be a shame too. If all her hair started to fall out like the boy's in the letter, what would Brigham and Brian have to say about that?

They weren't children anymore. Life came with tough choices and right now she intended to do what was best for all of them. There was no future. There was only today.

She looked at the second wine bottle and grinned, seeing that it was empty. Sherry had never opened a second bottle of wine in her life. It wasn't that she didn't like to drink. She just didn't like wine all that much. Maybe that was part of her newfound boldness. Maybe she'd gone a little heavy on the wine since she'd been thinking the entire afternoon how wonderful it would be to forget about Brigham and Brian and Monahan and secret weapons and gamma rays. How wonderful it would be to try something entirely new, to get comfortably drunk.

Sherry knew it was almost midnight and the remains of dinner were piled high in the kitchen sink. She had never done that before either. Never dared to prepare a candlelight dinner for a man. Not that there was anything complicated about making steaks on a countertop grill and vegetables in the microwave, but the idea, the accomplishment was out of character.

She was taking on a new role these days. She was acting out a fantasy she'd always imagined the rest of the world was playing. As long as she could see, she would decide what was worth having and taking. The world wasn't as complicated as she'd made it out to be when she was blind. There was just today and everyone knew you were supposed to live in the moment, live for today.

She considered that idea for a moment, wishing she had more confidence in it. Wishing she was relieved by her newfound liberation.

It felt uncomfortable, unsuitable to her, making her think it was dangerous right now to take chances, but that might go away with time. She could ease back into life a little bit at a time.

"I really should get to bed," she said.

"What, you don't like the company?" Troy pretended to be offended.

"The company is just fine," she said smoothly. He was sitting on the couch and she was lying on her back, head on his lap.

She reached up to touch his hair, brushed it aside on his forehead. "You know I'm not looking for a relationship." She slurred the words badly.

He nodded. "That's okay," he said.

"Really okay?"

"I'd be flattered if you thought otherwise, but no, it's really okay."

She nodded. "Good, I think that's best."

The only light in the room came from the dinner candles. She had CDs in the Bose, and the empty wine bottle was listing badly in a bucket of melting ice.

He leaned down and kissed her again, this time pulling her

shirt from the waist of her skirt and putting his hand on her stomach.

"Your hand is hot."

"Your body is cold."

"Better leave me dressed then," she whispered softly.

He removed his hand and traced her lips with his finger.

"You are truly beautiful," he said. "More beautiful than any woman I've ever met."

"Silly," she managed to say, but her head was spinning, and his hand felt good.

"Are you sure the front door is locked?"

"I checked it twice," he said. "Who are you expecting?"

"No one." She glanced guiltily at the clock, reaching up to undo the buttons of his shirt.

"I missed you yesterday," he said. "I called you at the house, before I tried your cell phone."

"I went back to Stockton." Sherry tugged his shirt out of his pants and pulled it open and just stared at his chest.

"Another reading," he teased.

"Yeah, another reading," she said, staring at his skin. It was the first bare chest she had seen in thirty-two years. "A journal, I'm reading a very, very old journal," she said sleepily.

He put a hand on her thigh and lifted her skirt a few inches. "Come on, we had a deal. You were supposed to tell me about the readings you do."

"Now?" She smiled wickedly, heady from the wine.

"Deal's a deal."

She shook her head like a stubborn child.

"I've had too much wine," she said.

"All right, then tell me about your journal."

"It's not my journal"—she made a face—"it's a soldier's journal." She turned her head and yawned. "He's dead. He died in an asylum."

"Is it a good journal?"

Sherry shook her head. "It's a sad journal."

"Why would someone want to read a sad journal?" Weir lifted her skirt another two inches, rubbing his thumb across her thigh. "There's too much sadness in the world already."

"There is." She nodded slowly.

"So you are interested in it from a historical perspective."

"History," Sherry whispered hoarsely.

"Where did you get it?"

"Friend," she said.

"Old friend?" he asked.

"Nah, I just met her once. Just last week, when I called you and told you I was out of town. She gave me the diary I told you about. It was her late husband's."

"How did you come to meet her?"

"Friend of a friend, as they say. I knew someone from up there and it was just some local people being nice to me."

"Did your first friend read the diary too?"

"Huh-uh, she just glanced at it."

"May I see it?" Weir asked softly, carefully.

"Brigham's," she said, opening her eyes and straining to look toward the door. She shook her head no, as if remembering something. "No, it's at my neighbor's," she said, starting to rise and feeling very drunk and wondering if Brigham was waiting for her guest to leave.

She looked at the door. He was, she thought. He'd be watching from his window. Looking to see if Weir's car was still in the driveway. And it was long, long past ten.

"I've got to clean up and get to bed," she said, sitting up and suddenly reeling. She buried her head in her hands and rubbed her eyes. Her hair was piled all around the sides of her face.

"It's very late," she said.

"All right." He rubbed his palms together and started buttoning his shirt. "Then I'll help you clean up."

"No, go, it's late. Maybe I'll just leave it all till morning."

"As you wish," Weir said.

Sherry stood and walked to the door and unlocked it.

"I still owe you a tour of my office and the museum." He slipped his arm around her and pulled her into a kiss. Then he undid his pants to tuck his shirt in.

Sherry turned the knob.

"Call me," she said, and pulled the door open to see Brian Metcalf.

"Brian . . ." she said, leaning with all her weight against the door frame to keep from swaying. "Brian, this is Troy, he's a . . ."

Troy was slowly zipping his pants and then he buckled his belt with a smile.

Metcalf turned and walked away.

23

"Moore says there is a journal. Monahan's journal."

Case let the pen fall from his hand and Troy watched the color drain from his stepfather's face. They were in Case's library, in the south wing of the Lancaster estate. The old man backed the wheelchair up to free himself from the desk and toggled forward, advancing to the windows and looking out, then back to his stepson.

He waited a moment before walking toward him. Outside the window, beyond his full white head of hair, there were gardeners pruning flowers and green hummingbirds leapfrogging the plumes of purple hostas.

"Where?" Case said at last.

"In Philadelphia, at her neighbor's house, he's a retired admiral."

"The older man she was with at the psychiatric hospital?"

"I can only assume," Weir said.

"How do you know? How do you know it's his? That it's Monahan's?"

GEORGE D. SHUMAN

"She said she's reading a soldier's journal. A soldier who died in an asylum."

Case stared at his stepson.

Troy Weir shrugged.

Case locked eyes with him, but the younger man didn't think Case was looking at him. He seemed somewhere far, far away.

"Doctor?"

Suddenly Case pounded the top of a serpentine tea table, snapping the top from the delicately carved legs. "Goddamn it!" he yelled with a fury that belied his eighty-three years. He tilted his head back and looked at the ceiling, all the muscles and leaders in his neck stretching like twine. He looked almost biblical for a minute, as if the backdrop of morning light that haloed his white hair was heaven-sent, to lift and deliver him from his agony. Troy knew right then that whatever else this journal held, it contained the ruin of Case's lifetime of achievements.

"I think it's time you told me what this is all about," Weir said.

Case was still struggling in the throes of this new reality, the knowledge that he had lost a sizable chunk of his armor, and was seriously vulnerable. Weir thought he looked like a man imploding, all the grace and swagger and authority he liked to project dissipating until all that was left was an old man in a wheelchair.

Case turned his head and gave the younger man a chilling look, his face white and empty as a death mask. Then he nodded, motored to the door and pushed it the rest of the way closed, then spun to face the leather sofa and chair.

Troy walked to the bar, poured an inch of vodka, carried it to the leather chair, and handed it to the old man.

Case was regaining composure, but only partially. He looked shaken. Troy would have loved to know what signals the old man's autonomic nerves were sending from the stem of his brain. Once upon a time he had studied the autonomic nerves' effect on heart rhythms during times of great stress. There was actually a percentage, albeit small, of people who died from heart arrhythmia due to sudden stress. The proverbial "died of fright" scenario. He had actually introduced the arrhythmia study to MIRA Project members from the Department of Defense. It was yet another means of close-contact assassination, he'd suggested, but that was a whole other story.

"You have come to know Case and Kimble's most closely guarded secret," Case said, "and not because of any particular knowledge you possess. I have no shortage of experts at my disposal. You were chosen to liaise with the National Security Agency because you think in a way that better serves my purpose. You do not limit MIRA's potential with a lot of unnecessary concern for risk.

"I was held in high esteem following World War Two"— Case swept an arm to encompass the many pictures on the walls—"one of the very few and youngest minds at the heart of the Manhattan Project." He nodded self-righteously, sat up, and the wheel of his chair made a splintering noise against an edge of his antique table.

"So when the army learned of a mind-control machine the Russians were working on in 1950, they came to me." He tapped the breast pocket of his jacket.

"I was promised anything. Money, home, laboratory, access to their latest nuclear data, test subjects to continue my work involving radiation, literally anything."

"We had the primitive hypothesis in those days concerning the effects of radio waves. Low-frequency sound being directed at human beings, highly concentrated microwaves in which we melded visual images and voices."

"LIDA," Weir said.

"Yes, LIDA." Case nodded, taking a sip of the vodka.

"The Russians," Case went on, "had their working model in Korea at the time and the army had proof they were using it on American pilots. Jason Kimble was at Princeton, that's where they sent the pilots who returned and that was how Jason and I first came to know each other. I was supposed to re-create the device based on intelligence smuggled out of the Kremlin. The army gave us test subjects, guinea pigs, from the front lines of Seoul."

"Disposable guinea pigs," Troy said.

Case shrugged. "I was told their absence could be explained, but only if things came to worse." He spread out his open arms. "That was part of doing business when you're at the cutting edge of science. Explorers, test pilots, researchers had always put their lives on the line." Case wore a look of disgust. "Had," he repeated. "Oh, the boys knew there was a risk. They knew they were walking away from all but certain death in Korea. Danger is synonymous with research. To find the threshold of a thing is to go out and touch its edge. Someone needed to do that. We didn't know about the long-term effects of radiation. We didn't know what exposures our boys could stand under attack. We didn't know how to protect ourselves from radio waves and being brainwashed into submission by the enemy. We needed to get out in front of the game. To find out what they were doing over there and contain it."

"But there never was such a thing as the brainwash machine, was there? The LIDA machine was a failure. Hocus-pocus. Soviet propaganda," Troy said.

Case shook his head emphatically "No, no. That was what we reported. I was on the inside. There were cases, many cases we could never explain. Those machines worked. They just weren't predictable. The brain was the unknown quantity in the equation. The brain's reaction to the frequencies was unforeseeable. Some men acted upon suggestion. Some who did not and seemed impervious went on about their business for days and weeks at a time and then suddenly something tripped their brain and they went on the attack."

"They were trained to resist?"

"Of course," Case said. "They were supposed to do every-thing in their power not to act on a suggestion."

"And the strongest motivation you could hope to overcome would be their reluctance to commit murder. To assassinate."

Case shook his head and a cruel smile formed on his lips. "We thought of one even stronger," he said. "Suicide."

Case raised his drink and Troy noticed that the doctor's hand was shaking.

"It was very dangerous stuff. We had to watch our subjects constantly. To make sure they weren't going to harm one an-other. A psychiatrist monitored them daily. We removed danger-ous articles from the dormitory. There was always an MP posted outside the entrance."

"But Monahan got out just the same."

Case looked at the young man. "Yes, he got out."

"How could he have kept a journal without your knowing it?"

"We knew. Hell, we encouraged them to keep diaries. Their writings were evidence of their state of mind before and after the tests. We went through their bunks while they were out in the labs. We knew what they were thinking. We wanted to know what was happening to them as the tests proceeded."

"Where did you think the journal was after all these years?" Troy asked.

"We didn't know. We talked to the security men from the asy-lum who had found him. We asked if the kid had anything with him. All of them said he hadn't. All but one had been together when they were with him. It didn't seem likely that four people would conspire to hide something as innocuous as a journal as fast as we got to them, and they were interviewed within an hour of bringing him to the asylum. They didn't have time to contrive a story."

Case sipped more of his drink. "We went up there on the summit many times afterward, looking for the book, but it never turned up. After that we could only hope it was lost to time and the elements."

"That doesn't sound like you," Troy said. "*Hoping* for something."

Case's expression remained fixed.

"This is where the all but one comes in, isn't it?" Troy added.

"The security chief. Jack McCullough. He was the one who found Monahan's body. He was alone with the boy for over an hour. He told the ER doctor he thought the boy might have intentionally jumped from the cliff wall."

"So you questioned him?"

"Not me, but the right people took him aside," Case said. "He was convincing."

"What happened to the kid afterward?"

"He was already in the asylum. Our best psychiatrists determined he was brain-dead. There was nothing we could do to make him go away so we decided to leave him there. Where better to tuck someone away than a mental institution in the Catskills? The government could pay for his interminable convalescence, and we could monitor his progress from time to time to ensure he was no threat. Standing orders were left for the administrator to contact our foundation should he ever awaken or pass away."

"And the security chief, McCullough?"

Case looked at his hands. "He committed suicide."

Troy looked out the window, the slightest smile forming at his lips. He shook his head in admiration of the doctor.

"It was I who laid the groundwork for MIRA. Block by block until what you have seen today is the most sophisticated mind-control device on the planet. A virtual library of human emotions, thirty years of EEGs catalogued and waiting for the moment they could be released in microwaves. Like a bullet they enter the body, with a complete set of blueprints, which guides the target's every move. In ten years we will be able to direct such a bullet at the masses. We will be able to turn armies on their heels and send them walking and after all the lives it cost to create it, we will win wars without a single shot being fired. We will save whole nations. We will turn dictators into apostles and terrorists into lambs."

Case spun in the direction of the bar and poured another tumbler of scotch. "No one can read that journal and live, Troy."

He studied the old man a long moment and grunted.

"Is that a problem?" Case asked.

"Not in the least."

"Who has seen it?"

"Obviously the security man who found Monahan had a wife or a child who kept his belongings. Sherry Moore found out about it somehow, so then there is Sherry Moore herself, and her neighbor."

"Troy, I think you now understand the gravity of the situation. This is why you have become so essential to what I do. I need this to go away, but with the finest touch. No clues, no loose ends, no inferences. Do nothing unnecessary, but end it. I want you to understand that. It must be very, very clean."

24

Sherry's mouth was dry, her head still pounding from last night's wine. She wished she could forget how the evening had ended, but she kept seeing Brian Metcalf's face at her door. She was reasonably sure she was dressed as she'd stood there, but Troy's shirt had been out and they both must have looked quite disheveled.

"You call him?"

"No answer," she said softly.

"You going to call him again?"

"Just read," she whispered.

Brigham, looking stern, put on his glasses and lifted the book.

Sherry closed her eyes.

November 16th

> *Well the other group is all gone and more arrived to re-*
> *place them. Tim Pollock and I are the two most senior guys in*
> *the barrack now. The replacements are straight back from the*
> *front lines in Korea. They couldn't believe we were in Seoul*

two months ago ourselves. They said we did the right thing getting out of there. They said Chinese soldiers were found amongst the North Korean dead north of the 38th Parallel. If Chinese communists decided to join North Korea they would overrun the American lines with millions of new troops.

Tim was beginning to suffer migraine headaches so they took him to the infirmary. I only hear the voices, but in time they begin to run together and the noise is overwhelming. Both of us look like we've been in the desert, our skin is flaking and red and our temperatures are running high. They say it will go away as soon as we get outside again. We haven't seen the sun or sky or breathed fresh air since the day we arrived. We were told it was necessary, both to keep the tests secret and to ensure the integrity of our results, whatever that is supposed to mean. They started giving us shots to counteract our symptoms. Just supplements they said.

November 19th, 1950

The machine on the table in R-lab has become my closest friend. I have talked to it more than to any human being in the past four days. Actually I haven't talked to anybody since Tim was taken to the infirmary.

I am beginning to get the headaches too, but with only five weeks to discharge I don't say anything to the doctor. I don't want to end up in their infirmary. I want to be home for the New Year and for good. I want to put this war behind me.

I have learned something about solitude while I am here.

Tim stopped talking for more than a day before he collapsed. I asked him what was wrong and I assumed it was the headaches, but he showed no sign of pain. He just lay in his bed and stared at the ceiling. And he was crying.

The number thirty comes to mind more often. Thirty is just before can't and on is just after thirty and there is comfort in the knowledge that can't and thirty and on precede the gun.

"This is really getting hard to hear," Sherry said.

Brigham nodded and laid the book on its spine. "Take a break?"

She nodded and went to check the answering machine. Someone had been calling her during the last hour of Brigham's reading.

"Your friend?" he asked sarcastically.

"Brian," she said distantly. "Wait . . ." and she held up a finger as more messages came through. After the fourth, a frown formed on her face.

She walked back to the chair as she punched numbers into the receiver. "Two calls from Kelly O'Shaughnessy in Wildwood."

"You guys still talk?"

Sherry shrugged, pushing Send and lifting the phone to her ear. "It's been awhile."

"Kelly," she said after a long moment. "Sherry. How are you?"

Kelly O'Shaughnessy had been a rookie lieutenant in charge of Wildwood, New Jersey's detective division in 2006, when a string of boardwalk murders brought Sherry to the oceanside resort—an incredibly sad time in her life. That's where she lost her best friend, John Payne.

Sherry could tell from the police captain's hesitation that it wasn't going to be good news.

"I'm sorry, Sherry. I didn't know who else to call."

"What is it, Kelly? Are you all right?"

"I'm fine, it's not about me," O'Shaughnessy said. "I just got a call from state police headquarters in Trenton. A trooper was killed an hour ago on the Garden State Parkway. His partner was taken hostage. They can't identify the shooter on the dash cam. There were no witnesses. Only the dead trooper could have seen who took her and what he was driving. The superintendant called me. Very privately, about you."

"Where did they take him?"

"Shore Memorial, Somers Point."

"They'll let me see him?"

"They'll turn their heads for ten minutes. You're supposed to call me when you get out of there."

"Can you get me a car?"

"I can do you one better. They've got a bird in the air. Your lawn okay?"

"No one's sued me yet."

"I'll tell them you're getting ready."

"I'll be ready when they land. I'll call you from the hospital, Kelly."

Twenty minutes later Sherry was on her lawn, boarding an Sikorsky S-76B, waving to Brigham and putting her hand to her ear to signal that she would phone.

She had been dreading this moment for weeks now, ever since New Mexico. She was scared of what would happen the next time she was asked to do this. Very scared.

Not that there had ever been a guarantee about her powers. There were just times that nothing came to mind. Even when she saw things, they were often out of context, the dying person's random access from a lifetime's archives of memories, easy enough to confuse with more recent images.

But this time was like no other. Never before had she been exposed to radioactive isotopes and then dosed with a dye called Prussian blue. Never before had she tried to do this when able to see with her own two eyes.

Whatever had happened to her in New Mexico and later, on that table in Nazareth Hospital, may have done far more than reconnect her to sight. There might not be any more images for

Sherry Moore—and so much was at stake. But then there was always so much at stake, wasn't there?

"Twenty minutes," the pilot said into her headphones.

Sherry nodded and looked at her watch. There had been a sixth message on her answering machine, one from Troy Weir, who'd called as Brigham approached her door and she'd silenced it on purpose.

They flew alongside the Atlantic City Expressway, then banked south at Mays Landing and crossed half a dozen golf courses before she saw the hospital on Shore Road.

It took less than a minute to enter the hospital with a cortege of stone-faced state troopers blocking her from public view and rushing her to the ER and a draped triage room guarded by wild-eyed police officers.

"In here," a man said. He had eagles on his epaulettes. He pulled the curtain closed behind her and she could smell the inside of the body cavity, the broken arteries and torn bowels, the room, the floor and counters strewn with bloody instruments and surgical sponges. She had never seen such a room, though she had visited literally hundreds. She made her way to a stainless steel stool with wheels and rolled up alongside the body. She lifted the hand, which was in a clutching position, and felt the gritty crumbs of dried blood pressed between his skin and hers.

She squeezed and closed her eyes and took a deep breath.

And nothing happened.

25

"Sherry?"

"I'm listening."

"It doesn't look like you are."

"I was just thinking about the trooper."

Brigham nodded.

"I could have saved her a month ago."

"You don't know that."

"I think Kelly was disappointed with me."

"Sherry, for God's sake. How can anyone be disappointed with anyone for not reading someone else's mind? You know, you really are caving in. You've got the bar so damned high no one could get over it. Act human, for God's sake."

"I'm not caving in."

"It's no goddamned different. I don't like it when you start to feel sorry for yourself."

"Well, I'm still sorry." She huffed, rearranging herself on the chair. "Tell me how it goes with your own gamma ray test next week. Maybe you're just better adjusted than I am."

He saw she was near tears.

"I'm sorry," Sherry said, putting up a hand. "Really, I'm sorry, I shouldn't have said that."

Brigham's hand moved to his jacket pocket and he had the oddest of urges just then. To remove the pack of Marlboros and light one, except that he'd quit smoking forty years ago.

Sherry knew Brigham had his own trials and tribulations. She knew he'd lost a wife and that cancer wasn't new to him.

"Forgive?"

Brigham nodded.

"Please, tell me what you've got."

Brigham looked out the window. He wasn't thinking about Monahan or the Korean War anymore. "Ever smoke?"

"Smoke?" Sherry repeated.

"Cigarettes. You ever try one?"

She shook her head. "No. Why do you ask?"

"You wouldn't understand."

He sighed and then he opened the folder on his lap. "They called it Bluebird in the beginning," he said solemnly. "The CIA's attempts at using drugs, isolation, and hypnotherapy to effect mind control. They also tried electroconvulsive therapy at a lab in Canada, which produced drug-induced comas. Patients were made to listen to recorded loops of tapes for weeks, even months, at a time. The longest one that was documented went on for a quarter of a year."

"Oh my God," Sherry said.

"There was also a study of probing brain centers using segments of hypodermic needles that were quickly pounded into the head with a hammer, so at any time—even years later if they shaved the head—doctors could find the needle openings and thread fine fiber leads, like fishing line, through the hypodermic needle and probe different depths of the cranium."

"Ugh." Sherry shook her head. "To find what?"

"To stimulate hunger, thirst, arousal, euphoria—we were

learning where the emotions came from and how to excite them on demand. This was back in the 1940s. Later the project was re-named MK-ULTRA, around the time young Monahan was in up-state New York. There was now officially a race for a weapon to control the human mind. MK-ULTRA was under the command of the deputy director of the CIA. There were thirty universities par-ticipating in the projects and untold doctors and scientists in se-cret labs around the country. They were dosing patients with LSD and sodium pentothal, among other things. Dosing without their knowledge, I might add, but this was to avoid symmetrized reac-tions. In fact, one of the most famous scientists attached to MK-ULTRA was a doctor by the name of Olsen, who took a leap from a New York high-rise hotel in 1953. His fellow scientists later ad-mitted he'd had a psychotic episode following high doses of LSD, but there is evidence that he was increasingly unhappy about the direction MK-ULTRA was taking."

"He may have been murdered?"

Brigham shrugged. "It was suggested often enough, but who was around at the time to investigate? The CIA?"

"So all these people were duped into using potentially lethal drugs?"

"I wouldn't say duped. There were a host of willing volun-teers around as well. The Unabomber, Kaczynski"—Brigham pointed at her—"participated in MK-ULTRA experiments at Har-vard. Kesey, who wrote *One Flew Over the Cuckoo's Nest*, volun-teered at Stanford. The list goes on."

"What does this have to do with radio waves?"

"The process," Brigham said. "The more we learned about Soviet advances on their LIDA Machine, the more our own pro-gram morphed from psychotic drugs to radio-wave frequen-cies." Brigham pressed his palms together. "There was a device created by a Yale physiologist, named Delgado, that could con-trol the implants in the brain with radio waves. He called it the stimoceiver."

"And it worked? Really worked?" Sherry asked.

"He stood in a ring with a bull in 1947 and stopped it dead in its tracks when it charged. He claimed his device interrupted the bull's aggressive tendencies."

Sherry was silent for a moment. "Which must have seemed like a miracle at the time."

Brigham shrugged. "There were skeptics. They thought the bull was turning away to avert the frequency of the radio waves, but I still think the experiment would shock some people today."

"The problem was that a human who had received the implants would know what was happening to them," Sherry said. "Which negates its use as a weapon."

"Exactly," Brigham said. "Which led to the next step in MK-ULTRA's research. The apparatus described in your journal. How to control the brain by beaming microwave bursts at it."

"Voices?"

"Images, voices, sure, but maybe more. Possibly the volunteers were shown videos meant to desensitize them to violence. Then they were given an idea, a suggestion. A subliminal message."

"Like suicide."

"It would be the extreme of the extreme emotions to resist. Men might be convinced to commit murder for a cause, but how much harder would it be to surmount our own natural instinct for survival? How much would it take to make a man kill himself?"

"This machine worked too?" Sherry asked.

"The Russians had some success, though we can't say how much. ELF waves emit extremely low ionizing radiation and very low heat. These machines were virtually undetectable."

"Invisible to counterintelligence technology," Sherry said.

He nodded. "It wasn't just intelligence signals that the machines delivered. ELF waves in themselves were capable of crumbling brick walls or vibrating the internal organs of a human body so violently as to alter their location. They could disrupt brain patterns and prevent organisms from functioning altogether. They were literally lethal."

"Grotesque." Sherry made a face. "This is what happened to Thomas Monahan? Brain damage? Possible suggestion of suicide?"

"I think so," Brigham said. "His writings mention a metal box. Fabric mesh could mean speakers, and you've seen the white dial and numbers he described. It had to be radio waves they were using on him. He talks about the sunburns they were experiencing, which sounds very much like exposure to microwaves."

Brigham shifted in his seat. "Sherry, I've said this before, but this journal could cause quite a stir for the people involved."

"The government?" Sherry said.

"The government, the scientists, the doctors, the patients' families."

"Maybe that's good."

"I'm just saying."

"I know," Sherry said. "I know. I'll be careful."

"You want to finish these last couple entries?"

Sherry nodded.

"You want me to fix you anything to drink?"

She shook her head.

Brigham opened the green journal.

November 20th, 1950

There are two new members in R-lab now. Radio heads we have begun to call one another. They were talking about food and one of them was telling me about his parents' farm back in Oklahoma. They raise a small herd of buffalo and he was saying how tame they all were.

I drew some sketches of the room we all sit in to do our

tests. The room is very narrow and has a long wooden table in it. At one end of the table there's this machine. It is very sophisticated technology we are told. It sends out radio waves that the enemy can't hear and that we can and that's what makes it valuable as a weapon. Our job is to try to understand what the radio waves mean. In other words, they want us to listen for any sounds and mark on a sheet of paper what we hear and when. Sometimes you can tell when a signal is coming because there is a gauge on the front of the machine with a needle that registers between zero and thirty. But the gauge isn't always reliable because once when it wasn't moving I heard voices talking to me and not like voices over a radio or outside the room, but right there in my head. I was the only one who could hear them. I think that maybe the needle is there to fool us. Cool, huh?

There is also a movie projector and it shows film reels from the war in the Philippines and Japan and Korea and it plays over and over until you know everything that is going to happen before it does. There is no need to tell you much more than how horrible war is and I guess they just want to impress that upon us as much as possible. Even though we are all getting out of the army in a month or so.

There is a glass window near the door. You can't hear through it as the walls are so thick. The doctors watch us through the glass while we're working to make certain that everything is okay. The one who is in charge is a lot younger than the others. We know his name but no one here is allowed to repeat it or write it down because the enemy might be using their own type of radio equipment on us. I can tell you, he wears a white hat and smokes a pipe like General MacArthur. I heard one of the military policemen telling another he's a brilliant scientist and we're lucky to have him on our side. I guess that's almost as good as saying his name, not that anyone will be reading this.

November 21st, 1950

We've started a new exercise in the radio room. Now, instead of recording the signals we hear, we are supposed to resist them. We were told we could use anything as a diversion to think about, old memories, our serial numbers, we could pick out objects in the room to focus on until we train ourselves to overcome the voices. It's a bizarre exercise because one of the voices is about a revolver lying on the table in front of us. The voices tell us to pick it up, but we're really supposed to leave it on the table. Very strange, but they obviously know what they're doing.

November 22nd, 1950

They've started increasing the supplement shots now that we're in our last month. I think I might have had a reaction to the shot because I passed out when I was in the can this morning. Next thing I remember someone was banging on the door and instead of opening it I tried to think whoever it was away. I know this makes no sense to anyone who hasn't been here, but it did to me and the next thing I remember is the captain's voice ordering me to get up off the floor.

They strapped me to a gurney and left me in the R-lab most of the evening. I saw the replacement guy whose family owned the buffalo farm. He was on a gurney as well and they were getting ready to move him somewhere. They said he tried to get out and that one of the guard dogs attacked him. His bottom lip was missing. All the skin around his nose was chewed away. I've never heard the dogs barking, but I guess they're up there to keep spies out.

They wanted me back in R-lab right away. They said I was very important and that they were getting ready to give me my final discharge tests so I could get out of here.

Can't . . . on, can't . . . on, I couldn't remember the numbers anymore. Can't . . . on, can't . . . on, it's all getting to be too much, too hard to hang on another day. I'm trying to remember all of you, to keep your faces in my mind. Sometimes I think of Shep. You know when I get old and die I'd like to be with Shep under the cherry tree in Grandpa's field. People don't do that much anymore, bury their kin at their homes, but if you could ask Grandpa how'd he feel about it, that's as nice a place as any I could think to be. I used to sit there and talk to Shep. I'd like to do that again. I'd like to tell her about all the things I saw and did and I know she'd understand in her own way in the end. When I was a kid and did something wrong she always licked my face and I know she didn't mind.

November 23rd, 1950
Thanksgiving Day

I can only imagine you sitting around the fire this morning having breakfast. I know Mom is in the kitchen with the turkey and Grandpa is reading the newspaper. Most everyone is gone around here. All the brass went home for the holiday. All the guards but one and he's been drinking whiskey heavy most of the morning. One of the docs wants to run tests and I'm supposed to be in the lab in ten minutes. I don't know how well I'll do today. I didn't sleep last night. I tried to remember the numbers and names, but they're all gone. I can't think of anything but the gun anymore. I guess this is what happened to Tim before he left. I don't want to talk to anyone anymore. I don't want to hear anything else. I don't want to think. I don't wa. . .

The rest of the pages were blank.

26

It was a busy night at Grant's Tavern, perhaps more than the usual number of locals were there, and the weather was improving daily, so tourists were out stretching their legs after a long, dismal New York winter.

The bartender was pouring beer and talking a new waitress through the beverage menu. Every table on the floor was occupied and those left standing congregated around a half-wall wooden ledge that separated the bar from the restaurant waitstaff station.

Troy sat at the end of the bar. He'd arrived in town in the late afternoon and ordered a vodka, rocks. It would have been preferable to locate the address and wait in his car, but in a town the size of Stockton you were more visible trying to hide than acting like everyone else.

"Business?" the bartender had asked.

"Family business," he said with an appropriate degree of gravity.

Troy knew that all kinds of people came to the hospital. Most wouldn't be expected to talk about themselves.

"Heard about that plane crash in Moscow?"

Troy shook his head.

"Ran off the runway and a fuel tank ruptured. Looked like Armageddon, but everyone got out. You don't see that too often."

"Nope." Troy looked at his watch.

The bartender walked down the bar to take an order and Troy used the time to escape, leaving an appropriate tip. Not too much, not too little.

Carla Corcoran was sitting in a rocker in her living room. Her house was one of the larger ones, six doors down from Grant's Tavern, on the corner of an intersection. The décor was predictable early American, but done with style. She was as meticulous as her first husband had been. Everything was perfectly arranged, from the flowers on the table to the pencils on her antique desk.

The windows were open this evening. It was the first chance to air out the house, and the warm spring breeze smelled fresh and wonderful. Colter was at the clubhouse, as usual. He was a good man, but absent more than not. He wasn't the kind of man who could sit still. He could have retired on a government pension, but the club kept him busy, and he liked the attention everyone gave him. He certainly wasn't a Jack McCullough, Carla thought; the two men couldn't have been more different. She wondered if it was like that with all divorced couples. Were they constantly comparing past mates?

She'd hate to admit it to anyone, but Jack would always remain the love of her life. She missed the real companionship he gave her. She could never resolve that he would take his own life. If something were so wrong that he couldn't live with it anymore, he would have told her. They were just like that.

She'd thought about him more and more since Betsy had introduced her to Sherry Moore. Not that she'd forgotten him, not by a long shot, but now that she'd dug out that old journal in the attic and gone through the photo albums, he was on her mind much more.

She had all his things, all still locked in her desk. Colter might have been surprised to know that, but then Colter would never have cared enough to look. Colter's world was outside the house. Carla's was inside.

She picked up a book and read two pages before she marked it and laid it down. She went to the kitchen and turned the gas on beneath the teakettle, took a paring knife, and brought an orange into the living room. She looked at the television and decided against it. She peeled the orange neatly, studying the parking lot outside Grant's Tavern. People looked happy carrying their packages and there was laughter in the air. When Jack was alive he'd sometimes take her there for a drink, but that was an exception to the rule. Mostly they sat at home and read and Jack would clean his guns while they talked, and she would make jars of jam from the berries he brought her. It was a simple life, but simple was good.

The curtain fluttered in the breeze. She felt weepy just then and wiped a tear from her eye. The kettle began to whistle in the kitchen and she laid down the orange and went to make a cup of tea. When she returned to her rocker she sat and reached for the knife and a drop of blood splattered on the orange in front of her.

Carla wiped her nose with the side of her hand and was surprised to see blood on it. How odd, she thought, reaching for the tissues on an end table. She dabbed at her nose, then she stood and went to her desk.

She looked confused for a moment, but then she took an old key from her pocket and opened the rolltop. It was dark now, she'd noticed, the last light of day having slipped behind Mount Tamathy.

She took out a piece of paper and a pen. The words came easy, fluently, as if they had long been bottled inside. "Colter and all my dear, dear friends, you could never know the pain I have lived with these last fifty-eight years. . . ."

When she was finished she folded the letter neatly, creased it with a thumbnail, and stood it tent-style upon the top of her desk. She took Jack's big .38 caliber revolver from the bottom-righthand drawer and the box of ammunition next to it, old green cardboard flaking away across the desktop as she opened the box to reveal tarnished brass shells. She removed a few and dropped them into the chambers.

There was a slight smile on her face as she put the gun to her head and pulled the trigger.

27

Troy Weir was hardly oblivious to the fact that he was acting out his childhood conflict. He was also keenly aware that his acts were, if nothing else, perilously close to premeditated murder.

He knew that his dark psychosis had as much to do with his stepfather's arrogance as with his mother's irritating submissiveness. In his mind the abused had become as loathsome as the abuser. He had watched the game play out from the perspective of a toddler and then later, as a teen, reinforcing again and again that all people are not created equal. That money and aggression trumped goodness and decency and compassion every time. That power in the right hands could bring the most enchanting prom queen or respectable congressman to their knees. That one man could forever change another man's—or woman's—life in the course of hours, minutes, even seconds.

He remembered the day that his stepfather changed his mother's life. The day he took away his name and money and left her to die in a nursing home. Left her with a pittance of his billion-dollar fortune and a smirk as she reminded him of his own words when she signed a prenuptial agreement nearly twenty years before; when he said that the entanglement of personal and corporate lawyers made life impossibly complicated and that she only need trust in his word and she and Troy would be taken care of for as long as they lived.

Now, in an ironic turn of events, his stepfather had come to interpret Troy's antisocial behavior as ambition. And ambition was to Edward J. Case what a Harvard business degree was to Wall Street. Here was a man who could put humanistic feelings aside, a man very much like himself. It was only fitting, Troy thought, that the Nobel Prize–winning laureate would see his own reflection embodied in a sociopath.

He also knew he had to be careful. The National Security Agency vetted every single person who had ever been assigned to the MIRA Project. They would not hesitate to resort to legal, even physical, intervention if they thought for one moment that their multibillion-dollar weapon might be compromised. Even by its creator. That should have been a strong motivator not to kill with it.

Even with all its complexity and sophistication, MIRA's microwaves, beamed at varying megahertz, could not help but leave telltale signs of its destructive biological incursion, which affected the victim's cellular structure, glands, visual systems, central nervous system. While it might be prudent to let an old woman shoot herself in the head in a hick town like Stockton, too many suspicious deaths and one scholarly medical examiner familiar with the capabilities of microwave diffusion would lead the NSA directly back to him. And that he could not allow.

Sherry would learn of the news about Carla McCullough Corcoran soon enough. Hopefully after he had time to get her house key and to see her suicide through.

He knew there was a possibility she might be tempted to

return to Stockton when she heard about Carla's untimely death, though it was doubtful they were close acquaintances.

For now it would be smart to wait a few hours and then call Sherry to ensure she was still going to Case and Kimble headquarters in the morning. That was where his last plans for Sherry Moore would unfold.

Tomorrow was going to be a very big day for both of them.

28

Sherry sat in silence in an Adirondack chair, overlooking the river. She wore a wool fisherman's sweater and a drab blue plaid blanket wrapped around her shoulders.

She realized how quickly she had thrown aside her convictions and common sense. A month ago she had had everything she wanted. How quickly the world's eye candy had dazzled and overwhelmed her. How quickly she had come to rationalize that she should be living for today rather than tomorrow. Why had she chosen to expect the worst, instead of trying to get her life back to normal?

It really was possible, after all, that in spite of all the excitement of being exposed to radiation and regaining her sight, that nothing else had changed. That there really could be good news in the future and that getting caught up in the drama of defeat was the thing that felt so wrong inside.

She remembered the time she sat here with John Payne. It was funny, she thought, the power of memories. After a while you could push them back down, put them where they couldn't hurt you anymore. But every now and then, and from the strangest places—a song on the radio, a face in the crowd, or a long shadow cast by a tree in the fall—and suddenly you were right back there and that wave of emotion passed through your body like an electric current full of melancholy and despair.

She wiped the tears from her cheeks and fixed her eyes on the bridge to the south. If she had said anything different two years ago when her friend John Payne was still alive he might not now be dead. She might not even be sitting here right now. Anything could have happened, good or bad, but it would certainly have been different, and being different by a minute could mean being different by a lifetime.

That was the audacity humanity was resigned to. To question why life worked out the way it did. She had been torn throughout the morning over the meaning of happiness. Had she been happier before she regained her sight? Was she feeling depressed today because she'd lost her gift and was unable to help find a missing trooper in New Jersey or was she depressed over being ungrateful for regaining her sight? Over the way she had been acting?

She just wanted to be herself again, to be in control, to have some conviction that this or that was true. And she didn't feel that way now. She felt cheap. Like she had learned to use her eyes as an alternative to her heart. That she could retreat from responsibilities to others, because she was damaged, ill, unlikely to be good enough.

Brian had never said a word about New Mexico in his earlier messages on the answering machine, but the question was always hanging there. He wanted to know what was going on with her. He wanted to know if she was all right. And if they'd had a conversation, he would have asked about her eyes and the tests and she would have had to tell him she could see again. And he would think it was wonderful.

What could she say to him now that he hadn't already seen

for himself? She had sight. She had a new friend and she was being unfaithful to Brian.

Maybe she wasn't thinking clearly, but yes, she'd considered the implications. There was no real excuse. Brian would never know now that she'd looked at his picture every day since she'd regained her sight. That she thought he was more beautiful than she had ever hoped for. That she loved his eyes and ears and dimpled chin and the shadow of his beard in the evening light. He was no pretty boy like Troy. They weren't even close. He was the big quiet bear and Troy was the eloquent fox, sleek and confident and mysterious. The kind of man she would have shied away from under other circumstances.

It was almost like being stabbed, the pain of seeing Brian. It was an image that she could not get out of her head.

Was there something psychological about her decision to pursue something with Troy? she wondered. Was she trying to sabotage her own happiness?

Sherry swore after the death of John Payne—and that troubled year that followed—that she would never again succumb to depression. And yet the mind was like a theater, with a penchant to feature episodes that we would most want to forget.

"Sherry?"

"Mr. Brigham." She smiled, wiping the last of a tear away with her sleeve.

"I thought I'd find you here."

"Just watching the sunset," she said softly.

"It's overcast," Brigham said.

She shook her head. "But there's still a sunset behind the clouds. I knew that not so long ago. I knew that when I was blind." She turned and looked up at him. "And I didn't have to see it to believe it."

He sat next to her. "How are you feeling?"

"Confused," she said honestly. "And bad."

He nodded and sat in silence and they watched the clouds getting darker.

"I'm heading up to Boston this evening," he said.

She nodded. "Breakfast club?"

"The FBI switched the records at Nazareth Hospital. Monahan's body is on its way to Walter Reed in Washington."

"You know, his brain might be wired exactly like mine?" She attempted to laugh, but the sound came out as anguish. "What about the journal?"

"The FBI is seeing me tomorrow night, after my meeting. They'll be doing the lab work on it themselves. We'll know for sure if it's Monahan's handwriting and blood within a day. If nothing else we have his body. Nobody can dispute the DNA."

"And your friends will pull the records?"

"The journal speaks for itself, Sherry. Once they match it to Monahan, they'll start to pull the army's records on Korea. There are half a dozen other soldiers named in Monahan's journal. You and I both know that they're going to turn up killed or missing in action."

"You said yourself that whoever did this has friends." Sherry looked at him.

"You mean friends who might intervene."

Sherry shrugged.

"The breakfast club"—he smiled—"remembers Korea. We all made mistakes, but I can assure you there is not a man in that room that's going to tolerate a cover-up of murder. If anyone is still alive that was involved in Area 17 and they went beyond the scope of their authority, they're going to pay the ultimate price. And if there are any more rogue researchers out there, they can bet the new vice president will be chairing a review of all military records of the Cold War."

"Jesus," Sherry said. "You know that already?"

Brigham shrugged. "There is also going to be some excavating going on around old Area 17."

"You know, it's funny that you turned out to be the one person in the world I most misjudged."

"What do you mean by that?"

"I don't know." Sherry smiled, looking up at the clouds. "I just always had this impression of you over in your big old home ironing shirts and sweeping your porch with a broom. Just a nice older gentleman with his memories, trying to keep busy."

"Aren't I?"

"I don't know." She made a face. "Why don't we call the vice president and ask him?"

Brigham laughed. "What about you?"

"One more day with Troy."

"Why?"

"He invited me to see Case and Kimble the day I met him. I figure it's a good day to tell him it's over."

"Your blood tests are looking good?"

"Salix is happy."

"You started the therapy early. You're going to show up negative."

Sherry nodded. "Maybe you're right, and trust me, I know I've been acting like a child."

Brigham remained silent.

"I've never been a pessimist before."

"Not since I've met you," he said firmly. He looked out over the river and the sun started to descend from the clouds in the west.

"I don't know what to say to him"—Sherry folded her arms and tucked her feet under her behind—"even if Brian does talk to me again." She sniffed. "I'm just so sorry."

Brigham turned to look at her. "Then tell him that," Brigham said flatly.

She began to cry again. "Life isn't easy, is it?"

"Nope," Brigham said.

"I was always going to be honest with him."

Brigham looked at her carefully.

Sherry looked back at him. "Mr. Brigham, he was standing right there looking at Troy in my living room. He doesn't know what happened in there."

"Sherry, you didn't sleep with the guy. Don't confuse guilt with right and wrong. Don't go trying to sabotage your future because you think you're not deserving of Brian. . . . What I'm trying to say is that Brian knows the pressure you've been under. Brian is smarter than that. Tell him everything. Don't leave anything out, and if it was really meant to be, you'll find him right back at your side."

"I don't know," Sherry said softly.

"Sherry, sometimes people feel bad about themselves and they go out and do dumb things to prove themselves right. They create a self-fulfilling prophecy."

Her cell phone rang and she wiped a tear with one hand. "That's probably Troy now," she said, sniffing.

Brigham nodded and started to get out of his chair. "I've got an eight o'clock flight. You be safe tomorrow."

"Aren't I always?" She waved good-bye.

29

"He won't be home," Troy said. "She told me he's in Boston."

Case wheeled his chair to the window and looked out at the darkness. "Everything is at stake, Troy. Do you understand what I mean? Everything of mine and everything that will be yours, all of it."

"Yes, sir."

"I want her dead, suicide, and I don't want to leave them anything to autopsy."

"What about the admiral?"

"I think you know what has to be done with the admiral."

"Sir?"

"Oh, don't think I don't know the little games you play with MIRA. Have him set his house on fire, I don't give a good goddamn what you do, but when this is over there will be no more games, no more attention drawn to this company or me. What about the New York State Police?"

"The old lady wrote a suicide note, in her own hand. What can they say?"

"They will say autopsy her and then some doctor will see that her sinuses are half cooked."

"She put the gun to her head. The coroner will run tox screens. He won't even give her skull a second look."

"He might if your friend starts making noise, and you can bet the day will come when they ask themselves the question."

"If anything, Sherry Moore will feel guilty about the old lady's death. I mean, she brought up the subject of her husband after all these years."

"Yes, today she'll be in shock, but tomorrow she might consider what she read in that journal and then put two and two together, between the journal and the fact that husband and wife committed suicide sixty years apart."

"She doesn't suspect me," Troy said. "That's what matters in the end. All I need is another day with her."

"I've worked too hard in this life to have some halfwit army private crawling out of the grave to haunt me. And mark my words. If Monahan's name hits the newspapers, there will be someone out there who's going to remember him from Korea. Once that happens"—he spread his arms—"these walls will come tumbling down."

"I will handle it," Troy said.

"You had better," the old man said. "You had better indeed."

30

The satisfaction he gained by humiliating women was only compounded by his stepfather's misconception that he shared his vision, that the gift to render generals and their armies useless was a crowning achievement.

Troy cared about none of it, nothing but the power he had so providentially achieved. He had always had his victims, and Sherry Moore would never have been among them if it weren't for his father's interest in protecting himself and the interests of Case and Kimble.

Sherry was a curiosity herself. He hadn't even needed MIRA to introduce them. She had simply walked into his life at the wrong time and place. He wasn't sure how critical the damage to her body was from the radiation exposure in New Mexico; the report had only begun to receive East Coast coverage, and New Mexico's governor was doing everything he could to downplay the incident. But Troy had access to Sherry's medical records. Something had happened out there, and Sherry was now taking daily doses of Radiogardase, a widely used brand of Prussian blue—3,000 mg doses of a very old but very complex formula of a dye that had but one known medical use: counteracting the effects of exposure to deadly radiation.

And, whether it was related or not, Sherry Moore had for some reason regained sight after thirty-two years. It was hardly remarkable that she might be acting out of character. It would have been all but impossible for any human not to. If she failed to question coincidence and improbable meetings with a virtual stranger such as himself, it was likely she was trying to think like someone she was not. Trying to mimic someone with sight, because for all Sherry Moore knew, the seeing world was far less complicated, far more obvious than the world of the blind.

It would be ironic, he thought, from all he'd read about the woman, that she would become handicapped only after she regained her sight. That he had walked into her world at her most vulnerable moment.

In any event, it worked in his favor. Sherry might have eventually found her way to Case and Kimble if she'd continued on her course of investigating Private T. J. Monahan. She might even have managed to blow apart the misconception of Edward Case, Nobel Prize–winning humanitarian. But providence had put her at his disposal, and while Troy would have enjoyed watching his stepfather's ruin, he had himself to look out for as well. Troy with the power of MIRA behind him was going to overshadow anything his egotistical stepfather had done. Troy was going to become a name in the history books.

He knew Sherry was wavering. He knew she was devastated when she saw that man at the door the other night. He knew she was reevaluating the last two weeks of her life and reevaluating the miraculous recovery of her sight. And he knew that he, himself, would be the first thing to go when she was ready to tell him. As close as they had gotten to having sex, she'd said no in the end. There was still some conflict in her mind, a moral dilemma perhaps. The boyfriend?

Which meant he needed to find the journal and fast. He needed to know what she had done with it, whom she had talked to, and he needed to destroy her.

And if Sherry was no longer willing to take the next step, then he would have to increase the output of **MIRA** and help her along.

The world would not be surprised if Sherry were to kill herself. She'd overdosed on sleeping pills after her friend John Payne had been killed, hadn't she? She'd just been exposed to radiation in New Mexico. Her boyfriend caught her with another man.

She was poised to die.

31

Troy brought flowers to Sherry's door. He suspected she would be embarrassed by how she'd acted the last time they were together. For the things she had allowed on her sofa after dinner the other night. No, it wasn't really much, not nearly as much as if he'd put the whole tab of roofie in her wine or turned the MIRA device on her. But he'd only wanted to loosen her up, to get her talking and feeling sexy, because if she was feeling sexy she might lead him to her room and the diary.

But Sherry wasn't naïve. Not by a long stretch, and he knew he dare not push this woman. From all that he'd read, Sherry must not be underestimated.

Which meant that he could no longer afford to be subtle with her.

Horticultural Drive was down to one lane because of construction. The day was warm, and the mist from lawn sprinklers made rainbows in the sunlight. Tony turned onto Industrial Drive, lined with cyprus trees and manicured lawns, and finally in front of the Case and Kimble headquarters, a six-story wall of onyx glass surrounded by a million dollars' worth of tasteful sculptures and pristine landscaping.

Troy parked the Porsche in a reserved space. The guard waved as he came around to open Sherry's door and led her along a concrete path that veered away from the main entrance and joined a pebbled rim of a sparkling blue pond.

"You like goldfish?" he asked.

She nodded as if she saw them every day, but it took all of her self-control not to exclaim how large they were. *Weren't goldfish as small as the crackers and come in glass bowls the size of your fist?*

"My office is in the courtyard, just around the back," he said.

It wasn't a lab, or at least it wasn't the variety of lab that came with white lab jackets and Bunsen burners. There was a full hand-scan security pad at the entrance. There were phone banks and a floor-to-ceiling movie screen, several comfortable leather chairs and the door to a stainless steel safe the size of two side-by-side refrigerators.

Sherry expected cases full of arcane books, but there were only a few magazines around the room. The space looked more like a place to entertain important guests than a working office.

"Doesn't look like what I expected," she said.

"That's because I'm in the main labs so much. They just gave me a place to rest my hat where they store all their records. Looks like a lot of security for nothing, but you'd be surprised how much industrial espionage goes on these days. You want to leave your purse, you can put it under my desk. They don't allow packages in public areas. The museum's a little cold, though, I'd keep your sweater."

She nodded.

They took an elevator up one level and walked through a curvy hallway with glass walls facing a pond surrounded by tulip trees. The dozen or so people who passed them in the halls failed to acknowledge Troy, which agreed with his story that he was new to town. Still, the placement and elegance of his office seemed so strange.

They stopped at a pair of golden doors and Troy pushed a paddle to open them. "Winston," he said to an impeccably dressed older man. "We have a visitor to see the museum."

Winston nodded politely, but avoided Troy's eyes. He handed Sherry a clip-on pass and ushered them into the placarded alcove, where hallways split into two directions.

"I always like to do it backwards," he said. "Start with the future and end up in the past. I think it's more dramatic that way."

"Lead the way."

Displays were well designed, some frozen in glass cubes, some mounted on golden pedestals. There were lots of neat lights that formed holographic screens and images. There were microchips that when implanted in the brain could cure epileptic seizures or manage remote limbs; capsules that when swallowed could perform an endoscopy; nano-medicines, robotics, regenerative medicines, zero gravity cures, and on to Case and Kimble's showcase of field research on HIV and West Nile virus. And as the time line of C&K's medical wonders showed each decade receding, so did the backdrops, the models' clothing and hairstyles, the furniture.

One room was devoted entirely to the evolution of antidepressants and antianxiety drugs in the latter part of the twentieth century, receding to models wearing pillbox hats of the sixties; then Valium, amphetamines, anticoagulants, specialized sutures, and birth control. In the fifties scene, there were children in wooden wheelchairs and oral measles vaccines, early research in radiotherapy by white bearded doctors in black suits, X-rays as a cure for cancer, and microwave treatments for subcutaneous heat therapy. Sherry looked at the old heavy machines in wooden or metal boxes, covered with archaic-looking dials and levers, and she thought of the rather modern-looking radiotherapy machine that had been destroyed by thieves in New Mexico, and it tugged at her heart that the poison was still in her.

The seats of the Porsche were sun-warmed when they left Case and Kimble. Sherry turned the air-conditioning vents away from her face and wondered why she felt so odd, so out of sorts.

Troy wheeled the car into traffic. "How about lunch?"

"Fine," she said, rehearsing in her head what she was going to say to him.

Sherry stared at the sparkling lake as they rounded Horticultural Drive; she had the most curious sensation of being divided in two. Part of her was in Troy Weir's Porsche heading for the interstate and part of her was remembering the day she met him, the book about Halley House Orphanage lying open at his feet on the steps of the Athenaeum. Perhaps even odder was the sensation that the two halves of her were coming back together.

Sherry put on her sunglasses and looked out over the water.

She kept wondering why his office didn't really look like an office so much as a heavily secured boardroom that avoided the public entrances to the building. What new biologist rated an office like that?

The company's museum was certainly worth seeing, but why was the trip so important to him? Was he only trying to impress her?

"Care to share?" he asked.

She looked at him, his blond hair whipping in the open air. He looked good today, tanned, confident, she noticed how the other drivers were staring at them.

"You're deep in thought." He smiled.

"Just thinking how beautiful the day is," she lied.

"Why don't we get sandwiches at the deli and sit on your lawn?"

Sherry nodded. "Sure," thinking it was as good a place as

any to give him the news. To tell him she couldn't do this anymore. To admit she had not been herself lately and that there was no place for him in her life.

She laid her head against the headrest. Troy really had tried. She had to give him that. She couldn't have been all that much fun, asking him questions all the time, trying constantly to find something wrong with him. He'd taken her to the aquarium not knowing how much that had moved her. He had made her laugh when she just as easily could have cried. He even wanted her to be interested in his work. He was clearly proud of his job. She could probably have acted more enthusiastic about his office and tour of the museum.

She thought about Brigham then. He would be in Boston now, some nondescript brick building with its own discreet parking lot full of black sedans and limos. There would be men in suits standing in the halls, telltale bulges of SIG SAUER or Heckler & Koch automatics under their armpits. Breakfast would be served quietly by uniformed staff, the table, most likely round, would look like a who's-who of the last thirty political years; former CIA directors, retired admirals and generals, former secretaries of defense, former presidents and vice presidents, not always the same perhaps, but enough to form a cohesive and extremely influential committee. Sherry had only learned of Brigham's monthly breakfast club after a perilous forty-eight hours in Haiti last summer, when her unassuming neighbor, gentle old white-haired Mr. Brigham, set off a political storm that rained paratroopers down on a drug cartel involved in human trafficking. Of course, he didn't come right out and say it, but Brian had hinted as much.

"Yours or mine?" Troy asked.

Sherry looked at him, and then heard the warble of her cell phone in her purse. She opened it and reached past where her key ring should have been and flipped the case open. *Where were her keys?*

"Betsy." She smiled. "I heard you're coming to visit?"

Sherry was silent a moment and the color drained from her face.

Troy glanced at her thinking this was the call.

"Because of me," she said. "Oh, my God, I'm so, so sorry."

"No, no, I know that, Betsy, but how are you? Have you talked to Mr. Brigham?"

"I understand. I know he will, but Betsy, you shouldn't be alone."

"No, and I understand that too, but I did meet her and I do owe her family a visit. I insist."

"Yes, I don't think I'll be able to reach him until this evening. He's out of town on business. Look, Betsy, I'm with a friend, can I call you right back?"

Sherry closed the phone and stared straight ahead at the windshield.

"Bad news?"

Sherry nodded, still unable to speak. She opened her phone and dialed Brigham, but it went to his answering machine. Brigham had planned a full day, first breakfast with the club, then off to meet the agent in charge of the FBI field office in Boston.

Sherry put down the phone, feeling the guilt that was beginning to well inside. If only she hadn't brought Carla into this. If only she'd been content to leave well enough alone. What good had any of it done? Monahan was still dead and Jack Mc-Cullough was still dead and now this sweet old woman was dying and about to be with them. She thought about the happy little woman in Stockton. The clear bright eyes that seemed to single you out of a crowd. She sure had missed that one. Just like she'd missed the memories when holding the hand of the New Jersey state trooper. Did the ability to see both dull her facility to read people and destroy her gift to commune with the dead?

"Troy," she said, "that was a friend of mine from Stockton.

She's the friend of a friend I was telling you about the other night. The one who introduced me to the woman with the diary."

Troy nodded.

"She tried to commit suicide last night," Sherry had a tear streaking her cheek. "She's in intensive care. They found her body this morning."

Troy took a deep breath and put his hand on her shoulder.

"Troy, I have to go up there."

"I'll take you," he said flatly.

"No, Troy, you've been a good friend to me these last couple of days, but I needed to tell you today that I have to stop seeing you."

"The man at the door the other night. It wasn't your neighbor." He smiled.

"No, it wasn't, but that's only part of it, Troy. I needed to do this anyway. I haven't been honest with you and I haven't been honest with myself. That wasn't me the other night. Not at your place, nor at mine. That just wasn't me and it's complicated, but you have to understand that."

Sherry looked at him. He hadn't said anything to offend her. If he was disappointed or even annoyed, he was hiding it well.

"I was going to tell you at my house. I appreciate your company and your kindness, but I've been avoiding some things lately and they need straightening out."

They rode in silence for a moment.

"You still need a ride to the Catskills," Troy said. "You said you don't drive."

"I'll work that out, it's okay. I just needed to say the part about us."

"Hey"—he put on a big smile—"you told me that first night at my place you weren't looking for a relationship. I took you at your word. I really did. You don't owe me anything. Really. I already took the day off, though. If you can stand a few more hours of me, I might as well make the trip easy for you."

"Oh, Troy, you know I don't mind you."

"Then let's keep going. We'll be back tonight and shake hands and leave it at that."

Sherry looked at him solemnly. "Really?"

"Really," he said sincerely.

It was dark to the north. More rain, spring rain, more things coming to life and more things continuing to die.

"We'd better put the top up," Sherry said, fishing through her purse and looking again for her keys.

He nodded. "Won't be long. We can make it to the tollbooth before it rains."

"You didn't notice my keys in your office, did you?"

Troy shook his head. "Lost them?"

"They're always hanging on this hook." She opened the inside flap of her purse to show him.

"Can you get in the house tonight without them?"

"Yeah, that's not a worry, I've got one hidden away. It's just so strange."

The sky grew dark and the rain came minutes after they started north on I-95. By the time they were on I-87 the temperature had plummeted eighteen degrees and the rain had turned to sleet.

Headlights came at them southbound like an endless string of diamonds, yellow, white, and blue behind the monotonous sweep of the windshield wipers.

"So you might as well tell me about the diary," Troy said.

Sherry, wanting to think about anything other than Carla Corcoran dying in the hospital, nodded.

"She was a sweet old woman," Sherry said. "Her husband, many years ago, almost sixty years ago, was a security officer for a state hospital up there. He found a boy of about twenty who had gone off a cliff on top of a mountain. The boy was from an army base that used to be up there. It's abandoned now, has been for decades. Well, the boy had a diary and the security officer kept it and gave it to his wife."

"This boy died in the fall?"

"No." Sherry shook her head. "But he never recovered. Head injury. He was in a semi-comatose state until he died last month."

"Jeez, all that time. Any family?"

"No, and that's why this lady kept the book. There was never anyone to give it to, I guess."

"How did you get involved?"

"Even longer story," Sherry said. "Suffice to say I heard about the boy and how he was found and someone introduced me to the guy's widow."

"And she thought you would like to read the diary?"

"She didn't even know what was in it." Sherry shook her head. "She had it sealed away ever since her husband died."

Troy let out a breath of pure relief.

"You said it was about a soldier, I remember. I'm a little fuzzy about the night you told me."

"Yeah, me too," Sherry said, feeling her face getting warm. "I don't usually get that 'fuzzy' myself, but yes, it was about the army back then. Strange times, that's all. I think they were probably doing some things at the army base that weren't all that proper."

"Like what?" Troy looked interested.

"Oh, I don't know, just stuff. Like maybe they were doing tests on them."

Sherry had no interest in having this conversation now. Not with a stranger. Not until she talked to Brigham. Not until she had a clue as to whether or not some general's or psychologist's name was going to pop up in his investigation and if so, how detrimental the news was going to be to the administration that was still in the White House.

The tavern parking lot was filled. Sleet covered the blacktop. A news van was sitting in the public parking lot across the street; a reporter was probably still interviewing neighbors. How much news could there be around a town like Stockton, or at least news that didn't involve the state's psychiatric institute?

"My friend Betsy will meet us in the tavern." She pointed to Grant's, where a man was sprinkling salt across the steps and sidewalk. "She said they took Mrs. Corcoran to the state hospital up the road. They have a trauma unit there."

"I'll wait right here in the car for you. Have a drink with your friend. She probably needs you right now. Take as long as you like. Really."

"You don't want to come in?" Sherry asked, surprised.

"No, no, I've got some calls to make and I'll be fine right here." There was no way Troy was going to chance that the bartender might recognize him.

The bar was packed. Betsy was against the wall talking to a trio of people. She waved and Sherry made her way through the crowd to join her.

Betsy put her arm around her and began to introduce everyone. "Everyone's out tonight," Betsy whispered, pointing around. "No one can get over what happened to Carla. Her son is on the way from Tallahassee. He's supposed to be in tonight."

"Her husband?"

"Up at the hospital."

"She's still . . ."

"Alive." Betsy nodded. "And they've upgraded her to stable," she added enthusiastically.

"What happened?"

"All we know is that her husband stayed in Ashokan last night—he keeps a room at the golf course—and when he came home this morning he found her lying on the floor. She'd shot herself at her desk, the bullet entered her head behind the ear, and there was supposed to have been a note."

"How in the world did she survive?"

"One of the doctors from the asylum just called his wife, Lynn, that's her over there in the black turtleneck. She said the ammo Carla used was pre–World War Two. It must have been corroded. She said the shell barely struck her hard enough to fracture her skull. Caused internal bleeding and swelling. That's what they're doing now. Trying to get the swelling to go down."

"But it will."

"He told Lynn she was going to make it."

"I'm so sorry," Sherry said. "You know that."

"I know and so am I, but we've all known Carla Corcoran a long time before you got here, young lady. There was nothing anyone could have said to that woman to unhinge her like that. Whatever happened to her over at that house had nothing at all to do with you or me."

Sherry took a deep breath and exhaled. She wanted to cling to that idea as long as she could.

"It's Sherry, right?" Mike the bartender called out, recognizing her. "You need a drink?"

Sherry shook her head. "No, but thanks anyhow, Mike."

"Here if you need me," he said cheerfully.

"I'm so glad you came up, but they won't let anyone see her. Not yet," Betsy said.

"You know, I'm just happy I'm not going to a funeral home. When you said she was shot in the head, I thought I was coming to pay my respects to her husband."

"Well, the weather is perfectly awful. You can stay at my place, if you like."

Sherry shook her head. "I wouldn't even have come if it weren't for a friend. We'll be driving back tonight."

Betsy looked at Sherry. "You sure?"

"Sure," Sherry said. "What can I do for you right now? Anything?"

"Well, I feel a hell of a lot better after talking to the doctor's wife, but if you talk to Garland before I do, please tell him to call me. I think I'll delay my trip to Philadelphia until Carla's home and her husband can take care of her again."

"Brigham," Sherry said. "I forgot all about him. You've been calling?"

"Right up until twenty minutes ago. He's still not picking up." Betsy shrugged.

"Betsy?" someone called from across the room.

Betsy put her arms around Sherry. "Okay. I'm sorry, but I guess I let you come a long way for nothing. If you're going to go back, get on the road before it's too dark. I'll tell Carla you were here, and don't you fret over her. I'm sure there's an explanation and whatever it is, we all have a chance to help her get through it this time. Thank you so much for coming." She hugged her. "But get out of here and I'll fill Garland in on the phone when I reach him."

Sherry turned to leave as Betsy started for her friend who was calling.

"Betsy?"

Betsy turned. Sherry had stopped and was coming back toward her.

"Yes, Sherry, what is it?"

"Can I ask you a quick question?"

"Of course, dear." The older woman smiled.

"How do you get to that old army base?"

32

Brigham laid the copies from his folio on the table beyond his coffee and pushed them forward. "I'm sorry this turned into a whole day for everyone, but you know our esteemed colleagues back in Washington would not wish to be blindsided if any of this were true. That is of course the last thing we wish to do."

There were murmurs of agreement. Clinks of spoons in coffee cups, ice cubes in one man's scotch whiskey, one woman's Bloody Mary being stirred.

"What we talked about at breakfast this morning," the woman said. "I don't think these things have been repeated outside of Washington and I mean not ever. It all feels a little dicey to me. This isn't exactly the CIA."

"I'll vouch for the security of this room," a former president said. "Tell me what they've got over there, Addie."

The woman nodded in surrender. "Its code name is MIRA," she said. "More synthetic telepathy, you've all heard it before, but this is exponentially sophisticated. Like nothing we've had in seventy years of research."

She stirred the olives in her Bloody Mary without taking her eyes from the men around the table. "The technology is the same, extremely low-frequency radio waves, electrical impulses—"

"I'm sorry." A very old man sitting next to her interrupted. "Can you just tell us what agency we're talking about?"

She nodded at him, lips tight. "DARPA," she said. "Defense Advanced Research Projects."

"Sorry, but thank you." The old man smiled.

She laid her stirrer aside. "So I'm talking about subconscious, microwave telepathy. We've known the effects of radiobiology since the early 1980s. We knew since long before that, that certain extremely low frequencies of radio waves could disrupt organisms and raise body temperatures. But neurological variations, the effects of radio waves on the central nervous system and particularly cells of the brain, remained a mystery until we decoded biorhythms and assimilated hertz and frequency to the human organism."

"Madam." The man with the scotch sighed.

She nodded. "I know, Jim," she said, "it's like this. The inventors of MIRA are following a course of known electroencephalograph patterns catalogued by computers, subtle characteristics of EEGs that occur when a person experiences particular emotions. We can now identify the concomitant brain waves that correspond to the act or emotion and duplicate it through microwave technology. We can introduce it into another human target. In other words, MIRA can put thoughts and words into your head that are indecipherable from your own. The target cannot possibly comprehend that the thoughts are synthetic and manufactured."

"The ultimate purpose being?" The old man raised his eyebrows.

"That would depend on the agency. I won't even say the first word that comes to mind, but I will stress the defense advantages of neutralizing an aggressive world leader in the interest of peace."

A distinguished-looking man across the room leaned forward. "There have been rumors of errors. Deaths in trials?"

The woman nodded. "Twenty-five GEC-Marconi scientists died in eight years working with ELF transmissions on the Star Wars project in the U.K. They were mostly suicides, auto accidents, nothing traceable. We were learning a great deal more about ELF at the time, the relationship between low-frequency fields and its recorded effect on the brain." She waved a hand and looked at her notes. "Humans couldn't perceive it, but in trials we learned that animals would intentionally try to leave an area that was being bombarded. We now know that the biobehavioral effects of ELF vary from human to human."

"Before MIRA came along."

"Precisely," she said. "MIRA compensates by using brain-based rather than computer-based models."

"And the accidents. I meant here. In the United States."

"None since this administration took office."

"Really," one of the men said.

"Really." She nodded.

"And before that?"

"Well, I believe that is exactly the Pandora's box that Admiral Brigham has just opened."

"Do you know who was there? In charge of Area 17?" the former president asked.

She nodded.

So did a former director of the CIA.

"What happens when we go public?" The former president tapped the table.

"Well, we certainly didn't know he was killing our boys up there. I mean, General Keith worked for Secretary Marshall. He must have known there were fatalities, Keith and both of his colonels from DOD. But killing soldiers and disposing of them on base to hide the fact, it's unbelievable! If this story were true, it runs darker than anything I've heard in fifty years of service."

The former joint chief of staff folded his arms across his chest. "And there are no records anywhere in Washington to support what you describe, I've seen them all, I can assure you."

"Well, the diary certainly exists. We have the names. We heard from the general just fifteen minutes ago that these boys named in Admiral Brigham's diary were not supposed to be in New York in 1950 and are still considered missing in Korea."

"And we've got this man Monahan's body under the knife in Walter Reed as we speak. If his brain suffered what our experts tell us to expect and his blood matches the DNA from that diary, then there is little else to conclude."

"Who was he?" the former president asked. "Who led the research team in the Catskills?"

"Edward Case," the woman said. "Case and Kimble Pharmaceuticals."

The former president nodded regretfully. "Yes, I've met the man, photograph's in the Oval Office." He squinted. "He's a goddamned Nobel Prize winner." He rubbed hard at his forehead. "How about military personnel? How many highly decorated war veterans are we going to smear that worked in Area 17?"

"All dead. Our people checked this morning. There isn't an officer over the rank of lieutenant still alive, maybe six or seven noncommissioned sergeants and corporals that took orders, but they can't be held to blame."

There was a moment of silence.

"Madam." The former president nodded. "Gentlemen, what do you propose?"

"We can't expose MIRA," the ex–CIA director said quickly.

"No," the former president agreed. "We can't do that."

"Neither can Case or his people. He's bound by the Official Secrets Act," the former defense secretary said. "If he threatens to talk he goes into isolation for the rest of his life."

The former president nodded. "So we can give these boys the honor and dignity they deserve?"

Brigham was looking down at the table, his hands out flat in front of him. He looked disoriented.

The woman next to him leaned toward him. "Are you okay, Garland?"

"Garland," the former president interrupted, taking notice of the pallor of Brigham's face. He reached for Brigham's arm. "Garland, is there something else we need to know?"

"I'm sorry." The retired admiral looked up. "Um, you just threw me a curve, is all." He began to rise from the table. "I'm afraid I have to make a very important call. Please continue. I'll join you momentarily."

Brigham ran to the door and down the hall to the exit to the driveway to get beyond the building's electronic audio scrambling systems so he could receive cell phone service again. He dialed Sherry's number again and again, to no avail.

Case and Kimble?

Troy Weir.

They had been onto her from the beginning.

33

"You really don't mind stopping there briefly?"

"Our last adventure." He smiled. "Why not? Your friend who gave you directions was who?"

"Betsy," Sherry said. "Same woman who introduced me to Carla Corcoran."

He nodded, satisfied.

"If it looks like any trouble getting into this place, we're turning right around," Sherry said.

"You said it's abandoned."

"Yeah, but the government still posts it and I have no intention of getting you or anyone else into trouble."

"Oh, I'm not afraid of a little trouble now and then." He smiled and elbowed her.

They followed the road they had taken to the asylum, but forked off on gravel before they reached the entrance.

"Betsy says this is a state road now. It ends at an outdoor range maintained by the game commission, about a hundred yards from the old base. She says we follow the path into the woods to the gate, turn right, and a hundred yards or so there's an opening in the fence."

The range was empty. It wasn't very sophisticated, a six-foot mound of bulldozed earth at one end of a small clearing. A steel drum brimming over with old beer cartons and perforated paper targets, one wooden picnic table at the open end where you could lean a rifle to sight in a scope before deer season. It was a place to take your son or daughter and plink at tin cans the rest of the year.

Troy reached across Sherry and took a small revolver from the glove box. "Just in case," he said. "Snakes and critters scare me. There's a flashlight in the emergency kit in the trunk."

Sherry wondered when genetic biologists began carrying handguns in their Porsches as Troy tucked the gun in his waistband and removed a flashlight from the trunk of his car.

"The path leads to the southern fence around the base," she said. "See the top of it over there?"

Sherry followed a path to the old steel mesh fence, twelve feet high and topped with rusting barbed wire. They left tracks across the ice-covered ground, their jackets and hair gathering tiny white beads of sleet.

"We'll just walk along the perimeter now until we find a place to get in."

It took less than ten minutes. The wire had been cut and pulled back several feet so that you could walk in without turning sideways. There was a well-beaten footpath inside the fence that eventually joined a dirt road and the scaffolding of an old radio tower.

The closer you got to the base, the more you could see of the buildings. Rooftops sticking up between the overgrowth of saplings and tall grass, a few metal chimneys from woodstoves, it looked more like some third-world country than a mountain in upstate New York. There was a cluster of rust-colored steel huts that must have collapsed under a half century of snow. A fallen tree had cracked a cement block building with part of a radar dish. A clearing the size of a football field was spotted with black chunks of asphalt that rose up out of the ground. It wasn't exactly a landing strip, but big enough to accommodate the immense tandem rotor helicopters the army would have used as equipment transports in the 1950s.

There were rotted wooden buildings on the far side of the landing pad, single-story barracks and some ground-level roofing with a variety of ventilation pipes over a large section of ground. Possibly a foundation of something meant to be underground.

Sherry pointed toward the hull of an old gasoline tanker truck on its axles in the trees. Two deer were standing in front of it, watching to see what they'd do.

There were beer cans in the tall grasses and hundreds of broken bottles. The barracks had not a windowpane remaining and the scarred gray walls were covered with profane graffiti. Appliances were strewn across the grounds, old refrigerators and stoves, marketable antiques if they hadn't been shot full of holes or beaten so badly with boards and old piping.

The grass grew tall and careless around the buildings. Roots from the forest had invaded open spaces. There were long shaggy vines of poison ivy, greasy leaves as big as fists. There was bracken fern and poison sumac and thickets of sleet-covered sedges.

Troy stepped ahead onto the long flat ground-level roof. It appeared to be an underground bunker, and it was easily fifty feet in length and twenty-five feet in width. The roof, once tarred, was either bare or peeling away.

Sherry made her way into one of the barracks. There was no door, just rubble from the crumbling plaster on the floor. There was a broken table, the barely discernible remains of a sofa, and a large fabric chair full of straw where mice once nested. She took out her penlight and checked each room.

On the second floor she found condoms and beer bottles on the floors, a pair of old sneakers, someone's discarded bra, a torn picture of the Empire State Building, an advertisement for Regent cigarettes.

Troy called from outside. "Here, I found a door."

Sherry retraced her steps, watching carefully where she placed her feet—many of the stairs were rotting through—as she made her way past the charred remains of a mattress to the foot-high roof Troy was walking across. "There's a stairwell here on the side," he said, pointing. "Let's look inside."

Sherry ran to catch up, but Troy had already disappeared below ground level. The deep stairwell was dusted white and covered with broken tree branches, weeds, and old leaves at the foot of the door. Someone had beaten one hinge off the frame and the door hung there stubbornly, a foot and a half open, and she squeezed past it into the dark.

Sherry caught a faceful of cobwebs as she cleared the door. It was windowless and pitch black but for their flashlights. She saw Troy shining his beam up and down the walls along a long straight hall.

"One way in, one way out," Troy called back. His voice was distant and it echoed off the walls.

Sherry saw that there were rooms to their right, each one a little different, offices perhaps, all cleared of furniture, floors bare and concrete.

The walls were scarred and spray-painted with graffiti like the outside of the buildings. Sherry caught up to Troy and saw a rat cross into the shadows in front of them. There was one steel plate from an old set of barbells. It read *20 lb*. Marks in the floor where tables had once been mounted, a half wall into a room full of sooty ceiling vents that could only have been a kitchen. This is where they once ate, Sherry thought, imagining an Italian cook who could not speak English.

Sherry walked down the hallway deeper into the cavernous foundation, leaving Troy to linger behind. Her light found a Campbell's soup can label with a cherubic girl, a glass aspirin bottle sitting on a ledge, a yellow marble, a red wooden checker.

There was a series of smaller rooms with adjoining doors and bathrooms. They must have been bunkrooms, she thought, looking at a long dried snakeskin in one corner.

The last door in the hallway was still in place, made of steel, the hinges welded onto an iron frame. It had a glass window in it, screened and double paned. Someone had cracked the glass but not completely shattered it.

The door was closed and stuck. Sherry wrestled with it a moment and it moved an inch, then another. She played her light around the hall and saw a section of lead piping at the very end that someone had torn from the wall. With it she was able to leverage the door several more inches until the sound of the old ceiling creaking warned her to stop.

She tried to squeeze herself through the open space and just managed to slip into the dark room.

She played her penlight around the walls, up and down the length of a long wooden table in a room that had once been painted white. The legs of the table were broken and it leaned precariously like a long dusty ramp toward the far side of the room. It was the only piece of furniture still left in the bunker, the hardwood boards too long to be removed. It must have been built in place.

Sherry's light found a square recess in the wall by the door, large and deep enough to accommodate a movie projector that could be operated from outside the room. She could picture where the chair would have sat at the end of the table, the chair that Monahan had been in. She could imagine the strange metal machine with its cones and dial at the far end of the table. She could almost hear the voices in her head.

"Can't . . . on, can't . . . on."

He was here, she thought. Right here. Fifty-eight years ago.

She bent over and brushed concrete and plaster from the

end of the table until she found the groove he had carved into the table with his thumbnail. She put her own thumbnail in it and rocked it back and forth as Monahan had done.

He would have been sitting here, war cinematography beamed by the projector to the blank wall on his left, bombs going off and people dying. He would have been looking at the machine at the opposite end of the room and hearing the voices telling him to pick up the gun and kill himself. He would have been trying to concentrate on the numbers on the gauge, the needle bouncing up and down, five, ten, fifteen, twenty . . . the gun would have been right there on the table in front of him.

Can't . . . on. Had he repeated those words over and over in his mind to block out the voices in his head? She concentrated and tried to imagine what it all might have looked like, in spite of her little experience with sight. She had never seen books or magazine or computer images of the period. In fact, the closest she had ever come to visualizing the era was at Case and Kimble's museum this morning. Like the exhibit of a long-bearded physician in a black waistcoat, administering vaccines in an old-time schoolhouse, or the room full of antique brain wave synchronizers that predated modern entrainment devices, the massive artificial kidney units, the iron lung, the LFP—low-frequency pulse—apparatus used on patients with psychological problems and neurotic disturbances.

And she stopped.

She remembered the LFP, the primitive-looking wood-and-metal box sitting at the end of this table, the large white dial with numbers in increments of five through thirty. And there at the bottom, the manufacturer's stamp. She remembered thinking it curiously familiar at the time. It read CANTON, OHIO, only the word CANTON was divided by the resting pin of the gauge's needle and it looked more like CANT!ON.

The numbers and then the letters. Monahan was trying to focus on the gauge and not the gun. It was the only other thing in the room to think about but the bloody films playing out on the wall.

She suddenly sensed something that she hadn't felt in quite some time.

Unequivocal danger.

She held her breath and listened. Something was terribly wrong, she knew. Something wrong, and she was in the middle of it.

Sherry catches vibes like spiders catch flies, a friend had once boasted, and in spite of her blindness, it was true. There was a time Sherry could accurately describe the guests of a party long afterward, just by hearing their names.

She couldn't describe them physically, of course. Voices don't always ring true. But a few minutes of conversation was all it ever took to discern someone's nature, whether aggressive or passive, proud or kind-natured, whether someone thought himself clever enough to hide a lie.

Sherry's intuition was without equal. Or better said, *had* been without equal.

Sherry had never believed in coincidence before, but wasn't it just a week ago that she had a chance meeting with a man in a hospital waiting room and then again a few days later, only this time across town and carrying a book about the orphanage she grew up in? And then he takes her to an aquarium in Camden that she had been to with someone she loved.

Oh my God, she thought. She wasn't just getting dull with sight. She was getting stupid!

Someone at Case and Kimble—and it would had to have been one of the two founders—had been here in 1950 with his antiquated LFP microwave machine. And Troy Weir was here to see that no one would ever know, to make sure that the story of Thomas J. Monahan was never told.

Her purse, she thought. Troy had specifically asked her to leave her purse in his office. He didn't shake hands with the curator Winston when he entered the museum, but he did when he left. She saw him straying slightly behind her until they were out the door. Had Winston given him her house keys?

And if Troy Weir had her keys, it was because he wanted the diary.

She remembered the gun he took from the glove box. He was going to kill her. She needed to get out of the bunker, and there was only one long hallway back to the entrance.

"Find anything?" Weir asked from the other side of the partially cracked door.

Sherry's heart was pounding in her chest. She shook her head. "Just an old table."

What was in his hand?

"You don't look so good." Weir cocked his head sideways, studying her face. He took the pipe and pried the door open further. Mortar and pieces of concrete rained down on them as he squeezed into the room.

"You know, I thought you and I were really going to get it on the other night." He brushed the white dust from his wet hair. "What a shame. I think you would have been good."

Sherry watched his face come into focus in the ambient light off the walls. He looked so very different all of a sudden. As if the layers of his physical attractiveness were shedding before her eyes. She could see him now as he really was. She could feel the cold chill of his presence.

He reached into his jacket pocket and Sherry began to arch her back, stepping to her left and setting her feet. A snap kick would disarm him, she thought. Then she would roll into a side kick aimed at his solar plexus and that would put her near the door. It wouldn't kill him, but it would be enough to immobilize him until she could clear the building, and once she was in the woods he might never find her again.

But it wasn't a gun that he drew, it was a pen, and she saw the floor and leg of the table appear on a cell phone screen in his other hand. She stepped to her left, and he moved to block her way. She saw her shoes and then her legs on the screen of his phone.

She felt a wave of nausea, the white lights coming again, and when her vision cleared she saw a chunk of concrete lying on the high end of the table.

"Don't worry. I won't leave you here," he said. "The friends of your friends might decide to come looking for you one day," he mocked. "Besides. I have friends too. Friends who can make it look like you shot yourself in your own bed." He laughed, the sheer evil in him coming to the surface.

Suddenly the table was gone, she could put it no other way. The table was gone and the room was gone and Troy Weir was gone. Everything gone.

She felt herself looking down the end of a long, well-lit hall. She felt herself walking toward the room she was now in.

. . . The halls were lined with olive metal file cabinets, illuminated by bare lightbulbs in heavy wire casings. There was a man in uniform at the end of the hall, sitting by the front door. He was young and he was in uniform and he was drunkenly raising a bottle of whiskey to his lips. There was a smaller man in a white smock, a weasel of a man, maybe sixty years old. He wore thick spectacles and a stethoscope around his neck and he was standing at the door with the glass window.

A–P, she noted on the tabs of a file cabinet to her right, P–Z on the next one. Another cabinet was labeled R-Iodine, R-Calcium-R-Iron, and in large capital letters, SUPPLEMENTS.

A dead mouse lay in a space between the next set of cabinets and these were labeled NUCLEONICS and LFP-ELF respectively. There was a cold black cigar stub balanced on the edge of the last one, and just beyond that, pushed against the wall, sat a metal hospital gurney on rubber wheels. It had restraining straps on it.

The small man in the white smock and glasses was beckoning her to the door with the glass window. She walked past him and through it.

Sherry had experienced dreams of residual memories before, the finer details of things seen or remembered by someone in those last eighteen seconds before death. Such a dream usually came unexpectedly, in the middle of some night, when the subconscious mind comes out to play. Having the recent experience of sight and television, she likened it to instant replay, those dramatic, slow-motion, time-stretched moments when things become evident that could not be seen in real time.

Only this time she wasn't sleeping and she wasn't dreaming. This was here and now. This was in the light of day. She knew that something had changed when she took Thomas J. Monahan's hand. That his distorted memories had thrown some cerebral switch in her head and opened a brand-new door.

She caught the peripheral images of light flickering on the wall to her left, a jeep approaching a spread-eagle woman in the medical corps uniform, the water buffalo, the mist of blood and brains as the grenade was pulled from her clamped teeth.

How many times had she, no he, been made to see it? How much violence had he been forced to watch to desensitize him to death? Was it over hours or days or even months?

The machine was there at the end of the table, the needle on its resting pin, and she knew it would remain that way until the weasel was safely outside the door. The pistol was there on the table where *he*'d sit. Everything in its place, everything ready to resume.

"Cant . . . on, Cant . . . on," she whispered.

She thought about leaping for the gun, wondering if it was loaded. She looked at it, studied the contour of its frame, the smooth curve of the trigger guard, the barest glint of light on the steel blue barrel. She caught the slightest whiff of cinnamon, the smell of good gun oil. She admired the walnut diamond-stamped grips. She could even imagine the weight of it as she raised it to her . . .

She took two steps forward and reached for it. She picked

the gun up and raised it to her head. "Are you there?" she whis-pered, and Troy Weir laughed, and as he did she spun and slammed it down on his forehead. It wasn't a gun, she saw, as she snapped back to reality, but a baseball-sized chunk of concrete. He stumbled as she hit him again and again and the last time she hit him she heard it break the cartilage of his nose.

His hand grabbed hers, wrestling for the weapon, but he was blinded by the blood running into his eyes and their hands were slippery with it as she pulled herself out of his grip and found the opening of the door, and squeezed through it. She ran down the hall, smelling the wet air in front of her as Troy Weir hit the door with his shoulder to follow her. There was a loud groaning sound and small chunks of ceiling began to pelt down on her head, but then she was beyond the door and the mortar began to give way and one of the interior walls of the bunker crumbled under the weight of the roof.

Sherry ran up the stairs and across the glistening ice, hop-ing she could put enough time and distance between herself and Weir to allow sleet to cover her tracks.

She found her way through the woods by a deer path, crossed a dirt road, and in minutes was at the fence where it had been torn from the ground by the roots of a massive tree. She got on her belly and crawled under the opening, pulling herself forward with her elbows until she was free. Then she stood and ran and it was as if she knew where she was going. As if every step had been predetermined. She saw the front gates of the State Psychi-atric Hospital to her left as she crossed a wide field. She began to ascend a ridge when she reentered the trees, rising like the spine of a sleeping giant to the neck of the mountain. A thousand feet higher she was looking out over the Catskills toward the jagged Delaware Water Gap.

The overlook road was visible just above her and she clawed

her way up a grassy embankment to a guardrail and followed the road to the top of the mountain.

There were picnic tables around the overlook. A wire safety fence prevented children from wandering out onto Chimney Rock, the most prominent formation overlooking the horizon.

She vaulted the small safety fence and walked out onto the top of the rock.

It was mesmerizing to watch the sleet falling around and beneath her, a haze of white filaments as spare and delicate as spider's silk. Why had she come here? she wondered. Why hadn't she run to the asylum's gates for help?

"Dramatic, wouldn't you say?"

She turned and saw Troy.

His face and shirt collar were crusted with blood. His hair was wet. Rivulets of pink water coursed beneath his collar.

"You're still in his head, aren't you?" Weir said.

Sherry just looked at him.

"You're going to end it just like he did, except my guess is you won't survive the fall." Weir put a hand on the wire fence and threw a leg over the rail.

"They'll call it that too," he said, moving toward her on the rock. "A copycat suicide. They'll say you snapped. Drawn to the grave by a dead man. Lots of magazines will sell that story, I would predict."

Sherry saw Weir's hands come out of his pockets. He was holding the cell phone with one and raising the pen with the other. She knew he would be looking at an image of her head on the screen of the phone.

He was going to finish it now.

Sherry raised a finger to her lips in time to catch a stream of blood running from her nose. Her vision began to blur until she could see only light and then broken fragments of Weir and the trees and the sleet, as if they were shards of a shattered mirror. It was happening again, she realized. Whatever he was doing to her was opening that same door and reversing what Thomas Monahan had done to her mind. Troy had created a link between them.

He was thinking, she realized, and then she smiled.

He was instructing her to step off the end of the rocks.

She turned toward the edge of the cliff and leaned forward, seeing glimpses of the rolling hills and showering white lights. She was in that place between sight and blindness again.

"Troy?" She heard his shoes grinding on the dirt behind her and she knew where he was and she turned and thrust out her hand and grabbed his fist clamped around the small device.

"Did you ever imagine MIRA working both ways?" He tried to wrestle his hand from her grip.

"Imagine that a defectively wired mind might mirror your own contrivance. What might happen in a moment of rare eclipse as the device performs in your hand?"

By squeezing the skin cell receptors of his hand, her most unusually configured mind was feeding the link back to him. He scratched with his nails to remove her hand, but she clamped her other over it as well and held on.

"Troy?" she whispered.

"No," she heard him say. "NO!" he screamed and she knew he was hearing her thoughts.

"Stop it!" he yelled, wriggling in her grasp. "Don't do this!" he begged.

Sherry pivoted to maintain her grip as he stepped to her side and then past her toward the edge of the cliff.

"Jump," she said softly.

"Don't!" he cried.

"Go ahead, Troy, jump." She was looking his way but could no longer see. She took a breath of fresh air. She had traded her eyes for her gift, for her life.

"Jump," she whispered.

And she released his hand and he leapt from the rocks and it was many seconds before she heard him hit bottom.

34

Dr. Salix put his feet on his desk and rotated his chair toward the window as he spoke to Sherry by phone. "I spoke with the technician in Boston this morning. The roentgen equivalent of point oh-one is negligible, Sherry. In fact, it was little more than a therapeutic dose a cancer patient might receive. Your lungs and bone marrow are clean. You are fine, young lady."

Sherry thanked him and put the cell phone back in her pocket.

"He says I'm negative." She laughed and put her face against Brigham's shoulder, tears streaming from her eyes.

She took Brigham's arm and they walked across the rolling lawn of Arlington National Cemetery. She could hear a jet ascending from Ronald Reagan National Airport, a siren somewhere in the city across the Potomac River.

Her thoughts wandered, with the clop of hooves on pavement as black horses drew the casket to the grave. She could imagine the last of the cherry blossoms swirling around the wind with the words of the chaplain. She heard the sharp click of heels as the seven-man honor guard presented arms. She winced as three volleys were fired across the grave. She cried as the bugler played Taps from the top of the hill. She shook as Brian Metcalf presented her with the triangular flag from Thomas J. Monahan's casket.

Then Brian put his arm around her waist and walked her back to the car.

She remembered thinking how thankful she was to have seen his face.

epilogue

Edward Case hung up the phone and wheeled his chair to the window. The office was cool, the air-conditioning lifting pages of documents on his desk.

Outside it was a beautiful sunny day. The kind that toasts the tips of knee-high wheat and spreads honeysuckle scents across porch swings and vine-covered rural road mailboxes.

He saw the limousine coming, far above the fields, it was black, and two Pennsylvania state police cars escorted it in a cloud of dust. There was one before and one behind, their solemn blue lights flashing in the grilles.

He lifted a picture from his desktop, a very young and a very sure-looking man with his meerschaum pipe in his teeth, smiling for the cameras, rakish tilt to his white homburg. Case nodded and set it back down.

The government had severed the contract for MIRA research and gathered all traces of equipment. They could afford to do that now. They had bought and paid for the technology. It was already theirs.

He watched the limo getting closer down the lane. Now

he was about to sign away his position as CEO of Case and
Kimble.

It wasn't really a choice. The FDA's approval for Alixador
was being held until the ink was dry on the document.

They were also going to take away his Lancaster estate.
That and assets totaling $880 million, which would be held in
escrow for settlements sure to arise from the government's imminent disclosure of what took place in Area 17.

And he did it all to avoid prosecution and what would certainly be a literal life sentence in prison.

The Nobel Prize winner would be permitted to retain his
brownstone in New York City.

And live out his life in obscurity.

ACKNOWLEDGMENTS

I wish to thank Cindy Collins for her patience and prodding and most competent critique of my manuscript.

To Barbara Collins for the test drive.

To all the people at Simon & Schuster, but especially to Michele Bové, Colin Fox, Nancy Inglis, Nicole De Jackmo, Marcella Berger, Louise Burke, and Kathy Sagan of Pocket Books.

To my agent, Paul Fedorko.

To fans everywhere.

About the Author

George D. Shuman is author of *18 Seconds*, *Last Breath*, and *Lost Girls*. A retired police lieutenant from Washington, D.C., Mr. Shuman went on to executive positions in the luxury resort industry and professional security consulting before settling in the mountains of southwest Pennsylvania to write full-time. He has two grown children, Daniel and Melissa, who live in South Carolina. To learn more, visit his website at www.georgedshuman.com.